PRAISE FOR FAITH MARTIN

'Amuses and intrigues in equal measure.'

—*Daily Mail*

'Brilliant characters that leap off the page.'

—*Sun*

'The perfect village mystery. A golden-age world with an energy that is totally contemporary.'

—J. M. Hall

'All the ingredients of a classic mystery . . . enormous fun.'

—Orlando Murrin

'A fabulous romp . . . witty, devious, fast paced and totally absorbing.'

—*People's Friend*

'A charming, cleverly constructed caper, chock-full of captivating characters. I loved it.'

—Matt Dunn

'A masterfully constructed page-turner of a murder mystery. Clever, compelling, and intriguing. An excellent read.'

—T. A. Williams

'Hugely entertaining with an ingenious solution! I loved it!'

—Clare Chase

THE OXFORD DETECTIVE SOCIETY

ALSO BY FAITH MARTIN

DI Hillary Greene Series:

Murder on the Oxford Canal
Murder at the University
Murder of the Bride
Murder in the Village
Murder in the Family
Murder at Home
Murder in the Meadow
Murder in the Mansion
Murder in the Garden
Murder by Fire
Murder at Work
Murder Never Retires
Murder of a Lover
Murder Never Misses
Murder at Midnight
Murder in Mind
Hillary's Final Case
Hillary's Back!
Murder Now and Then
Murder in the Parish
Murder on the Train
Murder Under the Sun

The Travelling Cook Mysteries:

The Birthday Mystery
The Winter Mystery
The Riverboat Mystery
The Castle Mystery
The Oxford Mystery
The Teatime Mystery
The Country Inn Mystery

Monica Noble Series:

The Vicarage Murder
The Flower Show Murder
The Manor House Murder

Ryder & Loveday Series:

A Fatal Obsession
A Fatal Mistake
A Fatal Flaw
A Fatal Secret
A Fatal Truth
A Fatal Affair
A Fatal Night
A Fatal End

Val & Arbie Series:

Murder by Candlelight
The Last Word Is Death
A Dangerous Train of Thought

Standalones:

The Lavendar Lady

THE OXFORD DETECTIVE SOCIETY

FAITH MARTIN

THOMAS & MERCER

Published by Thomas & Mercer, Seattle

www.apub.com

EU Product Safety Contact:
Amazon Media EU S.à r.l.
38, avenue John F. Kennedy, L-1855 Luxembourg
amazonpublishing-gpsr@amazon.com

ISBN-13: 9781662538407
eISBN: 9781662538414

Cover design by Will Speed
Cover illustration by Matt Saunders

Printed in the United States of America

THE OXFORD DETECTIVE SOCIETY

CAST OF CHARACTERS

Lyssa Moore – a recent widow, biographer, ghostwriter and unwitting sleuth

Bibliophile (Bibbie for short) – her cat. A hefty tom, he knows which side his bread is buttered

Amelia 'Monty' Montrose – the subject of Lyssa's latest book, a controversial 'wild child' 1960s icon who died tragically young during her own birthday party

Frank Tillman – musician and amateur film-maker, who took the only cine film footage of Monty's last party – and promptly sold his pictures to the press

Justin Tillman – Frank's son, who just might not live to regret his father's actions

Chloe Tillman – granddaughter of Frank, who tries to be more helpful

Glen Bannister – lead singer of the Lucky Cuckoos, a 1960s pop group and Monty's lover (who also died young in rock 'n' roll style)

Freida Jones – Lyssa's best friend

Carter Lansing III and Jason Howerd-Pitt – Lyssa's friends and neighbours in the same building

Neville Rickman – a good-looking but enigmatic new addition to the apartment building who is up to something

Elizabeth Grainger – Lyssa's new client, a relation of Monty who has an agenda of her own in wanting the book written and published

Jonas Bannister – a relation of Glen who is determined that some aspects of Lyssa's new book never see the light of day

Ian Gorman – Jonas' head of security. Not a nice man

Monica Joiner – the widow of Ron 'Racey' Joiner, lead guitarist of the Lucky Cuckoos, whose memories of those days prove very valuable indeed

Jennifer Joiner – the daughter of Monica and Racey – a daddy's girl!

Deborah Simmonds – the very shady lady who 'managed' a charity set up by Monty

Jack Flynn – a relative of Deborah who, half a century later, has inherited her 'me first' outlook on life

Janet Connor – a young mother who benefited from Monty's charity, and has only nice things to say about the much vilified 60s wild child

Luke Raines – the manager of the Lucky Cuckoos

Caroline Dixon-Hayes – Luke Raines' niece, who sets Lyssa on a road to discovery

Emily Bannister – the little sister of Glen

Alison Jameson – the helpful widow of the investigating officer into Monty's death

Prologue

Oxfordshire, England, June 1966

Amelia Montrose looked up at the moon and wondered what it made of humanity. All those years it had orbited the Earth, watching the dinosaurs come and go along with various ice ages and – who knew – maybe even aliens visiting and then going away again. It must have wondered what it was all for. And then along comes man, who thinks he knows everything and . . .

She broke off and gave a harsh bark of laughter. If nothing else, surely the moon found mankind entertaining? She raised her glass of champagne to toast it, drained it to the dregs, then poured out the last of the sparkling stuff from the bottle of Bollinger she was carrying carelessly in her other hand. She placed the empty bottle with drunken precision on the edge of a hideous sculpture that Glen had loved and had insisted on buying and installing in the grounds of Evergreen, their 'forever' home, in Oxfordshire.

They had chosen the house together because they'd hoped it would prove to be a sort of halfway compromise between Glen's squalid childhood home on a north London council estate and her own childhood stately-home upbringing in Gloucestershire. In the event, it had never quite seemed to suit either of them somehow.

Hah! Now there was another cosmic joke for her to contemplate, she thought, and felt a tear slide down her cheek, tickling her skin. Impatiently, she wiped it away. What was the point of tears now? Glen was gone, dead at just twenty-five. He'd left her, without warning, with only the recorded sound of his voice for company and his awful taste in art.

She laughed again and drank some more of her champagne. The garden looked lovely in the moonlight, but why wouldn't it? Full of hope and optimism for the future, they'd paid a landscape gardener to design and plant it out. She'd pictured their children playing here one day, chasing butterflies with a dog or two yapping at their heels.

So much for that.

Behind her, Evergreen was a blaze of colour and light and raucous with the sound of pop music and human voices. Built sometime just before the Victorians came into being (for which she was eternally grateful, not being a fan of their overly ornate style) it had a simple country-house elegance that not even her snotty-nosed family could jeer at. Not that any of them had accepted her invitation to tonight's party, of course, one and all having assured her that they wouldn't be caught dead at such an affair.

Only Glen's parents had accepted her invitation and were staying overnight with their little girl Emily, who had been so wide-eyed and overawed by Evergreen when they'd arrived.

Yesterday had been her twenty-third birthday, which she'd spent stubbornly alone. She'd only arranged to have this party a day later, when it no longer mattered, to please everybody else. They thought such weird behaviour was typical of her nowadays, but then what did they know? Or really care? So long as they could enjoy the free wine and food and music, they were happy.

As the Swinging Blue Jeans' latest single blared out across the moon-kissed peonies and roses, she bent double and gave way to a sudden fit of delighted, drunken laughter. It was the thought of her father's face, had he been there and been forced to listen to the heavy guitar beat and simple lyrics, that made her so helplessly giddy with mirth.

Daddy dearest, who only ever listened to classical music and opera! He'd have gone purple, making him resemble a bulldog as painted by Picasso! She could even see the painting forming right before her eyes, with the help of the teensiest bit of acid she'd taken earlier, of course.

She stumbled a little as she waded through the psychedelic colours and, looking down, realised that she'd reached the stone bench set in front of the ornamental pond, and her vision cleared, leaving her feeling bereft.

She paused, staring out over the dark oval shape. She hadn't wanted a fountain in the middle of the pond, but Glen had insisted. Glen, with his working-class ideas of what was right and what wasn't. 'Can't have a lily pond and not have a fountain, Monty,' he'd admonished her, a big grin plastered across his silly face as he'd draped his arm loosely around her shoulders and kissed her. He'd even got out of bed before noon to come down and watch as the workmen installed the stone monstrosity, complete with peeing cupids and dolphins vomiting water.

And suddenly she was crying again. When had their dream turned to stone as well? And not just her dream, but that of her generation?

When she'd finally escaped her parents' choice of private girls' school at the age of eighteen, she'd headed straight to London, where everything was beginning to happen. It was 1962, and everything was changing. She could remember hearing the Beatles' first single, 'Love Me Do', for the first time and how it had astonished and delighted her. Music had always been her passion, and after the conservative offerings of her school and parents, the raw new sound of the Fab Four had been a revelation. The astronaut John H. Glenn was the first American to orbit the Earth and anything seemed possible. In the cinema *Dr No* was playing, and along with a group of her friends, she'd watched avidly as the gorgeous Sean Connery had brought the impossibly cool and dangerous James Bond into sexy being. And the rowdy and salacious talk about the actor that had followed!

Oh, it hadn't all been wonderful, she knew that. The Cuban Missile Crisis had given them all thirteen days of pure terrifying horror in October, with everyone wondering if it would end in a flash of light that would kill them all before the sound of multiple nuclear blasts ever got the chance to reach their suddenly non-existent ears.

But their youthful optimism couldn't be repressed for long. London still led the world in women's fashion, new ideas and, most of all, pop music. And then she'd met Glen and his band, the Lucky Cuckoos, who'd been playing in some dead-end pub somewhere in Soho, and everything changed forever.

Monty began to sway dreamily with the sound of the music spilling out from the party behind her. Over the sound of voices and the laughter of her friends and all the inevitable hangers-on, she could now make out the Merseybeats, and she half hummed along with them. It wasn't a bad song, but not as good as any of the Lucky Cuckoos' songs.

She abruptly stopped swaying as she faced the fact that, along with Glen, the music might be dead now as well. The Lucky Cuckoos had enjoyed six hits over the last four years, one of them even making it all the way to number one. But with Glen gone, and with all the in-fighting and ill feeling that beset the group now, the band seemed to be falling apart. If they couldn't get their act together, and the fans got fed up waiting for the next song or turned their loyalty to any of the new groups that were always cropping up . . . Who knew if they would ever perform again?

But that was too much for her to deal with right now, and she pushed the thought aside. Besides, she would never let it happen. She couldn't let Glen down like that.

She walked forward and sat down on the edge of the brick path that went all the way up to, and then circumnavigated, the pond. Pale, slender, blonde-haired and ethereal-looking, she could have played the part of an elf or fairy in any Shakespeare play or child's fairy tale. Without bothering to take off her shoes, she thrust her feet into the pond's cooling water, laughing at the thought of how shocked her nanny would have been. Ruining a pair of shoes like that! That would have earned her a slapped wrist and no pudding at teatime, all right!

'Well, I can buy a hundred pairs of new shoes anytime I want, Nanny,' she jeered defiantly, gazing at the hideous fountain ten yards or so in front of her. 'And not with Daddy's money either, but with my own, so there!'

Money. With a snort of disgust, Monty put her glass down and spread her hands on the ground behind her. Leaning backwards with her weight on her arms, she lifted her head to stare once more at the moon. Her good friend, the moon. Idly, she kicked her feet lazily in the water, making the water lilies closest to her undulate like belly dancers on the ripples.

'At least you don't want any of my money, do you?' she murmured, turning her head to one side to contemplate the pale heavenly body. 'And you're probably the only one who doesn't,' she said sadly.

Even Deborah wanted more of the stuff, but she wasn't going to complain about that; after all, it had been her own idea to set up the charity, and any charity needed constant funding. Deborah was only doing the job Monty had set her.

The music changed to a Hollies song – the boys from Manchester. Glen had really liked them, but Monty admired the Stones more. She smiled a little, remembering how Glen had been secretly jealous of Mick Jagger's voice, and how she'd had to keep on reassuring him that his own voice was just as good. And that the Lucky Cuckoos would stay up there with the best of them for at least a decade.

Not that she or anyone else she knew tended to plan that far ahead. They had been too busy having fun, enjoying the fame and the music and the screaming fans, the all-night parties, the drugs and wine. Life was all about fun, right?

Until suddenly, it wasn't. People started dying of so much fun, and so many of them had been in the music industry. She had just never thought Glen would be one of them. Gorgeous, talented, rough-and-ready Glen, the good-looking and irreverent lad from the housing estate who her family so hated and distrusted.

'They thought you would sully me, sweetheart,' Monty said, leaning forward again, picking up her glass and toasting the fountain ironically. 'Taint me and lead me astray. And so you did, you lovely, lovely man, you. Did I ever thank you properly for that?'

Another tear ran down her face, and again she angrily wiped it away. How he'd jeer at her if he could see her now. Sitting outside in the dark, all alone and weeping at her own party like some silly girl in one of those awful, syrupy ballads the Americans seemed so fond of producing.

At least the Lucky Cuckoos had nothing to do with any of that! No, good solid rock songs with heart, that's what they were all about – a strong beat with a catchy tune, and Glen's gravelly, deep-timbred voice leading the way. But now his voice was gone, and they were faced with having to come up with a new direction and a new sound.

Perhaps it was a good thing that the pop world was always renewing itself, she mused fatalistically. Fans always wanted the next thing, something they hadn't heard before. But this time she sensed that the changes coming would be more drastic – perhaps moving away from solid heavy beats to something more . . . spiritual, maybe? There was a restless feeling beginning to sweep across the scene – she could feel it blowing in on the wind. She would have to . . .

She heard movement behind her and peered blearily over her shoulder. But no one was there, unless that was a shadow moving across the lawn . . . No, it was probably just the wind in the trees. Or maybe a fox was prowling around. Perhaps, if reincarnation was an option, Glen would come back to her as a dog fox – it would be just the sort of thing he'd do, for he'd often quarrelled with her father over fox hunting. Yes, that would be his idea of a joke all right.

If he did, she'd have to build him a comfortable stable and feed him only the best steak and maybe she could come back as a fox too . . .

Trying to imagine herself as a vixen, she leaned over and peered down at her reflection in the water. It was deep at this end, because Glen had wanted to swim in it. But, typically of him, he'd only swum in it once and then never bothered to do it again. Her face morphed and remorphed with the gentle movements in the surface tension of the water. It looked dark and deep down there – perhaps if she stared hard enough, she'd be able to see him looking back up at her?

Monty, like most young people, had never thought much about death. Not until death had come up and taken the love of her life from her. Now she found herself wondering about it a lot. Glen had died from a drug overdose – so presumably he'd just fallen asleep and never woken up.

Perhaps it was that aspect of it that made her so angry. It wasn't how he'd have wanted it – she was convinced of that. He'd have preferred to go out in a blaze of glory, crashing his motorbike or something equally spectacular. Not slipping away without even noticing it.

During his funeral, and all the bleak, colourless days that followed it, she'd had plenty of time to contemplate death and how she felt about it but had never been able to come to any real conclusion. Sometimes she longed to follow Glen, and other times she felt she still had so much she needed to do. Either way, surely, when death came it should . . .

Monty gave a surprised yelp as she unexpectedly found herself surrounded by cold water, her whole body going into spasm at the sudden shock of it. She gasped spontaneously, but instead of air filling her lungs, it was water – cold, dark water, chilling her to the bone and making her mind spin in panic. Everything was so black already. Then she realised that she'd shut her eyes for some reason, and she forced herself to open them – knowing that she needed to get to the surface. But she couldn't seem to tell which way was up. Where was the moon, her good buddy, the moon? Why couldn't she see his friendly light?

She thrashed feebly about but felt shockingly weak and lethargic. Once more she tried to breathe but only encountered water and choked even more. And as the water filled her up, sucking the remaining heat out of her body and replacing it with a chill that grew and grew, she understood, with a mixture of panic and awe, that she no longer had to wonder how death should be.

Death was already upon her.

1

Oxford, England, Present Day

Lyssa Moore saw the unfamiliar name pop up on her email listings and contemplated it thoughtfully. Nowadays, she was always slightly wary about opening a message from an unknown source, fearing viruses or unwanted solicitations to buy anything from dodgy timeshare flats to super-expensive coffee that had travelled through an animal's digestive system or some such thing. On the other hand, as a self-employed person, she couldn't afford not to check it out. Who knew – perhaps 'Elizabeth-intd' might lead to work?

She was sitting on the sofa in her third-floor flat in Riverside House, a small suite of apartments on the far outskirts of the Osney area, and through the open doors of the French windows that led out to a small balcony, she could see the River Thames (or Isis, as the university city of Oxford insisted on calling it) shimmering away in the warm June sunshine. Absently, she followed the progress of one of the small river-cruise boats, full of happy tourists, that was winding its way towards Port Meadow and Wolvercote.

For all the years she'd lived in the area, she'd never yet taken one of those scenic picnic cruises and made a mental note to do so. Freida would no doubt tease her about it, but her best friend would almost certainly agree to join her and probably bring along an illicit bottle of something to pep things up.

Tearing her eyes away from the attractive scene outside, she forced her mind back to business. Much as she wanted to go out and enjoy the brief British summer whilst she could, sunbathing or window-shopping wouldn't pay her bills. On the plus side, she'd just finished the first draft of the story she was ghostwriting for a television soap star who was clearly looking for a second string to add to his career bow. She had sent it off last night and now faced a nervous wait for his reaction. From her past experiences of ghostwriting, she was expecting the usual litany of complaints, woes and demands for rewrites, so any distraction from that could only be welcome.

Biting the bullet, she clicked on the email heading and opened it, relieved to see that it was indeed a legitimate message and hadn't sent her computer into some sort of meltdown. (One of her friends in London had recently been the victim of one of those hacks whereby she had to agree to pay a sum to get her computer unlocked, so perhaps she could be forgiven for being just a little bit paranoid?)

She tucked her long legs more comfortably beneath her and balanced the laptop on one bent knee so that she could read it more easily. As she did so, the cushion beside her suddenly indented as, with a flash of black-and-white fur, her cat, Bibliophile (Bibbie or Bibs for short) jumped up and landed beside her.

She reached out to stroke his furry back, which arched appreciatively, and was instantly treated to his usual lawnmower-like purr. A handsome tom, he was all black except for his two forepaws, which were white, and a white 'champagne glass' on his chest. She knew he wasn't hungry, as she'd filled his bowl that morning, and within moments he'd kneaded a comfortable spot on the cushion and curled up to go to sleep.

She turned her attention back to her laptop.

> *Hello, I got your name from one of your previous happy clients, so I hope you don't mind me contacting you out of the blue like this. I was hoping you'd be available for a project I've had in mind for quite some time now – it's a biography of a now deceased famous relative of mine. I read and really enjoyed the job you did for Helena Vernier a couple of years ago. I thought it was honest, powerful and moving, and I believe you'd be just ideal for what I have in mind. I'll be in Oxford tomorrow, and was hoping we could meet up for lunch. I've taken the liberty of booking a table for 12.30 at the Ivy in High Street – my treat, naturally. If you can't make it, that's fine, but I'm hoping that you can. If not, we can always reschedule. Many thanks.*

'Huh,' Lyssa said, staring at the screen thoughtfully, not quite sure what to make of it.

She remembered the biography she'd written for Helena Vernier, of course, the flamboyant opera singer who'd wanted her memoirs written shortly after retiring from the stage. It hadn't been the easiest of projects, for she'd sometimes found the singer's mood swings and temperamental nature rather overwhelming. But she'd stuck to her guns when she'd had to, and she thought the singer had come to admire her for standing up to her, when the occasion warranted it. The result had been a book that had been well received by both the singer's fans and literary critics alike.

And, naturally, it was very flattering to hear that the mysterious Elizabeth had supposedly read it and enjoyed it – if indeed she had done so. More likely she had just been buttering her up.

But there were several things about the message that made her uneasy. To begin with, why didn't she sign off with her full name? Was it so that she, Lyssa, wouldn't have the opportunity to look her up on the internet and check her out? And although she said she'd got Lyssa's name from a previous client of hers, why hadn't she mentioned who it had been? Again, was it so that Lyssa couldn't double-check the claim?

And why did she not mention the name of her deceased but famous relative? It all sounded rather secretive. Of course, it could be that the so-called 'famous' relative wasn't that famous at all – at least, not to a wider audience. Perhaps the unknown Elizabeth knew full well that his or her fame might be confined to a small and select number, and didn't want to put her off before she'd even had the chance to pitch her project.

Lyssa smiled as she remembered one potential client who was so enthused about a dead uncle's lifelong collection of biscuit tins that he'd been positive the public was just panting for a full-length coffee-table book about the novelty items, complete with lovingly rendered colour photographs. Luckily, a little tactful chat about the cost of self-publishing had dampened his enthusiasm.

She glanced longingly out of the window again, and putting the laptop down on her own (book-free) coffee table, allowed herself to be lured outside on to the small patio. The city centre would be crowded of course, but here, about halfway between Folly Bridge and the Osney allotments, it was much quieter. She leaned her bare arms on the sun-warmed railing of the balcony and looked out across the river. The green willows moved in a gentle breeze, and a family of swans was being fed by some students who were lazing about at the river's edge. Behind her, one of Oxford's many clocks chimed the hour.

Lyssa, at the ripe old age of thirty-four, now considered herself a veteran of the city and took it for granted that the clock would be either early or late and, with a smile, pulled herself away from the seductive scene outside and back to the sofa.

She retrieved the laptop and reread the message, still not sure about it. The Ivy was certainly not some shady down-at-heel eatery in one of the city's backwaters, so she had no serious worries about attending the appointment on her own; but that famous adage about there being no such thing as a free lunch niggled away at her.

What if it was just a hoax or a practical joke of some kind? She could turn up and find that there was no such reservation booked. Well, so what? It would hardly be a disaster. She could head for Blackwell's and browse for a few hours, surrounded by books, books and more books. Which was not exactly a fate worse than death. Afterwards she could head to Waterstones and have lunch in the café there – it would be no match for the fare at the Ivy, but, again, so what?

Annoyed with herself for vacillating, she clicked on the reply button and sent a brief message to Elizabeth-intd saying that tomorrow at 12.30 was fine, and that she was looking forward to meeting her there. She hit the send button with a flick of her finger and closed the laptop decisively.

If she tried hard, she could convince herself that she'd just taken the first step to securing her next project and thus could treat herself to a little time off. And a stroll down to her local café for a cappuccino and a salad sandwich didn't seem that excessive an indulgence. She might even save the crusts for the swans.

'I don't know, I think you're right. It all sounds a bit iffy to me,' Freida Jones said, some hours later. 'Want me to come with you as back-up?'

'Who do you think you are – Morse or Lewis?' Lyssa shot back, grinning.

Her best friend laughed. 'Neither. I see myself more as one of those fabulous women in American television shows who can shoot a grape off the vine at thirty feet, whilst wearing high heels and putting a good-looking man in his place all at the same time.'

'Multi-tasking. I like it,' Lyssa said approvingly, watching Freida from across the small dining table as her friend scooped up the last of the salsa. At the age of thirty-three, but looking at least six years younger, Freida looked as if she could indeed have auditioned for that television part, being black and beautiful and with a sing-song Welsh accent that captivated you the moment you heard it. Had she been an actress, of course, and not the owner of a small but flourishing estate agency business in St Aldate's.

Freida had come to live in Oxford after following her first serious boyfriend here. The boyfriend was now long gone (and, she maintained, blissfully forgotten) but her love affair with the city was still going strong and looked set to last. The two women had first met at a student party that Freida and the boyfriend had attended at Somerville College, where Lyssa had been studying English Language and Literature. They had bonded instantly, and Lyssa often thought that they were living proof that opposites did indeed attract.

Where Freida was loud and bold and gregarious, she knew she was quiet, introspective and was never happier than when she had her nose in a book – either one she was reading or the one she was currently writing. Whereas Freida was small and curvy, she was five feet eleven and slender. Whereas Freida preferred a very short haircut, Lyssa hadn't cut her hair in years, keeping it up in a ponytail on the top of her head, so that it swung down to the middle of her back. Freida's eyes were of a rich chocolate brown and full of warmth and humour, but her own eyes were dark blue and she had often been told that they gave nothing away.

Her husband Kyle had once told her that he could spend hours looking into them.

Now Freida sighed and noisily crunched the last of the crispbread that she'd used to scoop up the dip and licked her fingers supremely unselfconsciously, reminding Lyssa of a sumptuous feline. 'So, I take it you're going to go, then? To this posh lunch?'

'Yes,' Lyssa said firmly. 'Apart from the fact that I can't afford to turn down potential work, I'm really curious now.'

'You do remember what that did to the cat, right? Oh well, I know better than to argue with you when you've made your mind up. But do me a favour – call me just before you go inside and call me the minute you come out, yeah? I'll wanna know all the details. I bet this Elizabeth whoever-she-is is a seventy-year-old millionairess with masses of white hair and a facelift, who wants you to write about her psychic parrot who can tell the future by picking up certain tarot cards in its beak.'

Lyssa laughed. It had been Kyle who had invented 'The Most Out There Game', whereby everyone had to come up with the most ridiculous scenarios for things. She'd then taught it to Freida and then Carter and Jason, her next-door neighbours of the last six or so years.

'Nah, too tame,' she mocked her pal now. 'I bet she's a tall, blonde bombshell and a Russian gangster's moll who wants me to write a book so that she can encode secret messages in it, giving away bank details of some offshore account to her confederates on the sly – because, naturally, she's really a spy for the Russian government and a turncoat.'

'Oh, naturally,' Freida nodded solemnly. 'And no doubt has some nefarious plan to abduct you and make you write to her dictation.' She shrugged with faked nonchalance. 'Oh well, even more reason to let me know you've escaped her clutches unscathed, then.'

Freida's silly words came back to her the next morning as she walked along the High Street, making her smile. With the chimes of Carfax echoing behind her as she reached the doors of the restaurant, she couldn't help but think that anywhere less dangerous was hard to imagine.

All around her, tourists wandered about taking photographs, whilst the famous swifts of Oxford screeched high overhead as they darted like tiny black arrows around the city's dreaming spires. It was another hot day, and she had worn her second-best summer dress, a long, floaty, mainly white creation with tiny embroidered forget-me-not blue flowers that contrasted with her raven hair and complemented her eyes. She was wearing flat white sandals and the minimum of make-up. She wanted to look presentable and professional but also feel comfortable, and it was not as if she was on a hot date or anything.

In fact, she was not at all sanguine that she would be meeting anyone at all and was quite prepared to be told that there was no reservation waiting for her inside. She was proved wrong in short order, however, by the smartly dressed young man behind the lectern who ushered her into the main dining room and across to a discreet table in the corner.

The woman seated there and looking expectantly her way resembled neither a gangster's moll nor an old lady with a psychic bird, but a woman in her early thirties, with shoulder-length curly brown hair and brown eyes that were no match for Freida's. She was, however, small like Freida, but much thinner, and had an air of nervous energy about her that was not exactly restful.

'Hello, you must be Lyssa?' she asked, popping up to shake hands. Her grip was strong, and she really did shake Lyssa's hand, briskly up and down, not merely clasping it lightly and then letting it drop, as so many people did. It was perhaps because of this that Lyssa couldn't help but notice that, though her hands were well maintained and her nail polish was a bright red that exactly matched her lipstick, the fingers themselves were nicotine-stained and unattractively bony.

'Yes, and you must be Elizabeth?'

'Yes, that's me! Elizabeth Grainger. I'm so glad you could come – please sit down. Wine?'

Lyssa said no to wine but yes to a long cold lemon and lime with ice and settled herself at the table. 'Please, take your time,' her companion urged, handing over a menu and then fussing with a glass of mineral water. She fidgeted constantly, reminding Lyssa of a canary in a cage, moving and flitting about, trying to find a way out. She was dressed in a suit that screamed an expensive Italian or maybe Parisian maker that Freida would have been able to name in an instant, but which was beyond Lyssa, who tended to get most of her clothes from charity shops.

Lyssa opted for a salad option and once the waitress had delivered her drink and taken their orders, Elizabeth finally sat back a little and studied Lyssa thoughtfully.

'I really have read a lot of your work, you know,' she said earnestly. 'I wasn't joshing you or trying to get on your good side. I did my research.' She named a couple of Lyssa's contemporaries, and their best-known books, but concluded, 'In the end, though, I think you're just right for what I had in mind.'

Lyssa nodded happily but still warily. 'I'm looking forward to hearing all about it,' she prompted her hopefully, and Elizabeth smiled, revealing small, white but slightly uneven teeth.

'In other words, get on with it, woman,' she said, rolling her eyes. 'Yes, you're quite right,' she continued, before Lyssa could assure her that she'd meant no such thing. (Though, of course, she had.)

'All right.' Elizabeth took a deep breath. 'If I said to you Amelia or Monty Montrose, what immediately springs to mind?'

Lyssa blinked, fighting down an all-too-familiar feeling of mild panic. It had been just as she feared – the name rang only the faintest of bells. Perhaps something of her consternation must have shown, for Elizabeth quickly waved her hand in the air in a wait-a-minute gesture and added, 'Think 1960s pop culture.'

And with that, Lyssa had it. 'Oh! Yes – she was, er, associated with that band . . . the Lucky somethings . . . I keep hearing a song now in my head . . . About frightened hearts . . .'

Elizabeth very tunefully hummed a few bars of a melody and Lyssa nodded. 'Yes, that's it. It's coming back to me.' Although the 60s had been decades before her birth, a surprising number of the tunes from that era still lingered on into modern times, and not just the really famous ones from the likes of the Stones and the Beatles, but haunting songs like 'Nights in White Satin' by the Moody Blues, and of course, the iconic and unforgettable Procol Harum song 'A Whiter Shade of Pale'. And what with modern-day bands 'remaking' or 'remixing' the songs all the time, and with them popping up as advertising jingles or being given a new of lease of life when used as background music in films set in that era, she, like most of her generation, could probably name quite a few 60s hits.

'Yeah, "The Frightened Heart" was the Lucky Cuckoos' only number one hit,' Elizabeth said, 'but they had six hits in all. Then their lead singer died, and they never really recovered.'

Lyssa nodded. 'Was he one of the casualties of rock 'n' roll culture, or a car crash maybe . . . ?'

'Oh, drugs, I'm afraid. Like so many of them,' Elizabeth confirmed sadly. 'We lost so many great talents that way back then. And then Monty went the same way; well, more or less. She was only twenty-three. She was my great-aunt, I think. Or grand-great aunt? I can never figure these things out.' She took a deep breath. 'Let's see – Monty's older sister was Raine Montrose (or rather Cadman after she got married), and she had only one child, Felicity; and Felicity is my mother.'

Lyssa acknowledged how explaining that connection could be confusing.

'Exactly,' Elizabeth said, grinning. 'Anyway, Monty never lived long enough to have children of her own, but Granny remembered her, and always talked about her with love and some anger. Mummy, as a child, was sort of fascinated by her, but then I suppose to a little girl, Monty must have seemed like a sort of larger-than-life fairy-tale figure. She was rather beautiful and very famous in her own right, you see – here, let me show you.'

As she'd been talking, Elizabeth was scrolling on her mobile phone and now held it out so that Lyssa could see the screen. The photograph may have been old and in black and white, but even so, Lyssa could tell that the elfin blonde young woman depicted in it was indeed startlingly lovely and had an aura of tragedy about her. Even though she had been smiling, you just had to take one look at it to sense that the woman in the image was somehow doomed. Which only added to her charisma, naturally.

Lyssa gave a little sigh and leaned back in her chair. 'It must have felt like such a waste of a young life,' she said gently.

Elizabeth nodded, looked at the photograph of her dead relative for a moment, then shrugged and slipped the phone back into her bag. 'She was found in her garden, drowned in the pond, the day after her twenty-third birthday,' she said simply. 'At her own birthday party.'

Lyssa swallowed hard but said nothing. She knew what it was like to lose someone so young and unexpectedly, and for a moment she felt tears stinging at the back of her eyes and fought them back fiercely. To give herself time to pull herself together, she reached for her drink and took a slow sip.

'Of course, the press had a field day,' Elizabeth said bitterly. 'The vultures.' Then, catching Lyssa's questioning look, waved a hand vaguely in the air and forced a smile. 'Sorry – don't get me started on them. Let's just say that back then, they were less than sympathetic. It was 1966, and despite what we think now about the "swinging" 60s, the times were still not particularly liberal. And you can image what they made of a young girl from a prominent family living in sin with the long-haired singer of a pop band.'

Lyssa could well imagine. 'I expect "groupie" was the mildest thing they came up with.'

'And the rest,' Elizabeth said bitterly. 'To hear them talk, she was an immoral, drunken, drug-crazed, out-of-control nymphomaniac and nobody was surprised by her self-destruction.'

'They brought in a verdict of suicide, then?' Lyssa asked, keeping her voice calm and trying to bring down the emotional level a notch or two.

Elizabeth must have sensed what she was doing, for she took a long slow breath, drank some water, and visibly relaxed her shoulders. But then she was back to fidgeting again, and began restlessly tossing a small diamond-and-platinum cigarette lighter between her hands. With a small grimace, she pushed the lighter back into her bag.

'No,' she finally said in answer to Lyssa's question. 'The jury concluded it was accidental drowning, whilst under the influence of drink and drugs. The postmortem found a small amount of LSD in her system, and quite a lot of champagne.'

Lyssa didn't know what to say to that, so she said nothing at all.

That's when Elizabeth Grainger lifted her head defiantly, and levelled a long look her way. 'That's why I want us to put the record straight,' she said firmly.

It wasn't until they were at the coffee stage that Elizabeth brought up the sometimes tricky subject of money, and for that, Lyssa was grateful.

Although she wasn't worried that a woman who casually lunched at places like the Ivy and wore designer outfits that probably cost more than Lyssa's monthly mortgage rate would quibble at her fees. She just always hated to bring up the subject herself.

'Of course I'm happy to pay your going rate,' Elizabeth said. 'Perhaps a downpayment of 10 per cent up front, say, and then a monthly payment during the writing of a first draft, with a final payment and bonus on completion? Does that sound good to you?'

She then named a sum that made Lyssa very happy indeed – although she wouldn't start counting her chickens until her agent had gone over the contract details and the first deposit was safely in the bank!

'And this is for you,' Elizabeth said, reaching into her Gucci handbag and handing over a computer memory stick. 'It's all the stuff I've managed to collate about Monty from the family and my own research so far.'

'Thanks, I'm sure it will be very useful,' Lyssa said, slipping the small gadget into the internal, zippered part of her own (definitely not Gucci) handbag.

'There was also some cine film footage that was taken at Monty's birthday party, by one of the guests – you know, with one of those old handheld cameras?' Elizabeth screwed up her face in a wry grimace. 'Apparently, he was a bit of an amateur enthusiast – probably thought of himself as a potential film-maker or something.'

At this, Lyssa's heart rate shot up. 'I don't suppose you have a copy of it, do you?'

Elizabeth rolled her eyes theatrically. 'I wish! I was kind of hoping you might be able to find out more about it – who knows, maybe even track it down if by some chance it still exists. I remember Mummy telling me the swine who took the film went on to tell his experiences of the party to the press and also sold some of the stills from the film to the jackals for a tidy sum, but I haven't found out his name yet. I was hoping you might be able to identify him and see if he or his descendants might be willing to sell the film again – to us, this time.'

'I'll certainly do my best,' Lyssa said ardently.

'Right, then. I'll send over the contract paperwork via email as soon as it's all set up,' Elizabeth assured her, and with another energetic handshake, she was off. She walked fast, dodging around people and the waiters and waitresses as if anxious that they might slow her down. Lyssa, taking more time getting her things together, could only watch her with a sort of bemused wonder.

A few minutes later, she stepped out on to the High Street and, remembering her promise to Freida, texted her that she was now emerging, unscathed (and un-abducted) from the Ivy, and was heading home.

2

Back at the flats, she let herself into the small but thankfully light-filled and rather elegant foyer, glad to get out of the heat. The building was less than ten years old, but it had an art deco feel to it that sat well with the other beautiful architecture to be found in the city. White-painted, it was a modest but well-proportioned building, with black iron balconies, most of which housed tubs filled with flowers. These, and the small but shrub-filled front gardens, lent the place an air of distinction.

Inside, the dim light reflecting off the black-and-white tiled floor and cream walls gave her eyes a rest from the strong sunlight. (Typically, she had forgotten to take her sunglasses.)

Due to planning restrictions, Riverside House had only three floors with three sets of flats on each floor. She usually trotted up the two flights of elegantly curving wooden stairs to her own place for the sake of callisthenics, but today she was too hot to bother, so opted for the one and only lift. She was just stepping out of it when, a little way down the communal short corridor, a familiar head began to appear from the nearby flight of stairs.

'Carter! You're back early,' she said, making the American man swivel around on the top step to look at her, a smile instantly lighting up his features. Square of face and with a firm jaw, he had a smattering of freckles across his nose and cheekbones that were the bane of his life – or so he claimed. At five feet nine, he was shorter than Lyssa and had a mop of unruly sandy-coloured hair. He squinted at her through pale blue eyes rimmed with slightly gingery-coloured eyelashes, giving the impression that he might need glasses, but in fact she knew his sight to be excellent.

'Lyss!' he greeted her happily. 'Yes, I decided it was too nice a day to stay cooped up at the Bodleian.' He casually named the world-famous library as if it was as accessible to everyone as the local supermarket. 'Come on in, I've got a Chardonnay on ice, and Jason will only drink the lot if we don't get our dibs in first. And fast.'

Lyssa grinned and followed him into the flat. Every floor in the building had its one 'super-deluxe' flat, and two more run-of-the-mill offerings, and Carter Lansing III was most definitely one of life's 'super-deluxers'. The youngest son of a very wealthy American family, he wore his affluence easily and genuinely seemed to be unaffected by his privileged upbringing.

The flat was large and spacious and had been 'interior designed' to within an inch of its bricks-and-mortar life. On a cream-coloured corner sofa covered in impeccable natural fibres, a man lounged full length on one side of it, his head propped on the armrest and an open newspaper held out in front of him as he twiddled a pencil rapidly between his fingers and knuckles, the way magicians could. He was scowling ferociously at the crossword puzzle.

'What's a ten-letter word for . . . Oh, Lyss! Didn't see you there. Don't tell me, you've come to steal my Chardonnay?'

'*My* Chardonnay,' Carter corrected him tartly, with a wide grin.

The man on the sofa waved a hand dismissively in the air and threw down the paper and pencil on the coffee table beside him. 'Let's not quibble,' he said.

His voice was straight out of something you'd hear on an episode of *Downton Abbey*, which was not surprising as Jason

Howerd-Pitt's parents owned half the Berkshire Downs. Or was it half of Surrey? Lyssa could never remember which. She only knew that Jason was always moaning about his poverty, and the pitiful plight of the land-rich but cash-poor upper classes.

She took no notice of him.

Neither did anybody else.

About her own height, slim and dark, he had a brooding, tragic-poet air about him that he exploited shamelessly. He now walked, barefoot, to the large American-style fridge in the kitchen section of the vast open-plan space and opened it, extracting the promised bottle of wine.

'Sit down and make yourself comfy,' Carter said to Lyssa, waving a hand carelessly towards the massive sofa. 'Jase, if you give yourself a giant brandy glass and me and Lyss two sherry-sized ones like last time, I'll strangle you.'

Jason gave him a rude hand gesture along with a sly smile and, rolling his eyes, reached for three equally sized glasses.

Used to their lovers' banter by now, Lyssa sat back and relaxed on the sofa (it was so well sprung it was like floating on a cloud) and tossed her bag down on to the floor.

'Been anywhere nice?' Carter asked, coming to sit down beside her. He was wearing shorts, a plain sports shirt, and trainers without socks.

'The Ivy,' she said casually.

'Oooo, get her!' Jason mocked. 'You never take me to the Ivy,' he said to Carter.

'I can't take you anywhere,' Carter shot back.

Jason made a show of considering this, then nodded. 'Yes, that's true,' he acknowledged sadly. 'So, come on, then, fess up.' He turned to Lyssa. 'Who was he? And what does he do? And does he have a better-looking younger brother?'

At this, Carter snorted. 'You keep on threatening to leave me for another man and one day I might just let you. And then where would you be?' he mock-threatened. Totally unfazed by this, Jason blew him a loving kiss.

'It wasn't a "him", it was a "her", so sorry to disappoint you,' Lyssa corrected, cutting across their antics before the two jokers could really get into their stride. 'And it was work. It's beginning to look as if I've got my next project – all being well,' she added, holding up both hands and crossing her fingers.

'Do tell,' Jason said. 'I'm still reading that biog you did of that racing driver a couple of years ago.'

'You've been reading that forever,' Lyssa said, giving him a mock-angry look. 'What, do you only read a sentence a day or something?'

'He can't actually read, didn't you know?' Carter cut in. 'I blame his Eton education. So, who's the subject this time?'

'I don't suppose the name Amelia "Monty" Montrose means anything to you,' Lyssa said. 'Not your generation for a start, plus she was British and not American.'

'It's ringing faint bells with me,' Jason said, bringing two poured glasses of wine to the table and depositing them in front of each of them, before going back to the kitchen counter for his own. 'Wasn't she something of a notoriously bad girl back in the day?'

'Not according to her "sort-of" great-niece, she wasn't,' Lyssa said mysteriously.

'Come again?' Jason said.

Briefly, Lyssa went over her lunch-time date with Elizabeth and the story of the Lucky Cuckoos' unofficial fifth member.

'That's right, it's all coming back to me now. I think one of my more aged relatives might even have known her,' Jason said, slipping on to the end of the sofa and stretching like a cat. 'I vaguely recall an aunt who once mentioned . . . someone-or-other having a right old gossip session with her about the Montrose "problem child". You know how these pesky relatives will insist on descending on the family home at Christmas and then going on about the good old days when they've had one too many Campari and sodas, bless 'em. I think one of Monty's sibs was very bitter about the whole show – having the family name dragged through the mud and whatnot, and reporters besieging the estate and skulking about with cameras in the shrubbery and frightening the horses, etc, etc. Or was it the other way around, and they were complaining about how the press were treating her? I can't quite remember.' He shrugged his thin shoulders graphically. 'Either way, I got the impression that she was part of that whole wild-child 1960s scene they had going on back then. Wasn't she a noted "beauty", like Twiggy or "The Shrimp"?'

'The Shrimp?' Carter echoed in disbelief, giving them a double take. 'They named themselves after seafood?'

'She was a beautiful model in the 60s, and her last name was Shrimpton,' Lyssa corrected him with a grin. 'I only know that because, over our lunch, Elizabeth was waxing lyrical about all things 60s. The only things that came to my mind when I thought of those times were the kinds of stuff that everyone thinks of – Mary Quant and miniskirts, the Beatles, and London being the coolest place to be, and all that other good stuff.'

'Actually, there was a lot going on politically at the time as well,' Carter said. 'You had the big freeze in 1963 when you Brits were up to your necks in snow – quite literally – and then you had the Great Train Robbery, and over in the States, of course, JFK was assassinated. A year later Nelson Mandela was imprisoned for life, and your House of Commons suspended the death penalty in '65. And then Churchill died and . . .'

'Oh, put a sock in it,' Jason drawled, faking a huge yawn. 'We all know you're a walking encyclopaedia.'

'Anyway . . .' Lyssa cut in quickly, before the American could retaliate. 'Monty Montrose was never a model, but rather the girlfriend of the lead singer of a pop group called the Lucky Cuckoos.'

'Never heard of them,' Jason said, already beginning to look bored.

'Well, they might not have been as huge as the Who or Manfred Mann or any of the really big bands, but they had several hits before the lead singer died. Apparently, Monty and Glen Bannister – that's the lead singer – were one of the age's "golden couples". He was poor, working class and quirkily handsome, and she was a slender blonde daughter of the rich, landed gentry.'

'Cliché,' Jason sing-songed from the depths of his wine glass.

'Cynic,' Carter sing-songed back.

'From what Elizabeth said, the press wasn't kind to them at any rate,' Lyssa soldiered on, determined to keep the conversation on course. 'According to her, the conservative establishment that still ruled the press in those days delighted in putting them down whenever they could.'

'Jealousy,' Jason snorted. 'I hope they lived fast, died young and left good-looking corpses. That was the saying, wasn't it?'

'Well, they certainly did that,' Lyssa said sadly. 'Monty was only a day over twenty-three when she died.'

Carter whistled through his teeth in sympathy. 'Drugs, I take it?'

'Drowned in the pond in her garden. But with LSD and champagne in her system,' she corrected.

Jason opened his mouth, no doubt to say something cheerfully inappropriate, but subsided as both Carter and Lyssa shot him a sturdy look. Instead, he mumbled something and reached for the newspaper and began to study his crossword puzzle again.

'So, it's a whitewash job she's after, is it?' Carter asked, looking at Lyssa thoughtfully.

'Maybe, but I hope not,' she replied.

Carter nodded his understanding. He was unrepentantly one of the city's 'perpetual students' – one of those who came to Oxford to do a BA degree but then fell in love with academia and stayed on, doing degree course after degree course. His family back home had begun to despair of him, and from time to time used various bribes or threats to try and entice him back across the Atlantic and take a sinecure job in one of the family's many businesses.

Instead, he preferred to immerse himself in history – first taking his BA in History, but going on to do the MPhil on the Restoration period, whilst currently his DPhil thesis was covering the ancient British feudal system, back when King Alfred the Great had been trying to fight off the marauding Vikings.

He, unlike Jason, was a widely read man in many fields, however, and once he'd learned that his next-door neighbour was a ghostwriter and biographer, he'd read every word she'd ever written. Much to her profound relief, he had liked her work, and as such she often used him as an intelligent sounding board and valued his opinions highly.

Back when she'd first started out and needed all the commissions she could get, she had written a few biographies where it had been made clear to her that an unbiased view of things was neither required nor desired. However, she much preferred to write balanced and truthful books. And due to having a growing body of work and good critical reviews behind her, she was now beginning to find herself in a position whereby she could turn down a project that came with too many restrictions and wait it out for a few months to see if another, braver client came along.

'I'll have to see how my preliminary research goes. But even if only a few of Elizabeth's claims about the real Amelia Montrose are true, a book about her would certainly make for an interesting read.'

'What claims are these, then?' Jason asked, looking interested again, but Lyssa knew better than to discuss anything even slightly confidential with Jason. The man had all the discretion of a journalist spotting a politician at a seedy nightclub.

'You'll just have to wait and read all about it,' she teased.

'What? Don't you trust me?' he asked, clasping a hand over his heart, as if mortally wounded.

'She has far more sense,' Carter informed him crisply, toasting him with his glass.

Half an hour later, feeling refreshed and in a buoyant mood (nobody could be around Carter and Jason for long and not leave them without a smile on their face) she returned to her more humble flat and slipped off her sandals. She took a quick shower, and then after pulling her hair up into its usual high ponytail, wound it around and around in a bun, to keep it off her face and neck. It was much cooler that way.

On her way to her workstation by the window, she paused by a sideboard, on which rested a vase of freesias, a lamp and a large, framed photograph of a man. Even as a subject in a photograph, you could tell that he was a big man, with wide shoulders and a strongly corded neck. This was not surprising, since her husband had been a personal fitness trainer, and regularly worked out at the gym. A natural sportsman, he'd been able to hold his own on the tennis and squash court, play a mean round of golf, out-swim most and bench-press who knew how many kilos. Blond, moderately good-looking and with a wide, warm smile, he'd been a massive presence in her life and she missed him so much. She paused now to stare back at his image.

'Well, Kyle, what do you think about Monty Montrose? Wild child or Miss Understood?' She ran a finger gently over the glass-protected face and then forced herself to step away.

She walked to her work desk and sat down, opened her laptop and then reached into her handbag for Elizabeth's memory stick, and inserted it. With a click, she called up the first file and began to read.

~

About three and a half hours later, Lyssa suddenly became aware of a pain in her neck, despite the efforts of her prized, ergonomically designed swivel chair. Her shoulders also felt tight and rather sore. She knew what had happened, of course – she'd lost track of time, as she usually did whenever something engaged her whole attention, and now she was stiff from sitting so long in the same position without a break.

She sighed, reluctantly closed her appliance and, swivelling the black-leather chair a little to one side, glanced out of the window. It was that period sometime between late afternoon and early evening, when the sun, though still relatively high and bright in the sky, was beginning to change from bright white light to something just a little more mellow that forewarned you the night was coming.

It was the perfect time for a short run. Donning her jogging outfit and running shoes, she went through the warm-up exercises that Kyle had taught her, then headed out to her favourite route along the riverbank.

She wasn't what she thought of as a 'natural' jogger and had never even considered the activity until she'd met Kyle. He, of course, could have run a marathon, but she had never aspired to such dizzy (and exhausting) heights, content to merely keep him company for a mile or so, but unable to match his pace for any longer than that.

Nowadays she kept to a much slower time, little more than a fast-walking pace actually, but it suited her better, and meant she could go further, more comfortably. It always amused her when eight-men rowing teams sped past her on the water as if she were standing still, but she was content with the fresh air, moderate exercise and the de-stressing release of endorphins.

Her circular route completed, she returned home, took another quick shower, pulled on her oldest pair of leggings and a loose T-shirt then walked over to her small kitchen area to check out the contents of her fridge. They weren't particularly inspiring, but she had the makings of a mixed-bag omelette and set about chopping up some ham and slicing a large beef tomato.

As her hands busied themselves with her meal, her mind was going over all that she'd learned about her latest subject so far.

According to Elizabeth's view of things (and Lyssa wasn't going to take any of that for granted without independent research of her own), Monty had been no mere hanger-on in the Lucky Cuckoos camp; and certainly not just a pretty face whose sole role had been to keep Glen Bannister happy and amused. Instead, she claimed that her relation had been the fundamental force behind the band's success.

To back up this contention, Elizabeth had managed to find several documents and receipts establishing that Monty had used her own money to help fund the band's original efforts to hit the big time. (After inheriting money on her eighteenth birthday from her deceased grandparents, she'd raided the trust fund to buy the band new and better instruments and a comfortable touring van, and paid studio fees to get their demos cut.)

Not only that, it had been Monty who'd chosen – and initially paid – their manager, Luke Raines, for his services. And in a cut-throat industry notorious for dodgy management dealings, he had turned out to be one of the more trustworthy financial advisers who hadn't ripped them off with poorly worded contracts. This meant that the band had never been cheated of royalties, nor had they been forced, like so many other bands at the time, to sue in court for ownership of their own songs. He hadn't accepted backhanders from the more unscrupulous record company bigwigs or radio broadcasters either.

A shrewd, hard, canny man, he'd steered them straight and (from what Lyssa was able to tell on first showing) had successfully kept them in the spotlight for four years – which, in an era overflowing with talent, had been no mean achievement in itself. He'd also been something of a Dutch Uncle to the band, doing his best to try and keep them from the excesses to which young, working-class lads, on suddenly finding themselves flush with money and fame, must have been prone.

On these facts alone, Lyssa could tell that Monty Montrose had indeed been no mere pretty face.

But the one thing which had stood out most of all for Lyssa after spending an hour or so trawling through old newspaper articles about the Cuckoos – the one constant theme that the band had ultimately become most famous for – was the irony of their chosen name.

For although the Lucky Cuckoos did indeed become notorious for their luck, their luck was mostly all bad.

Very bad.

The first indication of this was obviously the tragic death of their lead singer, Glen Bannister, but it was as if his early death became a catalyst for the tragedies that were to follow.

Their lead guitarist Ron 'Racey' Joiner became severely alcoholic, perhaps partly due to the band's decline in the latter half of the 60s, but there was also much speculation that his father – who'd also been similarly afflicted – played a significant role as his enabler. The father died in 1972, but his son was not long in joining him and was dead by the age of thirty-five.

The next to suffer was the drummer, Micky Ventriss, who lost all of the money the band's manager had accrued for him, the victim of a clever conman who cheated many investors out of millions of pounds. As a result, he became increasingly bitter and self-destructive, and eventually his wife left and divorced him, and was awarded custody of their children. Forced to take menial jobs to support himself, he died aged forty-five, a bitter and resentful man.

But perhaps the one who suffered the most in this jaw-dropping run of bad luck was the band's other guitarist, Arthur 'Artie' Lowell, who lost both his wife and only child in a car accident in the late 1970s, and became a recluse, living on a small Scottish isle and never venturing out in public again. He died in his early sixties, never having remarried.

And, of course, although not an official member of the band, there had been the fate of Monty herself, the beloved or reviled (depending on your viewpoint) wild child and icon.

No wonder the Lucky Cuckoos had earned for themselves such an unenviable place in pop history as one of the unluckiest bands of that era.

And just how, Lyssa mused, should she tackle this aspect of the book?

3

As Lyssa began to eat her evening meal, at her own home in High Wycombe Elizabeth Grainger was standing on the patio overlooking her small but well-maintained garden. The view was spectacular, as her house was situated high in the valley, but she hardly noticed it nowadays. Instead, she had her mobile phone clamped firmly to her ear, awaiting the call she'd just punched in to be answered, and was restlessly tapping her foot on the paving stones.

In the garden's dwarf silver birch tree, a chaffinch was trilling heartily, and bees droned lazily around a colourful flower border. No gardener herself, Elizabeth nevertheless paid someone to keep the plot immaculate, for beauty in design and form were, and always had been, her passion. And since her detached home was also where she had her office, from which she ran her interior design business, everything about her residence had to be a showcase for potential clients. Anything less than an immaculate garden wouldn't cut the mustard.

She'd been in business for nearly fifteen years, now. A husband (or two) had come and gone in that time, but her love for colour, form, fabric and harmony in her surroundings had remained. And now, if things went well, she was anticipating being able to finally take her career up a notch or two.

Designing for wealthy friends and relying on their word of mouth for commissions from strangers was all very well, but if she wanted to make a real name for herself and be rated among the likes of Kelly Hoppen, Nina Campbell and Nicky Haslam, then she needed to up her game.

Born to relatively wealthy parents, she'd always been well heeled and used to ease and a certain amount of privilege, but she'd also been fiercely ambitious and competitive. It wasn't enough for her to live life in the slow and comfortable lane, when what she really wanted to do was soar. And it had become apparent to her over the years that if she was to make it to the big leagues, she needed serious money behind her.

Which was why she was intent on grabbing the opportunity to make the most of what had just landed in her lap. For once, her late and infamous relative was going to come up trumps – if she, Elizabeth, could just wangle it.

But she knew she didn't have much time.

In her ear, the ringing tone changed to that of a human voice, and one she knew very well. And after the usual, amorous greeting and whispered sweet nothings, she steered the conversation on to more practical ground.

'So, about my little scheme. Is everything in place? Did you manage to find someone?'

'Yes, it couldn't have worked out better for you, as a matter of fact,' the man on the other end of the line said, and Elizabeth listened in growing gratification as he explained what he meant by that. When he was finished, she nodded to herself, a small smile playing over her lips.

'You're right – that was a stroke of luck, and I'll get in touch with him right away. Let's hope it's a good omen. Now that I've got the ball rolling, I want to make sure that I know just where it is that it rolls.'

'You think she'll take the commission, then?'

'Oh yes, I think so,' Elizabeth said, casually crossing to a lounger and sitting down on the edge of it. 'She won't be able to resist. The research bait that I gave her will hook her all right.'

'If you say so, sweetheart. But I think you're putting a lot of faith in what can only be, at best, a long shot.'

Elizabeth sighed. 'Have a little optimism, darling. I did my homework, and Lyssa Moore is one of the best biographers around. She's an Oxford graduate, don't forget, so she's clever, and rooting about in the past and finding out about people and their lives is what makes her tick. She'll come through for me, I can just feel it.'

There was a brief silence on the other end of the line, and then a soft sigh. 'Well, let's just hope she isn't *too* clever, shall we?'

Elizabeth blinked for a moment, not following his meaning, then, when she did, gave a brief shrug. 'Don't worry about that. I'll make it part of the contract that she keeps me updated on her progress every other day, and if it looks as if she might cause trouble, I'll head her off and keep her on track.'

'If you say so,' the voice said doubtfully in her ear. 'At least I've paved the way for you with my contact, so you can get on to the man right away. He'll be able to help with anything like that, and he's expecting your call.'

'Don't worry, I'll do that right now, tonight,' Elizabeth promised. 'I'm not about to forget what's at stake, believe me.'

'Oh, I do! Well, good luck, sweetheart.'

'Thanks,' Elizabeth said, blowing 'kiss, kiss' noises down the phone before hanging up. She sat for a moment, frowning out over her lovely garden, but not really seeing it, as her mind whirled.

A long shot? Yes, she supposed commissioning the book was that. But after meeting her at the Ivy, she was confident that if anyone could find the proof she needed, it was Lyssa Moore.

She only hoped it was just there to be found.

The next day, Lyssa woke to the sound of rain pattering on the windows and thunder rumbling ominously somewhere in the distance. The hot weather of the past few days had broken – as it was wont to do in England – with a summer thunderstorm.

She rose, showered and dressed in thin white cotton trousers and a cool silk blouse the colour of moss. She put her long black hair up in the usual high ponytail and poured herself a cup of coffee. Outside, lightning flashed, and she moved to the French windows to look out over the river. The trees were swaying in the wind, and the river, sky and cityscape looked uniformly grey with only a few people scurrying about under umbrellas. But she knew the cloudburst would soon pass, and then the city's inhabitants and visitors would quickly come out again to go about their business.

She walked to her workstation and, setting her coffee to one side, quickly logged on.

There was another email from Elizabeth, which she opened and read quickly. The contract would be winging its way to her within the next few days, and she wanted to know how Lyssa would like her fees paid: bank transfer, old-fashioned cheque or even cash. (The last option came complete with a smiley face.)

'Wow, that's quick work,' Lyssa muttered.

The email went on to say how much she was looking forward to their collaboration, and how she couldn't wait to see her outlines for the book.

'No pressure, then,' she murmured to herself again, and shot off a quick reply. And with such a pushy client to keep happy, she decided she'd better get on with it and began to make a 'to do' list on a fresh notepad.

The first and most obvious task was to try and find anyone from back then who was still alive and willing to be interviewed for the book. Or, more likely, the direct relatives of those concerned. The trouble was, given the bad luck that had dogged the band members, she wasn't sure how any of them would feel happy about contributing to a biography that was bound to rake up so many bad memories.

Another priority was to find out who had taken the film footage of Monty's last party and see if it could possibly still be in existence. The first part of that shouldn't be too hard. The newspapers at the time would have published the film-maker's name in their interview with him, and if their back issues hadn't yet been digitised (which most had) she could always slog her way through some microfiches!

Resolutely, she set to work.

~

It was her rumbling tummy that eventually succeeded in breaking through her concentration, making her look up from her computer screen and check the clock. It was nearly one thirty, and seeing as she'd forgotten about breakfast, she was now in need of sustenance. On the plus side, her search engines and the various databases available to the public nowadays hadn't let her down, and at least she had a list of potential sources for the book.

Which reminded her, she was going to have to come up with a working title for it.

Thinking up book titles was her least favourite thing, since she found it almost impossible to reduce seventy thousand words or more to a single concept. Besides which, she knew from experience that any title she came up with would inevitably be changed either by the client themselves or the publisher.

Which was why she wouldn't spend much time on it. Nevertheless, she needed a working title beyond merely 'the book', and so she was pleased, when popping two slices of bread into the toaster, when her subconscious came up trumps by sending the Troggs song 'Wild Thing' hurtling into her mind.

'Perfect,' she said out loud, snapping her fingers. 'Right. *Wild Thing* it is.'

She cast a quick look over her notes so far. On it was a depressingly small list of names (as most of Monty's contemporaries had already made the obituaries) but it was a start.

So far, she had managed to track down and find contact details for Emily Bannister, the youngest sister of Glen, who must now be in her seventies. From her research, she knew that Monty had been putting up Glen's parents, as well as Emily, for the duration of the weekend when she'd held her fatal birthday party.

Although Glen's sister would only have been ten or eleven years old at the time, and had probably been put to bed long before the partygoer had discovered Monty's body floating in the pond, Lyssa still harboured hopes that she would be able to provide her with some much-needed, first-hand experiences of those days.

She had also tracked down Ron 'Racey' Joiner's widow, Monica, who had long since remarried and was now going under the name of Farley, as well as their daughter, Jennifer. Jennifer Joiner, Lyssa supposed, would probably have been much too young to remember her late father very well, let alone the band he had belonged to, but she might prove to be a treasure trove when it came to family photos. She might even have kept a scrapbook, or some other ephemera that could be useful.

Then there was Jonas Bannister, the son of Glen's younger brother, Robert. Jonas, from what she'd been able to glean from the social media posts of his own children, was a businessman of some wealth and standing. She'd gained the impression that he was a rather conservative and private man, and she thought it very unlikely that he would be particularly enthusiastic about a book telling the story of his long-dead rock-star uncle and his notorious wild-child lover, but sometimes you never knew.

She would need to find many more people to talk to, of course, both in the music industry at that time, and any of the reporters (or more likely, their children) who had written about the celebrity couple. But it was a start.

As for contacting various members of Monty's family, she thought she could safely leave that to Elizabeth – she would know who amongst her family would still be around and willing to talk about her. Although, from reading between the lines over their lunch conversation, she'd got the impression that her client's enthusiasm for the book wasn't widely shared. Still, once a project got off the ground, it sometimes gathered its own momentum, and Lyssa was nothing if not optimistic and determined.

She ate her toast minus any toppings (she usually had a tin of baked beans lurking about in a cupboard somewhere, but not today) and after taking a quick check outside to see that the storm had indeed passed, decided she would nip down to the nearest mini market and do some grocery shopping. Her mother might be a virtuoso of the weekly super-shop, but Lyssa had never quite mastered the art and tended to leave things until the cupboards were actually bare before venturing out in search of supplies.

Slipping her feet into some espadrilles and grabbing a light summer cardigan, she snatched her keys and bag and headed out the door.

After skipping down the stairs and crossing the hall, she was just about to reach for the communal front door when it opened in front of her and a man stepped inside.

'Neville!' Lyssa greeted him warmly. 'When did you get back?'

'The day before yesterday.'

'Carter mentioned you'd gone away somewhere – was it anywhere nice?'

'Oh, just a business trip, unfortunately.'

He lived in the super-deluxe flat on the ground floor and was a handsome man somewhere in his late thirties or very early forties. It annoyed Jason, who was perpetually nosy (especially about handsome men), that he hadn't been able to winkle out Neville's exact age yet, nor much about his background, or even what he did for a living. For all his apparent friendliness, it had quickly become apparent to Lyssa and her gang of friends that Neville Rickman didn't talk about himself much.

Six feet tall, with hair almost as black as her own and dark brown eyes, he was slender and looked fit. Jason insisted he could only be that toned through ruthless squash-playing, but he had no evidence to back this up – which was typical of Jason's theories.

Freida, who fancied him even more than Jason did, had been similarly unlucky in teasing out of him any titbits of information, and for all that he'd lived in the building for some years now, all they really knew of him was that he was probably single because he lived alone and kept odd working hours. That he could afford one of the big flats indicated that whatever he did must pay well, and he drove a nice, mid-range but unspectacular car.

Jason, who had tormented Carter into buying a flashy sports car, declared that it was the one thing about Neville that disappointed him.

Naturally, the gang had nicknamed him 'The Man of Mystery' and 'The Most Out There Game' had produced some real beauties about him. Carter, perhaps more stung by Jason's obvious drooling over him than he'd like to admit, had sardonically dubbed him 001-and-a-half, suggesting that he was a low-level intelligence officer for MI5, who was nothing more than a glorified clerk who liked to pretend that he was James Bond's sidekick. Freida had him down as a top-secret government scientist working on a secret weapon in a secret lab (this was Oxford, naturally, where science was always being done somewhere) and was working selflessly all hours of the day and night on something that would one day save the Western world. Lyssa had opted for him being a UFO researcher, who scoured the land for alien spaceship sightings, which Jason had leapt on and insisted on going one step further by saying that Neville himself was an alien in disguise.

Right at that minute, though, he looked human enough in a lightweight summer shirt and jacket combo over dark blue trousers. He appeared to be vaguely tired and maybe a little rumpled, though – perhaps he'd just got back from a long shift somewhere? The thought made her feel instantly guilty, and she stepped aside hastily so that the poor man could get past her and to his bed.

'Well, I'm just off out to the shops. Do you want me to get you anything?' she offered. Since he hadn't been back long, maybe his fridge was as empty as hers.

'Thanks, but I'm fine for the moment,' he said, giving her one of his nice smiles, the one that crinkled the attractive crow's feet at the corner of his eyes. 'Working on anything interesting?'

'Might be,' she conceded. 'I just got a new commission. Know anything about 1960s pop music?'

'The Kinks,' he said promptly. 'I'm a Kinks fan, personally.'

At this, Lyssa had to laugh, thinking of the look that would have been on Jason's face had he been with them. 'I'll have to remember that,' she said, and aware that she was still standing there like a lemon, gave a sudden nod. 'Well, I'd best get on with it, in case it starts raining again.'

Even as she said this, she looked beyond him out of the open door and saw nothing but sunshine and blue skies and felt like kicking herself. Of all the lame things to say.

'Yes, good idea,' Neville said smoothly and, so saying, moved past her and headed for his door. Her face feeling rather warm, Lyssa shot outside, cursing herself for her awkwardness.

It didn't take her long to do her shopping, and once back in her kitchen, she distributed her various purchases to the fridge, freezer and cupboards.

That chore done, she picked up her phone and notebook and made herself comfortable on the couch. Now, to try and track down the man who had filmed Monty's last party.

As she'd hoped, she soon found a website dedicated to 1960s scandals that had a section devoted to the Monty and Glen 'tragedy' and one newspaper interview with a partygoer named Frank Tillman.

He had been a bass player in one of the short-lived bands that had been around at the same time as the Lucky Cuckoos – hence the invite to Monty's party – but which had never achieved significant acclaim.

In the article, he confessed to filming some footage of the party, 'never realising they would be Monty's last moments'.

Ignoring the rather specious sentiment (given that he'd gone on to sell Monty out to the press), Lyssa set about finding any digital footprint for Mr Tillman. Not surprisingly, he had died some years before, but was survived by his only child, Justin.

And he, she was delighted to eventually discover, was not only alive and well, but living in the Northamptonshire town of Brackley. Which was not far away at all.

With a few clicks she found he had a profile on Facebook, and left a message, saying briefly who she was and what she was doing, and asking him to get in touch with her. She'd give it a day or two, and if she'd heard nothing back, she'd have to try a more direct approach.

That done, she started flipping through her notes, and came to Emily Bannister's details first. The youngest sister of Glen was now living in what had looked, online, to be a rather nice and upmarket care home for the elderly with more intensive nursing needs in Dorset. She was sure she'd written down the details, and sure enough, found it midway through her copious notes.

Punching the numbers into the telephone, she got through to the office, where a pleasant-voiced woman was able to confirm that Emily was indeed one of their residents. After Lyssa explained who she was and what she wanted, she was told that they'd speak to Emily and ask if it was all right for Lyssa to visit and then get back to her. Lyssa thanked them, gave them her own contact details and hung up.

She repressed a small sigh. She had been hoping that they'd simply confirm that Emily Bannister was living there and that whatever ailment afflicted the old lady, she was still mentally alert enough to talk to visitors. Most people enjoyed talking about themselves and the past, and even if Emily might have been a little uncertain at first, Lyssa was sure she'd have been able to put any of her doubts about the biography to rest. She certainly had no interest or intention of writing a prurient or inaccurate book, after all. As it was, Emily now had a very easy way out of it by simply telling her carers that she wasn't interested.

Next, she telephoned the head office of the company that Jonas Bannister ran. It claimed to support green and 'bio-efficient' businesses doing everything from manufacturing recycling bins to equipping incinerators. The website had leaned heavily towards stressing how 'green' the company's credentials were, and how it was 'helping the environment', but Lyssa (call her a cynic) had her doubts.

After having to select various options from an automated list, she found herself (naturally) talking to the wrong human being, who put her on hold, before transferring her (naturally) to another person who couldn't help her, before finally getting hold of a woman who said it was impossible for her to speak to Mr Bannister right then, but which energy company did she represent and would she like a business appointment? Patiently, Lyssa explained (yet again) who she was and what she wanted, and that it was a strictly personal matter, and was put on hold for nearly ten minutes.

Fighting the urge to hang up and swear, she forced herself to wait it out and was duly informed that Mr Bannister had been given her message and would think about it and call her back. Did she have an email address? Wearily, Lyssa gave it out and finally hung up.

She was not sanguine about ever hearing from Jonas Bannister (or any of his minions) again and made a note in her notebook to try once more in a few days' time and viciously underlined it.

Without much hope now, she tried Monica Farley's number next. As she heard the phone ring, she was quite prepared to discover that the lady was out, or had since moved, leaving no forwarding address, but after just a few seconds it was answered by a woman's cheerful voice.

'Hello, whoever you are. If you're trying to sell me double glazing, hard luck, I already have it, and no I don't want my loft reinsulated.'

'Oh, hello, is this Monica Farley?'

'I was the last time I checked,' the voice said breezily, and Lyssa couldn't help but grin.

Quickly, she launched into her little speech about who she was and what she wanted, fully prepared to receive a negative reaction, and so was pleasantly surprised when Monica gave a little squeal of delight.

'No! Really – you're going to write a book about Monty and the Cuckoos? That's great.'

Lyssa gave a little fist-pump of victory on her couch and finally began to feel more cheerful about her success rate. 'So would you be willing to give me an interview?'

'Oh, of course, darlin' – anytime, anywhere. I love talking about the good old days, because they really were, you know. Good old days, I mean. Woodstock, rock and roll, free love, the world was our oyster. Nowadays all we've got are computers that stuff everything up, bands that all sound the same and the world is going to a well-known hot place in a hand basket. Depressing, isn't it?'

Lyssa, quickly realising that she was going to have no trouble getting good source material from Racey Joiner's widow (and some probably quite sensational quotes!) got down to business. 'Where do you want to meet up? I can come to your home, but if that worries you, we can meet in public, at a café somewhere. You're in London, I think?'

'Barely.' Monica gurgled with laughter, but gave out her address without a qualm, and they set up a mutually convenient date for Lyssa to call on her at her home.

'I was wondering if your daughter Jennifer might be willing to chat to me as well?' Lyssa said, and for the first time there was a small silence on the line. Then, 'Well, she might,' Monica said slowly. 'I can always ask her. She was very close to him – hero-worshipped him, you know?'

'I'd be grateful if you would,' Lyssa pressed, sensing that for some reason she had put a small dent in the older woman's exuberant nature. 'And if you or she have any photos that you'd be willing to have copied for inclusion in the book, that would be wonderful. And would you mind if I took photographs of any memorabilia that you might have kept?'

'Oh sure, sure,' Monica said breezily. 'Help yourself. It'll be nice to see the band being remembered again.'

'The main focus of the biography is on Amelia Montrose, of course,' Lyssa felt compelled to remind her, 'but she was such a big part of the lives of the Lucky Cuckoos at that time, so of course, they'll all feature prominently.'

'Fine, fine,' Monica said nonchalantly. 'I'll get some wine and nibbles in. It'll be fun.'

Lyssa smiled. She had the feeling that Monica Farley, formerly Mrs Racey Joiner, still liked to live life to the fullest, and why not? Good on her! 'Sounds smashing,' she said. 'I'll see you soon then.'

She hung up with a happy sigh and wandered over to the window. This was going to be a great book – she could just feel it.

4

Positively upbeat, Lyssa turned to her laptop and revisited Elizabeth's notes. Now that she was feeling inspired, she wanted to tackle a major element of the book.

Lyssa knew that Elizabeth was keen to 'rebrand' Monty from her present status as a misunderstood self-indulgent wild child to someone far more well rounded and sympathetic, and was relying on her to do that through the medium of the first book to be written and published about her.

And one of the ways they could do that, they had both agreed, was to concentrate on the charity that Monty had set up.

At the time, sitting over their lunch in the fancy restaurant, Lyssa had been surprised when she'd learned of this aspect of Monty's character, and it had made her feel instantly uncomfortable and guilty. Without even realising it, she'd been thinking of Monty as a young and probably spoilt woman, living the hedonistic lifestyle with her rock-star lover, and totally immersed in the culture of drugs, drink and rock 'n' roll. Moreover, a woman intent on shaking off not only her wealthy family's credos, but also all the social shackles for which the 60s were infamous. A woman, then, who didn't devote much of her time to caring what anyone else thought of her.

So to be told by Elizabeth that Monty had founded a charity only a year before her death had forced Lyssa to confront just how unintentionally biased she had been. And now, still feeling guilty about that, she was determined to research this aspect of the dead woman with a chastened heart and a resolve to start to get to grips with the true character of Amelia Montrose.

Alas, Elizabeth's notes on this aspect of her late relative's life were rather meagre. She knew it had been called the YMT, short for the Young Mothers' Trust, and that Monty had asked someone called Deborah Simmonds to help her run it. To make matters worse, Elizabeth had been able to find very little documentation for it, and assumed, sadly, that it had all fizzled out after Monty's death. Nevertheless, Elizabeth insisted that family lore had it that Monty had used a good portion of her own money from her trust fund to set it up and get it going, but if she had actively campaigned for other donors, Lyssa might find corroborative proof that way.

Sitting at her work desk, Lyssa couldn't help but wonder if Monty's lover, Glen, had been a contributor as well? He would certainly have been in a good position to make a sizeable donation to the new venture. Maybe that was something that could ultimately be ascertained?

Putting that aside to be investigated for another day, she concentrated on what Elizabeth had managed to dig up, finding that the bulk of it consisted of newspaper references to the charity, which were nearly all as scathing as the references to Monty and the band. It was as if the media at the time was determined to find nothing good in the new, emerging youth culture of the day, and so had derided the YMT as yet another sign of Monty's degenerate nature.

Basically, the self-righteous editorials had argued, if this indulgent and wayward young woman genuinely wanted to do good, why didn't she support the perfectly valid and upstanding institutions that already existed? It wasn't as if there were a shortage of good causes to support, they'd gleefully pointed out.

Instead, Monty had set up a charity for unmarried mothers, with the aim of allowing them to keep their children instead of giving them up for adoption, whereby their offspring could be raised by decent families, with decent values. It was, they decried, typical of the increasingly degenerate ethos of the times that she should actively support the immoral behaviour of young unwed mothers.

Reading it now, Lyssa could only shake her head in wonder. The gutter press coverage was a mixture of the usual headline-grabbing rubbish, but the editorials written in the more quality broadsheets were in some ways even worse.

Abandoning Elizabeth's slim file, she went online, and eventually tracked down something more useful, in a *News of the World* (of all things!) interview with a young woman who had been one of the first to benefit from the YMT.

Janet Connor had been a fifteen year old with a baby son who had been kicked out of her family home by her outraged parents when her pregnancy had become obvious. She, at least, had nothing but praise for Monty, who had taken a personal interest in her plight. Despite the reporter's obvious nose for scandal and salaciousness, Janet Connor had still somehow managed to put across some of Monty's compassion and had vigorously praised her for the practical help Monty and the YMT had been able to provide for her and her son.

It took Lyssa nearly two hours online to track Janet down on social media. She'd married later in life, but had then divorced and reverted to her maiden name again, and now, aged seventy-six, she lived in a trailer park in a seaside resort in Hampshire. She had been surprised by Lyssa's phone call, but obviously had never forgotten the woman who had helped her all those years ago, and would, she assured Lyssa, be very happy to talk about Monty for the book.

They quickly arranged a suitable day and time for them both, and deciding she'd quit whilst she was ahead, Lyssa finally closed her laptop and rubbed her tired and now somewhat dry eyes.

She felt a familiar soft headbutt against her leg, and looked down at her cat. 'Hello, Bibbie – finished giving the sparrows a hard time, hmmm?' she murmured. Her cat liked to sit on the balcony, lying in wait for any birds that might land on the railings, and then give them the fright of their lives.

So far, he'd never caught one, for which she was heartily grateful.

He was a big and hefty cat, and as she lifted him up and put him on her knees, she gave a little grunt. 'If you get much bigger, I might have to consider cutting back on your treats.'

She rubbed under his chin, which was warm and soft, and his green eyes half closed with pleasure. She leaned down and rubbed her chin on top of his head and smiled when he started to rub his cheek against hers.

'Well, someone loves me,' she said with a smile. 'Or else, someone is trying to get around me so that I don't cut off his supply of fishy-wishes.'

It was at this time of the day, when it was drawing to a close, that she wished her husband would walk through the door as he'd used to, wondering what was for dinner, and asking how her day had been, and did she fancy doing something silly over the next weekend?

But the door didn't open, and Kyle didn't come through it, and Lyssa fought her usual battle against the ache of his loss as she put Bibbie down and walked over to the kitchen area. Opening the fridge, she reached determinedly for the salmon fillet that she'd bought that afternoon and put it under the grill to cook. Naturally, Bibbie wound himself around her ankles whenever she tried to move.

As she steamed some vegetables, she forced her mind to think about work again, this time focusing her thoughts on money. Money, it seemed to her, had played a major part in the Lucky Cuckoos' and Monty's story in one way or another.

Monty, of course, had always had money and had grown up secure in the knowledge that she'd always have it, whereas the working-class boys from the band, when they'd started out singing in the local pubs, hadn't a bean to their name.

When that had begun to change, Glen had bought his parents a house and car, as well as giving sizeable gifts of money to all his siblings in one way or another. So, it had undoubtedly come as a severe shock to them that, when he'd died so suddenly, his last Will and Testament had left all his estate, including all future royalties on his records, to Monty.

Even when it came out that Monty had made her own Will at the same time, leaving Glen all her worldly goods also, and that the couple had done it as a typically extravagant gesture of their love and commitment to one another, she'd still come in for huge criticism – most of it from Glen's parents, naturally enough, as well as from her ever-present foe, the hostile media.

Why should she, who already had a wealthy family behind her and access to a substantial trust, profit from the death of her lover, a working-class boy made good? And when Glen's parents, Frank and Joan, vowed they would fight to have the terms of the Will overturned in court, the press had been right behind them.

Monty had refused to make her thoughts on the threatened lawsuit public, perhaps knowing it would be pointless to try and get public sympathy behind her. Instead, she'd apparently tried to make every effort to mediate the problem herself and had been trying to come to some sort of compromise with her dead lover's parents.

Elizabeth had managed to find some letters written to Monty from one of her friends that confirmed all this, although in the letter her friend made it clear that she thought Monty was wasting her time trying to be nice, and that the Bannisters were a greedy bunch who wouldn't be satisfied until they'd got the lot.

But the fact that Monty had invited Joan, Frank and their youngest daughter to stay over in her house on the night she'd chosen to celebrate her birthday, certainly indicated that she had still been trying to keep things civil, and hadn't yet given up trying, even on what was to turn out to be the last night of her life.

But what must have been going through her mind about it all? Lyssa paused in the act of putting her plate under the grill to warm. Glen would have been dead for barely six months, and his loss must have been still very raw for her indeed. Plus, Monty must have remembered the reasons why they'd named each other as sole beneficiaries, and loyalty to his memory must have made her feel that if her lover had wanted her to have his legacy, then she shouldn't go against his last wishes. And yet, if she loved him (and Lyssa was already quite convinced that Monty had loved him fiercely) she must have been torn by the desire not to upset his parents either.

The acrimony and in-fighting must have been unbearable for her.

Had it been enough for her to want to end her own life? Was it possible that the verdict of accidental death had been the wrong one? Drunken, lonely and not thinking straight, might she not simply have decided that she'd rather rejoin her lover in the next life than stay and fight things out in this one?

Two floors below her, Neville Rickman was drinking a cup of coffee and contemplating his life in general – and one person in particular.

Lyssa Moore had always been one of his quieter neighbours, never playing loud music or pestering him for cups of sugar or intruding on him in any way, and for that he was grateful. The nature of his work meant that he valued his privacy, and maintaining a certain anonymity was par for the course.

So far, he'd had no reason to regret moving into the small, select block of flats in this quiet part of the city, and he only hoped it would stay that way, now that things had just got a little more complicated.

When he'd first moved into the building, it had taken him some time to get to know his neighbours and their regular visitors, and Freida's habit of flirting with him he found both flattering and amusing. He could do without Jason Howerd-Pitt's constant nosiness, however, but at least his immediate neighbours on the ground floor kept themselves to themselves. Jason's partner, the rich American student, was all right but tended to be a little suspicious of him, which was understandable, and he only hoped it wouldn't become a problem now.

He didn't normally allow his business to intrude on his home life, but in this instance it was both unavoidable and made good sound sense.

And of all the people in the building, the one who most intrigued and interested him, and always had, was Lyssa Moore. Which had now become rather ironic, really.

It was funny how life could twist and turn in ways that you never expected.

But he told himself that now was not the time to wax philosophical – he much preferred being pragmatic. With that in mind, he used his online banking app to check on the current status of his bank balance and saw that the agreed initial payment for his services had been paid into his account, as promised.

So, no cause for worry there, then. Not that Neville was a man given to worrying unduly; his business was thriving, he was living the good life in a lovely city and had no responsibilities weighing him down. And if he was beginning to feel as if there should be more to his life than this, well, that was just life, wasn't it? He was getting to the age when a lot of people begin to question their choices and wonder if mistakes had been made. Neville didn't think he'd made any – well, not any real howlers, anyway.

But running into Lyssa Moore in the hallway earlier had left him feeling a little restless and antsy. A vague feeling that he might be missing out on something important was niggling away at him, and he didn't like that.

He shrugged the vague feeling away and decided to order in his favourite Italian meal. But no wine. He would need to keep a clear head and be on top form from now on.

~

Someone else contemplating food – but without much enthusiasm – was Jonas Bannister. He was in his office in Gloucester, working late as usual, and was considering phoning his wife and asking her to meet him in town at a restaurant of her choice. It might go some way to appeasing her for yet again failing to return home in time for dinner.

He sighed and turned his swivel chair so that he could look out over the city. It was technically in the Cotswolds, and a lot of the buildings were made of the famous pale cream Cotswold stone, but it was still a city and therefore wasn't exactly the quintessential vista one thought of whenever the area was mentioned.

Whereas the village where he lived truly *did* enjoy the Cotswold vibe to the max, being surrounded by rolling green hills dotted with sheep, winding lanes and vernacular architecture, and it even had a stream running down the length of the main thoroughfare. Every front garden of every picturesquely quaint cottage frothed with colourful plants, and the village pub had a reputation for good food and local ales. And he prided himself that his home – a large Georgian mansion, complete with a century-old wisteria growing around it – was considered by many to be one of the pearls for miles around.

The only drawback to his choice of living quarters was the summer visitors who descended every year, snapping away on their mobile phones and invading the 'niche' shops that catered to their various whims. The locals guarded the parking spaces outside their homes like the settlers from the American Wild West, fending off outlaws. Not that he had that particular problem, naturally, for his home was set in its own extensive grounds, which were kept immaculate by an army of gardeners.

He noticed his wife never complained about any of that!

He gave a small grunt and turned his chair back to face his desk, a slight scowl settling over his brows. He was a slim man, with grey hair and eyes, and well-kept hands. He liked to swim as a means of relaxation, liked to dress well, and knew that his children called him 'fussy' behind his back.

He was by nature a complacent man, but right now he was feeling a little out of sorts, and had been ever since his secretary had told him about the nature of Lyssa Moore's phone call.

For the first half hour or so afterwards, he'd barely given it a thought and had simply carried on working, but as the afternoon wore on, he found his mind being pulled back to it, like an oyster that had found that a tiny but irritating piece of grit had somehow found its way into his shell.

Why would anyone want to write a book about Amelia Montrose of all people? he asked himself crossly. Just why did people feel the need to drag up the past anyway? What was the point? His uncle's band had long since faded into decent obscurity. The Lucky Cuckoos – hah, what a joke that name had been for all of them. Bad luck had followed them around like a bad smell.

But it had not, he had to admit grimly, been the same for himself. In fact, he and the rest of his family had done very well out of Glen's share of their fame and fortune.

He glanced around the office now, as if seeking reassurance. The building wasn't new, but wasn't old, and had style, and it lent status to the businesses that had their offices here. He made sure that the furnishings in their corporate offices were renewed every three years, and the décor the same. He was constantly expanding and growing the company, and over the last decade it had really hit its stride, and now their offices took up one entire floor. This was not surprising, since everyone was becoming terrified of global warming, and the public was getting wise as to which companies were trying to do something about their carbon footprint and those that were merely faking it. Never had the services of his Bannister BioSolutions been more in demand.

But even after successfully taking over his father's legacy upon the old man's death and turning it into a growing power and multi-million-pound concern, he could never quite forget what had made it all possible to begin with. And that it all harked back to the 60s and the death of his father's brother.

He tried to console himself that nobody nowadays would remember that or even care about it if they did. All that mattered – what had always ever mattered in the world of commerce – was success. And he was a success. No doubt about it. In every way, he could be counted as a man who mattered.

His children had gone to the best schools, his wife wore diamonds, they holidayed anywhere in the world they wanted. He sat on committees, he dined in clubs in London with the likes of private bankers, politicians and the movers and shakers in the City.

And yet, he could never quite shake off the little voice in the back of his head that sometimes mocked him whenever he felt particularly proud of some coup or other, a voice that laughed at him and reminded him that it was all based on some silly pop songs.

It was annoying because he knew it to be true. If his father's more handsome and talented brother hadn't formed the band, written the songs and sung them to adoring silly teenage girls who ensured they sold millions of copies, then his own father wouldn't have had the capital to start up the fledgling business in the first place, and Jonas' life would have turned out so very, very differently.

Would his own father, Robert, have managed to escape somehow from the vast housing estate where he and Glen and all the other Bannister children had been born? He doubted it. He'd almost certainly have got a job at the local factory, and married a local girl and had a brood of unruly kids just like everyone else they knew, and would have thought themselves lucky to have enough to pay the council's rent.

And when he, Jonas, had duly come along, it would have been off to the local no-hoper of a comprehensive; no smart grammar school and a decent education for him, no chance to make good social contacts that would set him up for the rest of his life. And who knew what would have happened to him after that?

One thing was for sure – he wouldn't be sitting in this smart office in Gloucester, with a home in the Cotswolds and a discontented wife and ungrateful offspring to keep happy.

His spiralling thoughts were suddenly interrupted by the buzz of the intercom and his PA's voice. 'Mr Gorman is here for you, sir.'

Glad of the distraction, Jonas told her to send him in and then leaned back into his chair as his chief of security came into the room.

Ian Gorman was a former soldier who looked as if he still felt vaguely uncomfortable out of uniform, even if he was wearing an expensive suit. But he was no Neanderthal and, after leaving the army in his early forties, had done several IT courses with a vague idea of setting up his own private security business. Luckily, a mutual friend of theirs had introduced them to each other, and Jonas had never regretted talking the man out of becoming self-employed by offering him his current position within the company.

Competent, loyal, canny and (when necessary) not too scrupulous about his methods, Ian was a decided asset, and one that definitely earned his keep. Which was more than could be said for Jonas' firstborn son, who came into the office whenever he felt like it and seemed to think that entertaining potential business clients with expensive lunches and showing them a good time in town was all that was required of him.

'Hello, Ian – I have something I want you to do for me,' Jonas greeted him, with forced cheerfulness. 'On the QT, mind.'

His security chief raised one dark eyebrow. He was not a particularly big man, but he was wiry and fit. His brown hair was slightly receding, his features were unremarkable, and he could pass in any crowd without anyone paying him the least attention whatsoever. Which had sometimes come in handy.

Jonas' company, like a lot in the 'green' industry, had had its fair share of environmental protesters who didn't believe that Bannister BioSolutions were doing enough to help save the planet, so someone who could infiltrate their groups and cause mayhem and disruption when necessary was essential.

'Trouble, sir?' Ian asked now.

'No, no, it's nothing really, but I do want to nip something in the bud before it becomes a problem. There's a woman called Lyssa Moore – she claims to be a writer of biographies and such. I want you to do a deep background check on her. See if she's legit.'

It was always possible that this initial approach from Miss Moore might not be as straightforward as it seemed and, before he met with her, Jonas wanted to know exactly who – and what – he was dealing with.

'All right. Anything else?'

Jonas hesitated for a moment and then sighed and shook his head. 'No, not just yet,' he said. There was no point in borrowing trouble after all, he told himself. 'But be as fast as you can and report back to me tomorrow. Some further action might be called for down the line.'

Ian nodded, showing no curiosity, and left as silently as he'd come.

Jonas watched him leave before swivelling his chair back around and staring out blankly across the cityscape.

He was probably worrying needlessly, but he was a man who liked to prepare for the worst, just in case. And he doubted that this Moore woman had just decided to write a biography about his uncle and his wild-child lover for no good reason. Someone must have commissioned it.

And it certainly wouldn't have been anyone in *his* family. Which meant it had to be someone in hers. Amelia Montrose.

He'd been aware of who she was when he was growing up, of course, and seen various photographs of her, and during his teenage years he might even have had a crush on her. His dead uncle's lost love. All very romantic and all that rot, but he'd quickly grown out of it.

It had been years now since he'd thought about her, or the Lucky Cuckoos.

But obviously someone was thinking about them now – and he had a good idea who. The question was – why? Why now?

The intercom buzzed again. 'Sir, your wife is on line one,' his PA informed him.

With a small grunt, Jonas leaned forward to depress the lit-up switch and forced a smile into his voice. 'Sweetheart, I was just thinking about you. How would you like to come into town, and we'll eat at that new place you mentioned the other day?'

5

When Lyssa awoke the next morning, she lay still for a while, listening to the muted sounds that leaked in from outside. A river boat hooted at someone – probably a student rower who hadn't seen them coming – whilst a blackbird was singing in one of the silver birch trees that had been planted in a nearby garden. The traffic noise, even during rush hour, was little more than a mild susurration, and she forced herself not to roll over in the double bed and touch the empty, cold side where Kyle had once slept.

Instead, she got up on her side of the bed, had a quick shower, checked on the state of the day outside – which was sunny and bright – and chose a white cotton skirt and a vintage cheesecloth top in rainbow colours that she'd discovered at a village fete many years ago. Putting up her long black hair in its usual high ponytail, on a sudden whim she tied a colourful orange ribbon around its base and let its long silken strands ripple down to her back along with her hair.

She made herself a cup of coffee, and was about to start work on the preliminary notes for the first draft outline of *Wild Thing*, complete with a first-chapter synopsis, when the doorbell rang, and she detoured on her way to her workstation to answer it.

'Hello sweet 'ums, you do look lush this morning,' Jason greeted her, walking in and holding out a bag that smelled of something delicious. 'I've been down to that deli on the corner and got a couple of bacon butties. It was either that or something really wholesome and vegan.'

'Bless you,' Lyssa said, almost falling on his neck to kiss him. 'I can't remember the last time I had bacon.' She walked to a kitchen cupboard and brought out two plates, a bottle of brown sauce and two paper napkins which she transferred to the kitchen table.

Jason pulled out one of the chairs tucked neatly away underneath it, and parked himself happily, taking a massive bite out of his bap. He then pulled up the top half of the bun, splodged in a dollop of extra sauce, and took another bite. Naturally, the sauce oozed out of the sides.

'Sheer bliss,' he moaned, then mimed pouring out a cup of coffee. Lyssa rolled her eyes at him but went to the coffee machine and obliged.

'I'll bet you're wondering what I'm doing up at this unearthly hour,' he said, dabbing at his lips with the napkin.

'It's gone nine o'clock,' Lyssa pointed out gently.

Jason faked a shudder. 'Is it really as early as that? It's Carter's fault – he's always up with the dawn and makes a hell of a racket. Anyways, I've come bearing more than one gift.'

'Should I be looking you in the mouth?'

'Undoubtedly! But in this case, I'm no knock-kneed old nag but a genuine white steed, the kind that knights are supposed to ride in on.'

'If you say so.'

'Remember I told you that I thought my family knew the Montroses, back in the day? Well, I was right,' Jason said, gaining Lyssa's serious and undivided attention now. 'Last night, I rang Mummy dearest, who demanded to know what I wanted, on account of my only phoning her whenever I want something.'

'Naturally,' Lyssa slipped in.

'Usually it's money, or the loan of the Bentley, or asking her to put up friends for a couple of weeks in the crumbling ancestral pile. I had to do that once when I was trying to butter up some Japanese business types, the kind who find ancient ruins quaint.'

'I can imagine your mother was delighted to have strangers foisted on her at short notice.'

'She didn't speak to me for three years, which was a real bonus,' Jason said, sounding genuinely pleased at the remembrance, then waved a hand in the air. 'Anyway, that's not important. You can imagine how relieved she was when I told her that this time all I wanted was to know if anyone in the old family lineage was still alive and kicking who remembered Amelia Montrose, and if so, could she tell me who.'

Lyssa felt her heart begin to beat a little faster. 'And since you're here now and looking like a cat that's eaten a whole smorgasbord of canaries, I take it that it means that your poor mother came up trumps yet again?'

Jason nodded. 'She did indeed. Apparently, I have an aunt called Edna – and before you ask, don't blame me. My family is rife with so many forgotten uncles and formerly unknown cousins and great-great-great-grand whatnots, that it's hardly a surprise to find I have an Edna lurking about in the family cupboards. Anyway, this particular aunt is now ninety-four apparently, but don't despair, according to Mummy dearest she's still as sharp as a pin. For some reason known only to herself, she married a chap called Frobisher who was something in frozen peas.'

Lyssa nearly choked on her coffee. 'Frozen peas?' she managed to repeat.

'Yes – he owned deep-freezing plants or something. I don't know, do I?' he said, his voice rising a few octaves as he robustly defended himself. 'You know me and commerce,' Jason said, beginning to look cross. 'The only thing I can do with money is lose it or spend it. Don't keep distracting me. Where was I? Oh yes, good ol' Aunt Edna. Anyway, according to Mummy, she knew Monty's sister very well and they spent a lot of time at the Montrose family pile when they were both giggling schoolgirls or whatever. And she remembers all the fuss surrounding Amelia's blackening of the family escutcheon by running off with a rocker. By the way – what exactly is an escutcheon? I've been accused so many times by various kith and kin of being a blot on it, that I've often wondered.'

Lyssa, who was nothing if not a wordsmith, opened her mouth to happily tell him, but seeing this he hastened on before she had a chance to do anything so terrible as actually educate him.

'Poor Amelia caused quite a stir, apparently,' he swept on. 'I got the feeling from reading between the lines that it rather tickled Aunty, even if it didn't quite have the same effect on the Montroses. Well, you wouldn't expect it to, really, would you? I daresay if Aunty Edna had been the one running off with a rocker, then my great-grandmother would have had a hissy fit too.'

'Just tell me your dear old aunty is willing to talk to me, and I'll loan you the use of my Bentley anytime you like,' Lyssa said fervently.

'You don't have a Bentley.'

'Don't nitpick.'

'Fine, fine, and yes, the dear old girl seems dead keen to chat to you. Says she likes to talk about the old times, and the Swinging 60s were a hoot. And that's a direct quote from Mummy dearest, who had it direct from the horse's mouth.'

'I could kiss you.'

'Please don't.'

'When can I see her?'

Licking brown sauce off his fingers, Jason pulled a rather grubby piece of paper from the pocket of his jeans and handed it over. 'Here are her contact details. It seems the frozen pea king left her well off when he popped his clogs, and she's now living in the lap of luxury in Basingstoke or Bracknell or something beginning with a "B" anyway.'

Lyssa, who was quickly jotting down the details in one of her ubiquitous notebooks, said mildly, 'It's Brockenhurst, actually, or a small village not far from there. That's the New Forest, I think.'

Jason gave another mock shudder. 'Rather you than me, darling heart. Personally, I wouldn't go into a forest if you paid me.'

Lyssa rolled her eyes at him. 'Go on, then, I'll bite. Why not?'

'Because I was frightened stiff by that song "The Teddy Bears' Picnic" when I was four years old. Never was able to stand teddy bears after that. I always insisted on having an Action Man figure instead. Well, that's what I told Mummy dearest anyway.'

Lyssa had to endure that and other nonsense for another ten minutes or so before Jason checked his Rolex (last year's Christmas gift from Carter), gave a little shriek of alarm, claimed that he was going to be late for a meeting with a man about a dog, and lit out.

Closing the door behind him with some relief, she instantly picked up her landline phone (since her mobile was still charging) and dialled the number Jason had given her. It was answered almost immediately by a young cheerful voice that couldn't possibly belong to a ninety-four-year-old.

'Hello? I'm hoping to speak to a Mrs Edna Frobisher? My name is Lyssa Moore. Mr Jason Howerd-Pitt, her nephew, says she's willing to talk to me about a book I'm writing?'

'Oh yes, that's right. His mother phoned last night and told us about it. Mrs Frobisher is very excited about it; she likes having a good old natter about the old days. I'm Cassy Dalton, by the way, Mrs Frobisher's live-in help. I'll just get her for you – she's still in bed.'

'Oh no, don't disturb her,' Lyssa said quickly. 'I was just hoping to set up a time and place for me to come down and talk to her. Will she mind if I record it, do you think?'

'I shouldn't think so for one minute,' Cassy said with a laugh. 'She'll probably demand that you play it back to her so she can hear it for herself. She's as curious as a cat about everything still. Marvellous for her age, she is.'

'And her memory is good, is it?' Lyssa asked, crossing her fingers.

'Oh yes. Well, about years and years ago it is. Just don't ask her what I cooked for her dinner yesterday though!'

'Fair enough,' Lyssa said happily. 'When will be a good time for me to visit?'

'Oh, anytime. We don't get out much nowadays.'

Lyssa gave a quick check through her diary and set a time and a date.

'See you then,' Cassy Dalton said cheerfully, and hung up.

Lyssa was about to do the same when she heard, above the disconnected sound coming from the other end of the line, a slight whine. It was high-pitched and short-lived and then abruptly cut off. It was a sound she'd never heard over the wire before and, as she hung up, she wondered if there might be a fault on her landline. She knew BT were in the process of changing from the old technology to digital, but she'd had no notification of it in her area yet.

Slowly, she put the phone down. It was an old model and had already been in situ when she and Kyle had first bought the place nearly six years ago. Then, not quite knowing why, she picked up the receiver again and put it to her ear. She thought she heard a faint click. But then just the dialling tone.

She put the phone back and told herself not to be so silly. She was acting like a heroine from a woman-in-peril film! Besides, she didn't have time to start getting paranoid about her phone line.

Today, she had somewhere she needed to be, and she needed to get herself to the train station within the hour.

She didn't often get up to London, and she wasn't totally sure where Monica Farley's home was situated, so she wanted to leave herself plenty of time to find it. If necessary, she could always get a taxi from the nearest train station in the general vicinity, for Elizabeth had assured her that she'd pay any necessary expenses.

~

In the end, the taxi *was* necessary, for Lyssa found herself not far from Kew Gardens before she got off the train, and even then Monica's home was still several miles away, set in a very leafy suburb-of-a-suburb which, by rights, probably couldn't claim to be in London at all.

But it was very nice for all that (maybe because of that?) and as she stood outside a well-proportioned terraced house in an affluent-looking street, she had to conclude that either Monica had done very well out of her divorce from the Lucky Cuckoos' lead guitarist, or her second marriage had been to a man with plenty of money of his own. Or maybe she had made it the good old-fashioned way, by working hard!

She knew from her research that 'Racey' Joiner had married young, and to a girl from the same poor neighbourhood as himself. What must it have been like for her to go from working-class poverty to the status of a celebrity's wife, and all the sudden affluence that came with the band's bigger hits?

Well, she supposed she was about to find out.

Walking up a smart front garden, she rang the bell set beside the conservatively black-painted front door and waited. This was one of the things she loved about her job. Like all ways and means of earning a livelihood, there were highs and lows no matter what career you followed, and in her case the isolation involved in working alone and the painstaking but necessary checking and rechecking of facts could get her down sometimes. But meeting new people and listening to their interesting stories was definitely one of the bonuses.

Lyssa knew that the woman who answered the door had married Racey Joiner in 1969, when she was just twenty years old, and that just after this the band had finally split up for good. Which, according to her mental arithmetic, meant that Monica must now be seventy-five or -six years old, but she looked a lot younger.

Slim, not too tall, with well-coiffured silver hair and pale grey eyes, her bone structure had stood her in good stead, for she was still a handsome woman. She was wearing a floor-length kaftan-style turquoise dress with lots of silver jewellery, and she gave a wide, welcoming smile.

'You must be Lyssa Moore?' she greeted her, thrusting out a bony hand. 'I was so curious after you got in touch that I'm currently reading a couple of the biographies that you've done. I must say, I'm enjoying them enormously – please come in. I'm afraid my daughter, Jennifer, couldn't make it today, though she wanted to, but I gave her your number and she'll be in touch.'

As she spoke, she ushered Lyssa through a spacious hallway and into an even more spacious lounge, done out in white, but with accent colours of turquoise (her favourite colour, maybe?) and different shades of green. The whole effect was cool and restful.

'But I'd better warn you now, my daughter probably won't be a pushover,' she added.

At this, Lyssa felt her spirits drop a little. 'Oh? I hope the idea of the book doesn't upset her?'

'Oh, lots of things upset her,' Monica Farley said with an attempt at a careless smile that didn't quite come off. 'She was an only child, and I think she felt lonely. I tried my best to reach her, but we found it hard to connect somehow. Perhaps that's why her father meant so much to her – though, to be honest, he never really spent much time with her. Too busy with his music – you know how it is with artistic types?'

She sighed, then indicated a large sofa. In front of it was a coffee table, upon which rested a large jug of something with a lot of ice cubes in it. 'Pimm's,' Monica said, catching the direction of Lyssa's gaze. 'I know what you're thinking – what's the former wife of an old rock-n-roller doing drinking such a posh drink? But I became hooked on it when I was with Racey, and it sort of stuck. Please sit down. I can get you something else if you prefer?'

Lyssa had never tasted the drink before but wasn't about to put her hostess to any trouble so early in the interview. 'Oh no, that sounds lovely, thank you.' She took out a digital recorder she used for such occasions, put it down on the table in front of her and turned it on. 'You don't mind if I record this, do you? I'll be jotting down a few written notes as well.'

'That's fine, go ahead,' Monica said airily. 'It's been so long since I gave an interview, I've almost forgotten the thrill!' She sat down on the sofa facing her and poured out the drinks. 'I think it appeals to my vanity. Mind you, by the time I married Racey, the Lucky Cuckoos were a bit of a spent force, but I'd been around a few years before we actually tied the knot, so I still remember the fuss about their last big hit, even if Racey and I weren't officially an item then. That didn't stop the press from pestering me for quotes though.'

'This would be their last hit song you're talking about? The one in' – she quickly rifled through her notebook and found the page she wanted – 'er . . . 1965, I think, "Take it All"? Is that right?'

Monica leaned back and nodded. 'That would be it. My, my, I haven't listened to that in some years now.' She hummed a few bars of the melody and then sighed. 'For a while, after Racey died,

I played the Cuckoos' hits a lot but . . . well . . .' She gave a shrug of her rather scrawny shoulders and spread her hands in a 'what can you do' gesture. 'Time goes on, doesn't it? I remarried, and now – what, it's been, what, sixty years? *Sixty years*,' she stressed, sounding mock-scandalised. 'How on earth did *that* happen?'

She shook her head and took a long sip of her drink, and Lyssa followed suit, almost choking when she discovered that Pimm's, whatever else it contained, certainly contained alcohol. For some reason – perhaps because it was a hot day, or perhaps because the drink came in a jug full of ice, she'd been expecting a soft drink.

She hastily put her glass down well out of the way. 'You must look back on those days with fondness,' she prompted.

'Yes, but so many people do, don't they?' Monica mused philosophically. 'Even those who barely remember them or hadn't even been born in the 60s still talk about them as if they wish they could go back there.'

'Perhaps that's not so surprising,' Lyssa replied. 'They were iconic times, after all. The fashion, the music, the emerging youth culture – it must have been a great time to be young and in the midst of it all.'

'Oh, it was! We had the time of our lives, I can tell you,' Monica enthused. 'I can still just about remember there being rationing as a kid – it didn't phase out until the mid-1950s, you know. Growing up in those dreary years just after the war with nothing to call your own – wearing my sister's hand-me-down shoes, which didn't quite fit and gave me blisters on the back of my heel. If you got an orange and some nuts in the Christmas stocking you'd be glad, and a bar of chocolate . . . !' She threw up her hands with a grin. 'Nowadays kids have all these fancy toys and gadgets and whatnots, and they still never seem satisfied. It makes me sad to see my great-grandkids so spoilt. Back then, we seemed to be happier with the little we had, but then we were all in the same boat, so we didn't know any different, did we? I went to the same primary school as Racey's kid sister, Valerie, that's how I met him, back when they first got together as a band. Oh, I was only a kid then, mind you, but even at the tender age of thirteen or fourteen, I knew that I wanted Racey!'

She gave a laugh, then shook her head. 'Drove Mum mad, me hanging around them, but it was so exciting, and actually marrying the lead guitarist . . . ? That shut Mum up, you bet! All that money, and a respectable ring on my finger. She soon changed her tune then – if you'll pardon the pun.'

Monica gave a gurgle of laughter and then sighed, the smile quickly falling away. 'Of course, we didn't know how things would turn out later – how could we? That bloody awful traffic accident, and Micky losing all his money to that rotten lying bastard, like he did. And Racey, drinking himself into an early grave . . .' She took a long, fortifying gulp of her drink, then shook her head and put another determined smile on her face. 'But why remember the bad times, when you can remember the good ones, eh? That's what I say. Whenever I look back now, I think only of the good things – the big hits, the riding around in fancy cars, the boys buying their parents homes and drinking champagne for the first time – and eating an avocado!'

Here Monica grinned hugely. 'Would you believe, we'd none of us ever heard of an avocado before. It was a big deal, eating one. Racey hated the taste but pretended he didn't. Bless him! Mind you, all the boys tried to pretend they were sophisticated and that the money and fame was just one long yawn. But they loved it. Why wouldn't they? Wouldn't you?'

Lyssa nodded. 'I'm sure I would. Tell me, who actually got the band together?'

'Oh, that was Glen and Micky, the drummer. Micky brought in Racey – him and Racey worked in the same factory, that's how they knew each other, and Artie Lowell was in the pub when he overheard them all talking about forming a band, and sort of auditioned himself into it. Not that they were anything to write home about for a while – just four good-looking lads, singing songs in pubs for the price of drinks and enough petrol money to keep them going.'

'Until Amelia Montrose came along? She financed them, didn't she?'

Monica slowly nodded. 'Yeah – I'd almost forgotten; that's why you're here, right? Because of Monty.'

'It's her biography, yes, but she died so young, and the Lucky Cuckoos were the biggest event in her life, so they're bound to feature prominently. That and her relationship with Glen, of course. From what I've been able to tell, he really was the love of her life.' She paused. 'Or was all that so much moonshine?' she asked softly. 'Sometimes, legends can build up that have little basis in reality, and it's hard to tell fact from fiction.'

She was watching Monica's face closely as she said this, for if there was one thing that Lyssa had learned whilst writing for – or about – other people, it was that everyone liked talking about themselves, and they also loved it if they could put you right if you made a mistake. And she was curious to see how her interviewee would react to the bait she'd just cast upon the conversational waters.

Monica slowly frowned. 'No, I don't think you're wrong about them,' she said cautiously, maybe even a little reluctantly. 'I know I was just a young teenager back when Monty and Glen were around, but I had eyes in my head, and I could see she was genuinely crazy for him. Whatever else Racey thought of her, even he had to admit that she loved Glen.'

Lyssa felt her heart rate rise but made sure none of her excitement showed. 'What do you mean? You make it sound as if Racey and Monty didn't see eye to eye.'

At this, Monica snorted inelegantly. 'You might say that, yes.'

'What *did* he have against her, then, do you think?' Lyssa prompted mildly.

Monica shot her a shrewd look, then smiled. 'Don't worry – I won't hold back on you. Why would I? They're all dead and gone now, aren't they? Nothing can hurt them any more.'

'I'm so glad you see it that way,' Lyssa said, relieved that she wasn't going to have to use all her skills to drag information out of someone who was becoming reluctant to talk, now that things were getting really interesting. 'And if you've read my books, you'll know that I'm not a sensationalist. I don't go out of my way to drag reputations through the mud – but I don't flinch from looking things in the eye either.'

She made sure she was maintaining good eye contact with the other woman as she continued to talk. 'Monty's relatives have commissioned the book and, obviously, they want a truthful but mostly affectionate account about those days and times. For myself, I also want my readers to get to know the real people behind the myths and icons. For instance – Monty's Wild Child image. I've seen some of the newspaper reports, and to me they seemed to be way over the top.'

'Oh, hell yes,' Monica said, nodding vigorously. 'The press really had it in for her. And, to a certain extent, the band as well. But you're right, she seemed to get the brunt of it. I never thought it was fair, even back then, as a self-obsessed teenager who was only interested in getting and winning her man! She got a raw deal, no two ways about it.'

'Perhaps because of her background?' Lyssa suggested. 'It's one thing to see working-class lads making the big time, but the establishment doesn't like it when their well-brought-up daughters go rogue.'

Monica grinned widely. 'Sod 'em, is what I say. And good on her too! Give the woman her due, Monty never wavered in her commitment to Glen and the band, though some of the things they said about her in the papers must have hurt. I can remember her laughing it all off, but still . . . Pity. They got her in the end though, didn't they?' she mumbled.

'Got her?'

'Well, you know, dying young the way she did. I suppose drinking and whatnot was a way of blotting it all out for a bit. She was only human, after all, and it must have got her down, secretly like.'

'Yes. In a way, though, it sealed her status as a legend, didn't it? Dying young and still so beautiful,' Lyssa said, playing devil's advocate.

Monica sighed. 'I suppose so. But I'm glad I got out with my skin intact,' she said, with another of her cheeky grins. 'I was one of the few associated with the Lucky Cuckoos who did!' Then she instantly sobered again, and Lyssa began to wonder if the reason behind her swift change of moods might have something to do with the fact that the jug of Pimm's was already half empty when she, Lyssa, had first arrived.

'My poor Racey never recovered from losing the band, I know that for sure,' Monica said now, sounding mournful for the first time.

'They finally split up just before 1970, didn't they?' Lyssa clarified.

'Yes, they limped on for nearly four years after Glen died, but they never could get themselves sorted out without him. Racey was absolutely livid about that. He felt that they should have gone on and become an ever bigger smash without him.' Monica reached for her glass of Pimm's and took a long swallow. 'And he always said that the reason they didn't was Monty's fault.'

6

'*Monty's* fault?' Lyssa couldn't help but yelp a little at that. Catching Monica's look of surprise, she hastily apologised. 'Sorry, I didn't mean to sound so judgemental. But how on earth could it have been Monty's fault? She died only months after Glen did, didn't she?'

'Ah, that's true,' Monica said, playfully wagging her index finger at Lyssa before smiling slowly. 'But she was making trouble long before then.'

Lyssa knew that Monica was enjoying herself enormously now, but she didn't begrudge her that. Especially as it was becoming clear that she was going to spill everything that she knew – and by the sounds of it so far, some of those details might well prove to be sensational.

'I'm all ears,' she said with a grin of her own, turning the page on her notebook, and surreptitiously checked from the corner of her eye that the recorder was still on and working properly. She didn't want to miss a single thing that was about to be said.

'Well, you have to understand, I got most of this from Racey after I married him, and the Lucky Cuckoos were more or less defunct by then,' Monica began. 'When they were in their heyday, I was around, but only as a young girl, a friend of his little sister. Nobody took me seriously or paid any attention to me – certainly not Racey. Not then. I don't want you getting the wrong ideas about him or the other lads in the band. It wasn't until I was over eighteen and began to fill out that he noticed . . . well, you get the picture.'

Lyssa nodded.

'So, most of what I'm about to tell you has been coloured by Racey's point of view. For myself – well, to me, the band were just the most exciting thing in my life, and I was so made up to be on even the fringes of it all. And Monty was this glamorous figure with a rich daddy – she wasn't like anyone I'd ever met. The way she talked with that posh voice of hers, and her clothes, and the way she swore and didn't care! My mum would have washed my mouth out with soap if I'd come out with even the least of the swear words she used! She fascinated me, but not in the same way as the band and the music, so my focus was always on Racey. And to be honest, I wasn't old enough or mature enough to come to my own conclusions about the dynamics going on within the band.'

'I understand. Please, go on.'

'Well, OK, just bear in mind what I've said, then,' Monica admonished. 'Anyway, according to Racey, when the band began to form in the early days, their roles weren't so clear-cut as they became after Monty appeared on the scene. Both he and Glen played guitar, but they took it in turns to sing songs.'

'And these were their own songs?'

'Oh, hell no! Most of them were cover versions of past hits, either from here or over from America. You know, Elvis songs, or whatever.'

'OK, thanks. So, basically they were taking it in turns to sing "Blue Suede Shoes" down at the local Dog and Duck or White Horse?'

Monica laughed. 'You've got it. Glen's voice was deeper and stronger, but Racey had a higher tone, and sweeter, so it really worked out well for them. Anyway, slowly, they began to gather a following – you know, older teenagers than me, both girls and boys who liked their sound. Word would get around where they were playing, and the pub would be packed. Racey, Glen and Artie were all real lookers, and Micky – well, bless him, he wasn't quite so handsome, but he had personality, if you know what I mean? Some of the fans saw him as a big brother, I suppose, and cute in a funny kind of way. Anyway, according to Racey, that was how things stood when Monty showed up at one of the pubs and began to pay attention to them. With Racey and Glen sharing the spotlight equally as lead singers.'

Lyssa nodded cautiously. Thinking back to all the songs she'd heard the Cuckoo's singing since taking on Elizabeth's commission, she could remember clearly Glen Bannister's well-known deep-timbred voice but couldn't recall hearing any other one that had stood out. Surely there had been only a general harmonising in certain parts, usually in the chorus. Like most hits in the early 1960s, the band's song formats were straightforward – chorus, verses, maybe with an instrumental bridge, repeat and so on. The lead singer usually sang the verses solo, and then the band would join in on the chorus. Occasionally you'd get groups where two men would sing together, but she didn't think the Lucky Cuckoos had ever favoured that arrangement.

'I've listened to all their big hits now, and some from the albums, and, sorry if this sounds insensitive, but I don't know that I could pick out your husband's voice,' she confessed.

Monica nodded. 'Yeah – that's the point I'm making. Or rather, the point that seriously pissed off Racey. Once Monty got involved, it was Glen's show all the way. She said he had the bigger and more individual voice, and it was that that made them stand out from all the other groups.'

'She had that much power?' Lyssa asked, genuinely surprised. 'I wouldn't have thought, back then, that a young woman who wasn't even a member of the band would have been listened to, let alone been taken seriously.'

'Ah, but she was calling the shots, wasn't she, because she was the only one of them with this,' Monica said, rubbing her fingers together in the familiar gesture that suggested money. 'And lots of it. Before she came on the scene, even their instruments weren't paid off, and they were still making monthly payments on them. Then Monty shows up, loves their sound, and begins splashing the cash. A new touring van – poof, there it is. Studio time? No problem! Getting their records played on the local radio station – "Oh, I know the DJ, my cousin went to Eton with him, he'll do me a favour and play it for you" and next thing you know – airtime.'

Lyssa understood her perfectly. 'Yes, I get it. She must have seemed like a dream come true.'

'Or a nightmare, according to Racey.' Monica snorted a laugh. 'Yeah, she bought them top-of-the-range instruments, and got them airtime, and all the rest of it. But what she said went. Take the recording studio – whenever Racey sang a song, it somehow got relegated as a future album track – never a single release. Glen's voice "registered" better, or Glen's voice could be heard better over the beat, and so on and so on. By the time they came to cut their first record, there was no question as to who was going to be the lead singer.'

Lyssa nodded, not without sympathy. 'That must have been tough for Racey to take.'

'Oh, believe me, it was. He never got over being bitter about it, and who can blame him? It was his shot at the big time she was trampling on. At first, he put up with it because he could see that the band needed her. Back then there were so many groups of good-looking lads chasing the same rainbow, and nine hundred and ninety-nine out of a thousand never made it. How could they? They were mostly working-class lads like Racey and Glen, and they didn't know the industry. Unless they caught a lucky break – a really lucky break – they didn't stand a chance.'

'And Monty was their lucky break.'

'Too right she was, and she knew it,' Monica said. 'And Racey was no fool – he could see that, and so could the others. She swore that she believed in them and would do everything to get them to the top of the heap, so they were willing to go along with her at first. And to give credit where credit's due, she was as good as her word. Within the year, they had their first record cut, and it was a hit.'

Lyssa glanced at her notes. 'This would be "A Lovely Face" if my memory serves me right. Got to number five in the charts? Early in 1962, I think?'

'That's the one.'

'And that was written by Glen, right?'

'Sure. Well' – she hesitated and gave Lyssa a knowing look – 'let's just say it was his name that appeared on the record label,' Monica said dryly. 'But according to what Racey told me years later, he reckons that he and Glen came up with it between them one drunken night.'

'According to Racey?' Lyssa repeated, gently raising one eyebrow.

Monica nodded, refilling her glass of Pimm's. 'Yeah, well, personally, I think it a bit unlikely. When he drank, he really drank, and it used to make him nearly comatose, bless him. I doubt he'd have been able to write his own name, let alone musical notes. But I never argued with him. And I know for a fact that lyrics were not his thing. His sister used to laugh about how bad he was at English at school. But maybe he might have come up with some of the rhythm – although, again, from what I could tell, that was really Glen's thing. Let's just give him the benefit of the doubt and say that his memory of those days was sometimes a little hazy. And biased.'

Lyssa smiled. 'Fair enough. I don't recall that the Lucky Cuckoos were ever particularly notorious for their drug use – not like some famous bands we could mention. Even so, Glen did die of drugs, so they must have been readily available to the boys in the band. I was wondering if Racey's bad memory . . . ?' She trailed off delicately.

'Oh, I wasn't thinking of that so much,' Monica said quickly. 'And I don't want you quoting me, saying that I ever saw anything really heavy like that going down.' She glared at Lyssa.

'I won't,' Lyssa promised. 'Seriously, I don't lie to my sources, and I won't publish anything that I can't back up by solid research and proof. Besides, Elizabeth wants Monty's real story told, and that means an honest assessment of the times and her life. Nobody's interested in muckraking just for the sake of it.'

'Well, OK then, so long as that's clear,' she said, mollified. 'And don't get me wrong, we weren't whiter-than-white little plaster saints. We all smoked a little weed back then, but it was nothing excessive. Anyway, where were we? Oh yeah, the band putting up with Monty calling the shots.'

She cradled her drink, her rings chinking against the glass. 'The way Racey told it, the boys discussed how things were going, and the three of them – Racey, Artie and Micky – all agreed that once they'd got established and had another hit or two under their belts, that they'd ease Monty out and take over the reins for themselves. As they figured it, by then they'd have their own money to splash, and they could get back artistic control of their music and sound. Book their own studio time and mix songs how they wanted to, and Monty would be out.'

'I couldn't help but notice that you didn't include Glen in that line-up,' Lyssa said.

Monica gave an elaborate shrug of her turquoise-clad shoulders. 'Well, no, you couldn't expect the bloke to agree to that, could you?' she said, clearly determined to be fair. 'Almost right from the start, Monty laid her claim to him, and he didn't exactly fight her off!' She gave a little gurgle of laughter at the thought. 'Well, you've seen pictures of her – blonde, lovely, loaded, posh, what working-class bloke from the slums was going to make a fight of it if she dragged him off to her bed?'

'Weren't the others jealous at all?'

'Probably!' She gave a big grin, then shrugged. 'But Racey would have bitten my head off if I'd ever suggested that *he* was. Though, for my liking, he always protested *too* much about her, you know what I mean? Men don't talk down about a beautiful woman unless they're a bit obsessed with her as well, do they? Not in my experience they don't. Of course, I was safely married to him by then, so I wasn't that worried – and she was dead, of course,' she added with brutal matter-of-factness. 'But even so, her ghost lingered. He still talked about her a lot, years after she'd gone, and with a passion that was genuine hatred all right, but even so . . . I didn't really like it, you know what I mean?'

'Yes, I think so. A living flesh-and-blood rival is one thing, but it must have been hard to compete with a beautiful dead girl,' Lyssa mused. 'Especially one who had developed a legend around her, like Monty did.'

'Yeah, exactly – you've hit the nail on the head there, Lyssa. You can tell you're a writer.' She nodded approvingly. 'Racey always said Monty was the worst thing that happened to Glen and the band, but I never got over the feeling that if he could bring her back and replace me with her, he would. Just like that . . .' She tried to snap her fingers but didn't quite make it.

Lyssa found herself feeling rather sorry for the now tipsy older woman and wasn't surprised that their marriage had ended in divorce. No doubt Monica must often have wondered what would have happened if Monty had made a beeline for Racey instead of

Glen. And, like Lyssa, she must have suspected that Racey wouldn't have fought her off either.

'So, the band always intended to go their own way, once they'd made it?' Lyssa brought Monica back on track. She needed to get the bulk of her story down before Monica became too befuddled with Pimm's to talk straight. 'But Glen and Monty were still very much together when he died – and by then, it had been . . . what, four or five years? So what happened?'

Monica sighed. 'They underestimated her, I guess,' she said, beginning to sound a little weary now.

Lyssa was uncomfortably aware that her hostess was well into her seventies – and a tiny bit the worse for drink – and was worried that she might be tiring. 'We can always wrap this up now if you like, and I come back another day?' she offered gently.

'What? No, you don't want to have to track back down here.' She waved a hand dismissively, indicating to her to carry on.

'I don't mind, honestly,' Lyssa assured her.

'No, no, I'm fine. My hair might be white but I'm not quite in my dotage yet. What else do you want to know?' She made an effort to sit a little straighter and squared back her shoulders.

'You said the band underestimated her. What do you mean by that?'

Monica gave a wide yawn and then apologised. 'Sorry, don't know where that came from! Well, like you said, Monty was still in the picture right up until Glen died. And by the way, that was a real shocker, I can tell you. I know you probably don't believe me, but it's true. Like I said, the boys didn't really indulge in drugs much – perhaps that was the problem,' she said, her voice sad now. 'Glen wasn't that savvy about pills and stuff like that and only indulged now and then. He just didn't realise he was overdoing it. Anyway, none of us were expecting him to die like he did. So young. It absolutely floored Monty, I can remember that much.

Even as a callow young girl, I could see she was devastated. And so was Racey, in a different way, of course. He and Glen were best mates, and he loved him like a brother. Far better than Glen's own flesh-and-blood brothers did, let me tell you. To them Bannisters, Glen was just a walking pot of money. When he died, all they cared about was getting their hands on his fortune. It was Racey and the band who really mourned him.'

Monica's tone dropped a little now, as if remembering back to that day had sobered her. 'I came home from school and went straight to Valerie's house – the new one that Racey had bought for them. I loved going there because it was so much nicer than Mum and Dad's council house back on the estate. Racey wasn't still living with his parents, of course, he had his own place by then. I used to love going with Valerie to Racey's pad, especially because he had a pool and everything. And all these famous people would saunter along for a party and a singalong. Anyway . . .' She took a fortifying breath and sighed.

'That day, as soon as we walked into her mum and dad's house, we knew something was up. Racey's mum had been crying, and she looked nervous about something. You know, the way grown-ups did when they had to tell kids something unsavoury and didn't really want to do it. Anyway, she sat us down and told us that "Uncle Glen" – that's how grown-ups back then always referred to close friends of the family, as aunty or uncle . . . anyway, she just said that Uncle Glen had passed over. At first, we didn't really know what she meant, because we'd never heard that phrase before, but then Valerie's dad put it much more clearly. Of course, they never told us it was an overdose or anything – we only knew about that later, when it came out in the newspapers . . . He just said that Glen had been taken very ill and had died suddenly. Me and Valerie just cried our eyes out.'

Lyssa remained respectfully silent as a tear made its way down the older woman's face.

Impatiently, Monica brushed it away with the palm of her hand and, with a visible effort, pulled herself together.

'The next time we went round to Racey's place, everything was so different. Quiet. Sad. It had always been a habit for the rest of the band to go to Racey's to drink and socialise and have fun – well, not Glen so much, because he and Monty had Monty's Mansion – that's what they all called their place, behind Monty's back. I thought that was a bit mean and petty, even as a kid. I can't for the life of me remember now what the real name of the place was. It was just always sneeringly known as Monty's Mansion.'

'I think it was called Evergreen,' Lyssa put in quietly, glad that she remembered the name from her research. For some reason she couldn't have explained, it felt important to her that Amelia Montrose's home should be given its true name – the name that the two lovers who had lived in it had given it. Evergreen. Had they chosen it because they'd believed that their own love story would also remain evergreen? If so, it only made the tragic end of their story all the more poignant.

'Yeah, that's it. Evergreen,' Monica repeated prosaically. 'Anyway, that's where he died. Monty found him – you know the story around that, right? She'd gone out with friend to a show and was back late. Glen hadn't wanted to go – he was tired after working in the studio all day. And she found him . . . Well, gone. Poor woman – I can't imagine it . . .'

Monica shook her head. 'Let's not talk about such sad things, eh?' She forced her voice to become brighter, as if she could shake off the past that way. 'Have another drink?' She glanced at Lyssa's still-full glass and grimaced.

'I'm sorry if this is bringing back bad memories,' Lyssa apologised. 'We were talking about how Monty was still such a big part of the scene still, even though Racey and the others wanted rid of her.'

'Yeah, that's right,' Monica said. 'They never did shake her off, did they? Now why didn't they . . . ?' She paused, obviously thinking back, and sighed. 'Let's see – after the first hit, they had another hit the same year, "Lying Lips" – which got to number three, I think, which was a few places higher than the first one, but still didn't manage to get to that all-important number one spot. Perhaps they just thought they needed to keep her and her money around a little while longer, just to be safe.'

'But by then they had their manager, didn't they?'

'Luke Raines – that's right,' Monica said. And snapped her fingers. 'And, of course, Raines was Monty's find, wasn't he? So maybe that's why they couldn't shake her off? Raines must have been grateful to her for bringing him and the Cuckoos together and so he supported her whenever the band took against her.'

It sounded a little weak and unlikely to Lyssa, but she was wise enough not to say so.

'I understand he did a good job for them,' Lyssa said instead, wondering if the glowing accounts she'd read of the Lucky Cuckoos' and their manager's good working relationship was all so much pie in the sky, and Monica was about to come out with yet more proof that not all was as it seemed.

But she was quickly disappointed.

'Oh, yeah, he did,' Monica agreed at once. 'He was one of the good guys – even Racey had to admit that. He got good deals for them and didn't take the lion's share for himself, like so many of the buggers did back then. Ripped off bands left and right, they did. Not Luke. And he battled the record companies when he had to, really argued the band's corner and threatened legal action if the companies didn't come across with the contracts he wanted. And he always got the boys good gigs and better television coverage and what have you. But he and Monty were tight, all right, and agreed on almost everything. Monty was good at things like choosing the Cuckoos' costumes and creating their look, pleasing their fans, running the fan club and promotional stuff and all that sort of thing. Racey said between them, they had the Cuckoos all sewn up.'

'It sounds as if Monty was a major asset, and yet still couldn't do anything right.'

'Yeah – I did warn you, Racey's views on Monty were a bit cockeyed. I think he just really felt cheated, you know? Sure, the Cuckoos were riding high, and he had the money and the fame and screaming teenage girls chasing after him, and all that. But like I said, when he and Glen started out, they were on a level footing, and yet by the time they made it really big, it was Glen who was the one standing in front of the mike and in the spotlight, whilst Racey was just one of the lads, doing harmonies and playing guitar. You can't blame him for resenting it.'

'I promise you I'm not. But . . . forgive me if this sounds rather hard-hearted and a little bit ugly . . . I don't mean to but . . . didn't Glen's death, well . . . I mean, his sudden absence . . .' Lyssa struggled to find a way to put things diplomatically, but luckily for her, Monica was happy to help her out.

'What you're trying to say is, wasn't Glen's death Racey's opportunity to finally take over as leader of the band?'

'Well, yes.'

Monica nodded. 'Yeah – you'd have thought so, wouldn't you? But it wasn't that simple, was it?'

'Why not?'

'Because Monty had other ideas.'

For a moment, Lyssa said nothing; she was too busy trying to sort out her thoughts. Seeing her confusion, Monica gave a rather wan smile.

'Want me to explain?' she asked, sounding once again rather tired and dispirited.

'If you wouldn't mind,' Lyssa said, humbly.

'OK. You have to know a bit about the times back then. The music trends were always morphing. In the USA they went from Bill Haley and the Comets to more hard-rock bands, and then along came the Summer of Love and Woodstock and all the hippy-dippy stuff, right? So you had the likes of Bob Dylan rubbing shoulders with Jimi Hendrix. Talk about diverse.'

'Yes, I'm with you on that. The range of music in that decade is mind-blowing.'

'Exactly! And back here in the UK it was no different. We had the Beatles and "Love Me Do" which morphed into more hard-rock bands like The Who and what have you. Now the Cuckoos sort of started off in the Beatles mode – catchy rock songs, but hardly edgy, like the Stones, say. But by the time Glen died, times were getting "softer" if you like. The Moody Blues weren't far off producing "Nights in White Satin" and Simon and Garfunkel in the USA would later come up with "Mrs Robinson" so it's not surprising that the fans were starting to get tired of the Cuckoos' "old" sound and wanted something new and fresh. Or at least, that's what Monty was saying. And she was the one who always seemed to have her finger firmly on the pulse of what the fans wanted. Even Racey had to admit to that.'

'And she was right,' Lyssa mused pensively, thinking back to how the music from the mid-to-late 1960s was so different from that of the earlier years.

'Oh yeah, turns out she was right. As ever – good ol' Monty,' Monica said with a bitter twist of her lips, reminding Lyssa that her ex-husband wasn't the only one who was hardly Monty's biggest fan. 'But back then, the Cuckoos just didn't want to hear it. Well,

Racey certainly didn't, and neither I think did Micky. Artie might have been more on the fence though.'

'And Glen?'

Monica shrugged. 'Who knows? Maybe he agreed with her, maybe he didn't. But from what Racey told me, Monty was already trying to change their sound. Less "I Want to Hold Your Hand" and into something far more lyrical and gentle. She said that Glen's deep-timbred voice could easily make that transition – just think of the Walker Brothers or the Righteous Brothers. They had great, big voices, but they weren't necessarily belting out catchy pop tunes, preferring to mix them with ballads as well.'

'All right. It sounds like she had a valid point,' Lyssa said, careful to keep her tone neutral.

'Yeah – but Racey didn't agree. He said the band had a loyal following already, and that they were happy with their songs. Even though their only number one hit, "The Frightened Heart", was the least catchy pop tune of them all. And their second biggest, "Going Nowhere", which got to number two, had a similar set-up.'

'He still wanted to carry on with the old vibe?' Lyssa clarified, then added casually, 'I take it that that sound played to his particular strengths as a singer? After Glen died, he would want to sing songs that he could handle well?'

Monica's lips twisted in a wry smile, and she cocked a finger at Lyssa and crooked her thumb, like someone pointing an imaginary gun at her and pulling the trigger. 'Spot on.'

'No wonder he and Monty didn't get on.'

'Yeah. No wonder,' Monica agreed flatly.

'So after Glen died . . . I still don't see why Racey didn't take over,' Lyssa said, puzzled. Something here just wasn't adding up. 'He was the obvious choice. The other band members knew him, the fans knew him, he was a known quantity, and you just said he sung those kinds of tunes well enough to take over. So what was the problem?'

'Monty was, just like always,' Monica said scornfully. 'According to Racey, she wanted to bring in a total outsider to replace Glen. A new singer, with the kind of voice that would be right for this new sound that she and Luke Raines wanted to press on with. Some good-looking blond-haired kid. There were huge fights and arguments about it, I can tell you. Luke Raines went so far as to have a demo made of the kid's voice . . . I can't remember his name now. Anyway, it never happened, because then Monty died, and Racey got the group behind him and they persuaded Luke to go on with Racey taking the lead and them bringing in some other green kid to take over his guitar spot and . . . Well, the rest, as they say, is history. The band never had a major hit again.'

Lyssa leaned back a little and digested all of this. 'And Monty was trying to do all this right after losing the love of her life? And whilst fighting Glen's parents over his Will, and all the drama that was causing? Not to mention the press being after her blood? Some of the articles I read stopped only a millimetre short of accusing her of being responsible for Glen's death by introducing him to drugs in the first place! Although, from what you say, none of them were really into drugs big time.'

'Yeah,' Monica said sadly. 'She said that she was doing it for Glen's sake. That he'd have wanted her to help the band continue to grow and prosper and would expect her to make sure that it happened. But it must have been beyond even her to cope with, mustn't it? It's no wonder she drowned herself in the pond, is it?'

7

'You think it was suicide, then?' Lyssa asked sharply.

'What – you think it was an *accident*?' Monica said, arching an eyebrow waggishly. 'Come on! Monty could swim – you should have seen her doing laps in their indoor swimming pool. And she wasn't totally out of her head on drugs – she'd only taken a tiny amount of acid, I can remember hearing Racey telling his mum that the doctors who cut her up said so. Yeah, she'd been drinking champers, but so what? You think she wouldn't have sobered up pretty damn quick if she accidentally toddled into the pond and found herself neck deep in cold water?'

Lyssa noticed that her words, whilst not quite slurred yet, were beginning to sound a little . . . tired now. Just how much, she wondered wryly, did Monica really believe her own words? It seemed to her that she rather liked being dramatic. On the other hand, that didn't mean she didn't have a valid point.

'You think she was that depressed, then?' she asked calmly.

Monica sighed. She took another alarmingly large gulp of her drink and then shrugged, her bony shoulders going up and down. 'Who can really say? The coroner and the jury said it was an accident. Who knows, maybe it was. I just never really believed it, that's all. You gotta remember that that night was the day after her birthday, and Glen wasn't there with her. Instead, his parents and his kid sister were, and the parents were only there to see if she was gonna come 'cross with Glen's money. How depressin' must that-a-bin?'

Monica leaned back more comfortably on the sofa, her eyelids beginning to sag. 'Them Bannisters were already seeing solicitors about overturnin' the Will. Put yourself in Monty's shoes . . . Her big love, gone – *poof!* The band was split down the middle about the new sound and arguing constantly. Yeah, they went to her party, but they were only doing it 'cause it would look bad in the papers if they didn't. Her parents had disowned her – or as good as. Her birthday, and all the people around her were either hangers-on or downright hostile to her. She's wandering outside because her own party's gone sour on her and she sees the pond . . . Perhaps she did slip to begin with, but then, once she was in there, just thought . . . you know, well wazza' a point in goin' on . . .'

Slowly her eyes closed, her head fell back against the headrest, and Lyssa reached forward and turned off the recorder. This was the first interview she'd conducted where her source had drifted off on her into a tipsy catnap, and she wasn't quite sure of the etiquette. Did she try and wake her to say goodbye? Or just tiptoe out, like an embarrassed guest?

In the end, she wrote a note, thanking Monica for her help, and asking if it would be all right if she came back another time to chat again, and left it on the table, where she couldn't fail to see it. She then gathered her things together and did, indeed, tiptoe out.

The train route between Oxford and London had a stop at High Wycombe, and it had seemed to her that the opportunity to call in and see Elizabeth on her way back shouldn't be missed, so she'd arranged to visit her client's home later that afternoon.

She took a taxi from the station, and was, as always, impressed by the deep wooded valley where the town had been established, and the hilltop views presented to those who lived higher up the valley slopes. She was not surprised to find that Elizabeth was one of those who liked to live up high, although her house, though large compared to your average house size in the UK, was not unduly impressive; even so, given its location and accessibility to the capital, it was probably worth a mint.

But still not, Lyssa thought, in the same bracket as those that Monty's immediate family must continue to enjoy. She'd done a little background check on Elizabeth before signing the contracts, and knew that she was the daughter of a daughter of a daughter in the Montrose family lineage, which almost certainly meant that she wouldn't have inherited anything like the wealth that the male line would have, given that the rules about female equality in these matters had only very recently changed.

As she walked up to the (by most people's standards) very desirable residence, in the very pleasant and leafy part of town, she couldn't help but wonder if Elizabeth resented not inheriting an estate in the country, or a London townhouse, or whatever it was the upper classes had considered a 'must-have' back in the 60s. Did she consider herself hard done by because she didn't have the family millions to fall back on, like her luckier, male cousins?

She rang the bell, and it was answered almost at once. Elizabeth, small, chic, smart, grinned widely back at her.

'Hello there. How did it go with the widow?' she asked, pulling open the door and ushering her inside. 'Go right on through – we'll sit out on the patio, shall we? It's such a nice day.' Just as that day at the Ivy, she seemed to almost buzz with a nervous energy that Lyssa was beginning to suspect was her natural state of being.

She followed the little pocket rocket through a stunningly decorated lounge area and then out on to a small but very pretty back garden, where a jug of what she hoped was just plain mineral water (untouched by vodka or gin!) was set out on a white wrought-iron table. Two matching chairs sat either side of it, and as Elizabeth sank down on to one, Lyssa gratefully took the other.

'Water? Hope you like it sparkling?'

'Fine,' Lyssa said, and for the next half an hour the two women talked, mostly about Monica but also about the progress she'd made on the book so far.

'Monica sounds a hoot,' Elizabeth said with a grin, when Lyssa had finally finished her tale about her earlier activities. 'And she does make a good case for suicide, but I just don't buy it somehow. I know I never knew Monty in person, but I was very close to those who did, and from what they say, she just wasn't the kind to chuck in the towel.'

Lyssa nodded, watching her client carefully now. 'I don't want to be indelicate, Elizabeth, but it seems to me that one of the pivotal issues that any book about Monty has to tackle is the manner of her death. Just how do you want me to handle it? Do you want us to slavishly follow the official version and leave it at that? Or do you want to incorporate other points of view from those around at the time – like Monica?'

Elizabeth shook her head, sending her riotous brown curls dancing, then reached out for her packet of cigarettes and lit one up, puffing on it energetically. 'No, don't worry – I don't want a whitewash,' she said firmly. 'If you want to include Monica's opinions, go ahead. Who knows, you might find others that think the same. Just don't give any bias to one opinion or the other. Let's face it, we're probably never going to know for sure what happened that night. Even the official police investigation of the party didn't really help much – except to show who was drunk or high, and who never left the party at around the time Monty must have died. Which was helpful, sure, but only in a negative sort of way.

The police at the time investigated Monty's movements thoroughly and questioned everyone, but no one saw what happened to her after she went out into the gardens. Or if they did, nobody was owning up to it. The coroner's inquest went through all the facts, and even that couldn't come up with any definitive answers. The jury returned an accidental verdict, but who can say if they got it right or wrong? If they couldn't do it then, I don't think we can be expected to succeed where they failed. Just write up what you find honestly and in a balanced way.'

Lyssa let out a slow breath of relief. 'I'm so glad you said that. That's the kind of book I prefer to write.'

Elizabeth grinned. 'Publish and be damned, eh? I can never remember who said that or why, but he was my kind of guy. Or gal. So yes – I want you to find out as much as you can, about everything that you can, and put the whole lot down in print. Good, bad or indifferent. Whatever the truth is, there'll have to be more to it than the generic "Oh, she was a bad 'un" rubbish that's been floating around out there about her for over fifty years now. And speaking of which' – she stabbed out her depleted cigarette with quick, vicious little jabs, and then held up a hand with one finger pointing upwards in a 'just wait' gesture – 'I found these . . .' She was rooting around in a voluminous bag that was already sitting under the table, and brought out a small set of old, cracked-leather hardback notebooks and a few loose sheafs of paper.

'I didn't hand these over to you at the Ivy because I don't want to let them out of my possession, but I'm sure you'll find them interesting. These first, I think,' she said, handing over the loose pile of yellowing paper.

On them, Lyssa was surprised to see, was written a series of about ten poems. The handwriting was faded but still legible, and was easy to read in a loose, flowing, feminine hand. Lyssa read the poems with growing pleasure. They were all love poems, some angry, some sad, some longing and mournful, others playful. The syntax was idiosyncratic but very individual, and it was clear they'd all been written by the same person.

She looked up at Elizabeth hopefully. 'Are these . . . ?'

'Monty's? Yes, you betcha! Aren't they great? I found them in my grandmother's attic. My great-uncle gave me permission to root around up there for anything I could find on Monty when I told him I wanted to go ahead with this project. He wasn't that keen on it, really, even after all these years, but his son told him that he was being an old fogey, and that got his goat all right. So he gave me permission. I wasn't really sure I'd find anything at all up there, but boy, did I hit paydirt. What do you think of them?'

'They're wonderful,' Lyssa said sincerely. She'd doubted that Monty would ever have found a publisher for them, since they were more personal than professionally written, but the emotion in them was undeniable, and her use of words memorable. 'You're sure they were written by her and not someone else in the family?' she said, sounding a word of caution.

'Oh yes – the handwriting is definitely hers. I know that, because of these,' she said, tapping the leather-bound books significantly.

Lyssa's heart began to pound. 'Are they what I think they are?'

'Diaries? Yup!'

'Elizabeth! Why didn't you tell me about these at our lunch?' she yelped.

'Don't get too excited – they're not journals or anything. Monty didn't spill her heart out on paper. Most of what's in here are just everyday reminders about dates and appointments, and a few notes about various ordinary things. You know, "Found a dress in Bond Street – nobody else will wear it, the chickens," that sort of thing. Nothing earth-shattering or revelatory. Except for one thing that really caught my eye.'

Lyssa, whose heart had plummeted at Elizabeth's first words, picked up again with her last. 'Oh?'

'Here . . . read this. This is dated November 1962. Remember that date, it's significant. You'll see why in a minute.' Elizabeth manoeuvred the book around to face her, holding it open at a certain page. 'You can see she had a hairdresser's appointment, but see what she jotted down just underneath it?'

Lyssa read it aloud. 'Meeting Glen at the Mad Hatters, 9.30 p.m. Must show him the latest line I've thought up for the end of "Scared Witless".'

She frowned. 'It's a bit out of context, isn't it?' she said, looking at the notations above and below it, which were indeed, as Elizabeth had warned her, merely mundane references to other meetings, and a memo to herself to get more birth-control pills.

'Yes – and no,' Elizabeth said, drawing the diary out from under Lyssa's reluctant fingers, and turning it back to face her. 'Remember what I said about the date?'

'November 1962 – yes?'

'Right. And what song came out in March, just four months later? Their biggest hit of all, the one that got to number one?'

'"The Frightened Heart",' Lyssa said promptly.

'Right. Don't you see?'

Lyssa frowned slightly. 'Sorry, perhaps I'm being a bit dim . . .'

Elizabeth grinned at her. 'No, you're not. You just haven't been living and breathing Monty and the Lucky Cuckoos like I have these past few months. It's in the file somewhere that I gave you, but I dare say you haven't got around to it yet, or if you have, it didn't mean anything to you at the time.'

'Er, Elizabeth, I still haven't a clue what you're talking about.'

Elizabeth leaned back in her chair, her eyes glowing. 'What if I were to tell you that before "The Frightened Heart" got recorded, they were calling it "Scared Witless", after one of the lines in the second verse?'

'Oh,' Lyssa breathed.

'Yeah. And now take another look at those poems. Doesn't the style and the way she rhymed things remind you of anything?'

'Oh,' Lyssa said again. Then slowly nodded. 'You think Monty helped Glen write the songs?'

'Help? Hell, I think she wrote all the lyrics. And he wrote the music. I think that's why he left her the money in his Will. He believed she'd earned it and deserved to have it!'

'That's . . . That's . . . If it's true, that's a major discovery, Elizabeth!' Lyssa gasped.

'I know – which is why I want you to put all your efforts into proving it!'

On the train ride back to Oxford, Lyssa's mind whirled. She'd been bombarded with too much information all at once and she needed to get things sorted out in an orderly way in her mind. As ever, she reached for pen and paper to do so. Sometimes a laptop and keyboard were just too impersonal and awkward for her.

Pressing down the top of the pen with a sense of satisfaction and familiarity, she pulled the notepad towards her on the train's small tabletop and began to write.

Firstly, she thought about Elizabeth, and her instructions after she'd dropped her bombshell. Lyssa was still smarting a little about her holding the diaries and poems back for a few days, but supposed reluctantly that she could understand why Elizabeth didn't want to let them out of her possession. At least Lyssa had managed to get her to promise to photocopy all that she had and send it to her, so that was something.

And Elizabeth's excitement over the possibility that Monty was actually one of the songwriters for the band's biggest hits was understandable. After all, it would be a major weapon in their bid to get Monty's legacy seen in a very different light.

If it was true.

But was it?

Lyssa paused in her note-taking, and ringed the last three words.

So far, they had the poems and the one reference in Monty's diary. Elizabeth had assured her she'd gone through the diaries obsessively and that it was the only reference there was, but until she got her hands on the photocopies, Lyssa was forced to take her word for it.

The poems would have to be investigated thoroughly. Here, Lyssa's old English tutors would be a vital source of help – they would be able to tell for sure whether they were all written by the same person.

Next, Lyssa quickly jotted down a note to remind herself to print off all the written lyrics of everything ever sung by the Lucky Cuckoos, so that the academics could make a comparison with the poetry. This was Oxford, after all, and she had the best of the best when it came to experts who could dissect and critique literary works. And if they all came to an expert's conclusion that the poems and the lyrics were written by the same hand . . . well, that would go an enormously long way towards giving Elizabeth's theory credence.

She made another note to get a reputable handwriting expert to check that the poems and known examples of Monty's handwriting were, in fact, a match.

What else?

Yes. Monica. And the things that had been revealed at that interview.

As the scenery sped past the windows, Lyssa felt some of the intense excitement over the possibilities Elizabeth had just raised slowly drain out of her. And after a while, as she sat staring pensively out of the window, she began to feel distinctly uneasy.

For, no matter how she looked at it, Monica's account of things had raised more questions in her mind than she'd bargained for. The picture she'd painted of Monty's last night on earth had been so vivid and showed so clearly how fraught it must have been, that she now couldn't help but wonder.

It was as if, now that the question of her death being an accident had been so thoroughly challenged, another, even darker suspicion had been born in her brain.

And one that she didn't like. At all. Because there were generally only four ways a person could die. Natural causes. Suicide. Accident. Or murder.

And the more Lyssa forced herself to think about it, the more she felt a chill sweep over her.

Monty had been alone, in the darkness of her garden. She could have fallen in the pond and died accidentally. She could have committed suicide. Either of those had to be taken seriously.

But she had also been surrounded by people who had a motive for wanting her dead.

Glen's parents were fighting her over the terms of their son's Will. Just how desperate had they been for the money that would secure their future, and that of their children? They must have felt enormous anger and hurt over Glen for leaving all that money to a woman who already had so much. Might they not have, in a moment of anger or madness, done something they might later have regretted?

And, Lyssa reminded herself, feeling her body chill even more now, they were not the only ones with a motive. Monica had confirmed that all the members of the Lucky Cuckoos had been at that party also. And one, in particular, had had a very good reason for wanting Monty dead.

Racey.

The man who'd been denied the spotlight by Glen and his rich lover in the first place. Racey, who, if Monty was to have her way, was about to be replaced with a handsome newcomer, whose voice she preferred to his. Which meant that his opportunity to finally step up and take Glen's place as leader of the band was in danger of being thwarted yet again. Had he been unable to take the rejection a second time? Had he turned to drink in his later years not merely out of a sense of disappointment at the band's failure to thrive, but also because he had something to feel really guilty about?

As the train carried her back to Oxford, Lyssa began to feel distinctly tense. She was determined to write a thoroughly researched, honest and truthful account of Amelia Montrose's life and death. But she had to wonder.

Just what had she got herself into?

8

'Who do you think you are – Miss Marple?'

The question came from Freida, but it might just as easily have come from either Carter or Jason, as all three of her friends were looking at her as if she was off her chump.

'Well, if you're not going to take me seriously,' Lyssa began, half laughing herself, 'I might as well chuck you out.'

They were grouped around her coffee table, Jason doing his usual lounging act in the biggest recliner chair, with Carter and Freida sitting on the small settee, facing Lyssa, who was in the second biggest chair placed opposite them.

They'd been drinking wine and catching up, and when the talk had come around to what she'd done with her day – and she'd told them – they'd all leapt on her like ravening wolves, demanding to know what she made of it all. And when she'd finally got to the part when she was on the train coming back, and her thoughts had begun to turn to the question of murder, they had all but erupted.

'Well, you have to agree, it does all sound a bit Agatha Christie-ish and "anyone for tennis?"' Jason drawled from his supine position. Lyssa was sure that if she tried to drape herself over the furniture like that, she'd have backache for a week. He was absently eating the grapes out of Lyssa's fruit basket, and he had a definite twinkle in his eye. 'Please, can I play Watson to your Sherlock?'

'That's Arthur Conan Doyle, you philistine,' Freida shot at him, and Lyssa laughed.

'You lot are as far removed from fictional sleuths as it's possible to get!' she told them firmly.

'Hey, I resent that,' Carter said mildly. 'I'd like to think I have as good a brain as any of *them*. In fact, if we put our heads together, I reckon we could solve any whodunit going.'

'To be sure,' said Jason. 'We could call ourselves "The Oxford Detective Society" and set ourselves up in business. Finding lost pooches and nefarious villains a speciality.'

Freida threw a cushion at him, which he fielded expertly, and promptly turned her attention back to Lyssa. 'Seriously, though, are you honestly thinking there might have been foul play involved?' she asked.

Lyssa sighed and shrugged helplessly. 'I've just told you all the basic facts that I've managed to amass so far. Your guess, at this point, is as good as mine.'

'Do you think it's possible that you might just be getting a little bit carried away though?' Carter, always the voice of reason, asked tentatively. 'I mean, you'd just had a long session with a tipsy rock chick, and then Elizabeth throws you the curve ball over the question of who actually wrote the hit songs. Your sense of drama was probably off the scale by that point.'

'Yes – don't forget, we all rely on you to be the serious, level-headed and sensible one,' Jason said, delicately spitting out a grape seed and leaving it in his cupped palm. 'When Freida lost her head over that Neanderthal of a bouncer, who pulled her irons out of the fire?'

Freida threw a rather wrinkle-skinned orange at him, which he deftly caught.

'And when Carter . . .' Jason swept on, then stopped, looked at his beloved and made a face. 'Yes, well, we know Carter never puts a foot wrong. But when I had a meltdown over that Flemish Rabbit incident, who calmed me down and found a vet and made sure everything was sorted? You did. Otherwise, my besties might not be speaking to me, even now.'

Lyssa didn't want to contemplate the foolishness of people who asked Jason, of all people, to babysit their pets when they went abroad on holiday.

'All right, all right,' she said, holding up her hands in surrender. 'Maybe I am going over the top a bit.'

'Just a smidge,' Freida grinned, holding out a finger and a thumb, showing a gap of barely a couple of millimetres between them. 'I shouldn't worry though; even if it does turn out that this groupie chick was pushed instead of fell, who's going to worry about it all these years later? Practically everyone concerned at the time is now dead, right?' But there was just a trace of anxiety in her voice.

'Yes, I suppose they are. But there are the families of those concerned still to consider,' Lyssa pointed out stubbornly. 'Just for the sake of argument, what happens if I do start to find things out that look a bit . . . er . . .'

'Murderous?' Jason said, lowering his voice dramatically.

'I was going to say iffy,' Lyssa said, with dignity. 'What then?'

'Call the police,' Jason said with a grin. 'Why is it, in all the films you see, whenever a woman finds herself in a tricky situation, she never just calls the police?'

'Maybe because most of the scriptwriters are male?' Freida suggested sweetly.

'Cut it out, you two,' Lyssa said sternly. 'I'm serious.'

'Well, what are *you* thinking?' Carter asked, coming to her rescue. 'As a biographer, you've undertaken to write a memoir of

Amelia Montrose. If you find evidence that questions her death, are you really going to suppress it?'

'No,' Lyssa responded instantly, without even thinking about it.

'Well, there you are, then,' he said, somewhat smugly, and leaned back. 'You've already decided, haven't you? You'll publish the truth.'

'And Super-Carter strikes again,' Jason said sardonically. 'Honestly, does the man have no faults? Good-looking, rich, brainy and reliable. No wonder I have to keep fighting off rivals with a stick.'

Carter held out two hands in a 'what can a guy do?' sort of gesture, and they all burst out laughing. It was Freida who got serious first, shooting Lyssa a long, careful look.

'Really, Lyss, are you genuinely worried about this? I mean, are you feeling that uneasy about it all?'

Lyssa looked at her friends, who were all now – Jason included – examining her closely. She shook her head helplessly. 'I just don't know. It's simply too early to say, at this point. I need to do way more research before I can answer that. Right now, the mystery of how Amelia died is just that – a mystery.'

'Well, if you come up with something really alarming, you have to let us know,' Carter said firmly, leaning forward a little on his chair. 'We'll do whatever we can to help.'

'Yes. And from now on, let us know where you're going,' Freida said, then added quickly, as she saw the look on her friend's face, 'Oh – nothing major, just give one of us a ring whenever you head out somewhere on the hunt so that we know where you are and who you're seeing. And a rough time of when you expect to get back. Just as a precaution.'

Lyssa laughed. 'Now who's going over the top? Who do you think *you* are – Inspector Morse?'

Freida gave her a hurt look. 'Please – I'd be somebody-or-other of the Yard. And a Chief Superintendent at the very least.'

Jason gave a mock shudder. 'Perish the thought.'

'Yes, but Freida's right about letting us know your movements,' Carter insisted. 'If only to stop us worrying about you. Please?'

Lyssa, feeling humbled to have such good friends, thanked them and opened another bottle of wine. And when they finally began to make going-home signs, she dutifully informed them that tomorrow she was going to Hayling Island to talk to the unmarried mother who had benefited from Monty's short-lived charity, the YMT. And that she expected to be back before dark.

Once they'd gone, she checked her phone and saw she had a notification on Facebook. Logging in, her heart fluttered to find it was a message from Justin Tillman, giving her his telephone number and saying he'd be happy to speak to her.

Within moments she was calling the number, feeling almost breathless with anticipation.

'Hello?'

'Hello, Mr Tillman? This is Lyssa Moore.'

'Who? Oh, the writer. Yes, hello. I must say, I was very intrigued by your message. And yes, you were quite correct – it was my father, Frank Tillman, who was at that party where that poor woman died.'

'Oh, I'm so relieved to hear that,' Lyssa said in massive understatement. 'As I mentioned, I'm writing Amelia's biography and, as you can imagine, when I found out there had been actual film footage taken at her last birthday party, I've been hoping against hope that it might still be in existence?'

She was now perched on the edge of her seat, her mouth feeling dry. Realistically, she was expecting him to give her bad news, but there was still that little spark of hope in her that had her mentally crossing her fingers.

'Well, you might just be in luck,' Justin said, his voice thoughtful. 'I'm pretty sure my dad's old stuff – cameras, music memorabilia and all that – is still up in the loft. My mother packed it away carefully when he died, and then when she passed I just moved it from her loft to mine. You know, the way you do with family things. You can't bear to throw them out, can you? Do you want me to check and see?'

Lyssa bounded up from the sofa, fists clenched in jubilation, then had to force herself to sit back down again and get herself under control.

'That would be marvellous, if you're quite sure it's no trouble?' she said as casually as she could.

'Not a bit,' he said promptly. 'Now that you've jogged my memory, I wouldn't mind taking out his old films and looking at them again. It must be thirty years or more since I last did. I just hope the film hasn't perished.'

So did Lyssa! They agreed that Justin would have a 'sort out' tomorrow and then he'd ring her back in the evening to let her know how he'd got on.

Hanging up the phone, Lyssa gave a little squeal of delight. Bibbie, alerted by the sound, came soft-footedly across the carpet and headbutted her in the shins, to remind her it had been at least an hour since he'd last been fed.

~

As Lyssa put the television on and settled down for the evening (a well-fed cat settled on her lap), in her own home Elizabeth was also sitting alone in front of the television, but she was not really concentrating on the antics of some rich youngsters on an island somewhere in the sun.

Instead, she was going over her recent visit from Lyssa Moore.

She thought she had played it well. The writer appeared to have risen to the bait as expected, and was now, hopefully, putting the question of who wrote the Cuckoos' songs at the top of her list of priorities.

Elizabeth knew that she'd have to make sure to stay on top of that, of course, and whenever Lyssa got in touch, she'd push that aspect thoroughly. But she must be careful not to overdo it. The Oxford graduate was nobody's fool and the last thing she wanted was for the biographer to start suspecting that her client had a hidden agenda.

She turned off the television and began to climb the stairs. A long hot bath, and then she'd read a few chapters of her book and get off to bed. She had a full day ahead of her tomorrow.

As she poured her favourite bubble bath into the water, she went over in her mind all the things that could go wrong with her plans. Apart from the obvious one, of course – that even Lyssa Moore's painstaking research didn't bring to light the evidence that she was hoping for – there were several other hiccoughs that might arise.

She didn't *think* that Lyssa would hold back on her and fail to reveal all that she might find out about Amelia. But she had put in place safeguards against that anyway, just in case.

And then there was just the remotest of chances that one of the Bannisters might get wise to what was going on – but surely that was so unlikely, the risk was negligible?

Elizabeth shucked off her silk dressing robe and slid with a sigh of appreciation into the warm, scented water. She'd always been a bit of a gambler; with everything except money. She'd gambled on her own talent as a designer, and that had paid off. She'd gambled on both her husbands, and that too had paid off. Their alimony payments were lovely.

And now she was gambling on poor, long-dead Amelia. And something told her that was going to pay off too.

The next day, Lyssa decided to drive down to Hayling Island. There was no real direct train link, and besides, the drive was a relatively simple one – driving more or less straight south, through the lovely Berkshire Downs, and on into Hampshire. Best of all, she didn't have to go anywhere near London, and so didn't have to negotiate the various ring roads and the traffic hassles that would inevitably occur.

She set the satnav before leaving Oxford at just after ten o'clock. She wasn't the most confident of people behind the wheel and hated rush hour and never drove in it if she could possibly avoid it. She didn't much like really busy roads either, but she made it a point of honour to not let that stop her.

Of course, Kyle had always been the one to drive whenever they'd taken a trip anywhere together. He'd loved being behind the wheel, and right from the start of their relationship, he'd taken it for granted that he would chauffeur her around. It was one of the many things she'd loved about him – his courtesy.

Every Valentine's Day there would be flowers, her favourite chocolates and a book. He wasn't much of a reader himself, but he knew how much she loved books, and he would scour Oxford's second-hand bookshops and dealerships, trying to find first editions of the authors he knew she loved. Or signed editions.

Except for that last Valentine's Day before his death, which he'd inexplicably forgotten. She'd noticed he'd been rather distracted for a while and he had reluctantly told her there was a temporary shortfall in his client list which had him worried, so she'd made light of it. Nevertheless, he'd been so upset that the next day flowers and chocolates were once more heaped upon her.

He'd cooked the meal too – nothing too challenging, but she didn't care. It was knowing that he cared enough about her to try not to burn some chops, or to cobble together a salad, that touched her heart. He himself always ate so healthily that most of his food was raw, organic and brimming with nutrients. It made the way he died so inexplicable. Sometimes, she found herself wondering if the medical examiner had made some kind of mistake, because it just didn't make sense.

Now, of course, Valentine's Day meant nothing to her.

Realising where her thoughts were wandering, she quickly nipped the feelings of grief and pain in the bud, pushed them back before they could swamp her and concentrated instead on the task ahead.

The day was intermittently sunny, the sky was blue and she was off to the seaside! As a kid, she'd have been over the moon with excitement and happiness. She must remember her New Year's resolution to live in the moment and enjoy it.

She turned on the radio and deliberately fiddled until she found a station that played 1960s pop – what could be more appropriate, under the circumstances? Who knew, maybe a Lucky Cuckoos song would make it on to the playlist.

She found what she was looking for, and listened to the Hollies asking someone to 'Stop, Stop, Stop' all the dancing, as she went along at a steady sixty miles an hour through the pleasant, rolling and green English countryside.

Naturally, all the cars whizzed past her at what seemed to her to be an excessive speed, all except for one – a nondescript dark-coloured hatchback that seemed to hang back behind her all the way.

When she left the motorway, she felt just a slight sense of foreboding when the hatchback did the same, but after she'd negotiated some roundabouts and got through some traffic lights, she couldn't see it any more. But the traffic was fairly heavy. Perhaps it was hidden behind the white van, three or four cars behind her?

Then she had to laugh at herself for getting carried away. Was she seriously thinking that someone was following her now?

'Lyssa, girl, you really need to get a grip,' she muttered to herself.

~

Janet Connor lived on a plot of permanent static homes or caravans on a site a little outside Hayling Island itself. The beach at Hayling, Lyssa noticed as she drove past, was all pebbles and hardly the comfortable sand so beloved of holidaymakers. But the farmer's land where the site was based overlooked a sparkling sea, awash with pleasure boats and windsurfers' sails.

Some of the residences were settled down in a hollow in the field, whilst others straggled up the inclines towards the better view. Lyssa suspected that those on the top rows had to put up with the winter winds as the price to pay for the splendour of the panorama.

She slowly trawled through the narrow little 'lanes' of the camping compound in search of Janet's address.

The site was very pleasant, with lots of small, non-intrusive trees dotted here and there, and the homes were all painted cheerful colours and looked well maintained. Small plots were full of plants – most of them in various tubs and planters – and several people, all of whom looked to be around retirement age, were out walking their dogs. She had to stop to ask one of these – a slender man walking two vociferous Yorkshire terriers – where she might find Janet's home, and he happily pointed the way towards Cherry Street.

Lyssa found the right number, parked and climbed out of her car – a mid-range, five-year-old Volkswagen that she had christened 'Mary-Jane' for no particular reason that she could think of.

She stood for a moment, stretching and looking around. Janet Connor's home was, like all of them, raised up on blocks, and had three wooden steps reaching up to the front door. It was painted a pleasant mint-green, with white trim around the windows and doors. Floral curtains gave it an even more chintzy appearance.

When she went up the steps and pressed on the doorbell, she could hear chimes ringing out somewhere inside. The tune was vaguely familiar – oranges and lemons, she thought, which, if her memory served her right, were the bells of St Clement's?

The door opened slowly, and Lyssa found herself looking at a well-padded woman who was bent forward just a little, making her wonder if Janet Connor suffered with back pain. She had a short cut of grey, straight hair, and blue eyes that might have been grey, or grey eyes that might have been blue, depending on the light.

She was wearing black trousers, black slippers and an oversize man's check shirt in black and red.

'Hello? Miss Connor?' Lyssa said.

'Yes,' the woman said. 'You must be the writer lady?'

Lyssa nodded. 'Thank you so much for agreeing to see me, Miss Connor.'

'Call me Janet. Or Jan. Come on in,' she invited.

She showed Lyssa into what felt like a surprisingly large lounge area. The walls were painted a pale peach and there was dark brown carpet flooring. One large settee and two matching armchairs faced each other over a small oval table, and a few landscape prints of famous paintings hung on the walls. A sideboard was lined with family photographs, and the room smelled very faintly of fish, leaving Lyssa to suppose that the older woman had not long finished having her lunch.

'Can I get you tea or coffee?' Janet asked.

'Maybe later?' Lyssa said, settling herself on the sofa and pulling out her notebook and setting her device to record. 'Do you mind?' she asked, indicating the device.

'Not at all. Not that I think I can tell you all that much – not really. Like I said to you when you first called, I can't promise to have anything good enough to say that could go into a book.'

'Please don't worry about that,' Lyssa said, with her best professional smile. 'All we're going to do is chat about the old times. Don't worry about trying to think of anything important to say – just say what you can remember. A biography is only a way of telling the everyday story of the life and times of someone, so believe me, simply talking to someone who knew Amelia Montrose is a treat. And it'll be up to me to pick and choose what I want to write about. Is that OK?'

Janet gave a brief smile and sat down, wincing a little as she did so, making Lyssa think that her theory about her having a bad back was probably right. 'Oh, I think I can manage that all right. Just so long as you don't expect anything fancy.'

'Nothing fancy – tick,' Lyssa said, miming ticking off something on the blank page of her notebook.

Janet smiled and slowly leaned back. 'So – where do you want to start?'

'Well, perhaps you can tell me how you came to learn about Monty and her charity in the first place? I know you were a young girl with a baby imminent, is that right? Did someone in social services give you their details?'

Janet shook her head, a wry smile causing the wrinkles in her face to deepen. 'Don't make me laugh! No, social services in them days was all about trying to get you to agree to having your kid given up for adoption. And I was never going to agree to *that*. No, it was some woman in a café who gave me the nod. She could see what a state I was in, and she said she'd seen a flyer somewhere about the YMT, and luckily for me remembered the name. It was good of her to take the trouble – most didn't. They saw a young woman "in trouble", as they said in those days, and they took it for granted you were no good and wouldn't be seen dead talking to you. Everyone goes on about the Swinging 60s and how liberated we all were, but that didn't come until much later – the Summer of Love and all that. Back in the early 60s, believe me, everybody judged you, and didn't bother to hide it, neither.'

Lyssa shook her head gently. 'That must have been very hard on you. Society rejecting you like that.'

'Yeah, well, they weren't the only ones. My mum and dad chucked me out the moment I started to show. At first, Dad threatened to beat up whoever was responsible and make him marry me. Don't make me laugh – he was married already. When I refused to name him – that were it. Out!'

'It must have been tough. What did you do?'

'Yeah, it was scary. I hitchhiked my way out of town and worked temp jobs until I was too big to do even that. That was when I had that stroke of luck in the café.'

'And that led you to the Young Mothers' Trust,' Lyssa mused. 'Sounds as if they might have been your last resort. Tell me, what did you make of them?'

Janet shrugged. 'To be honest, I wasn't expecting much. Call me cynical if you like – at the age of sixteen I felt older than I do now! I went along to this little office above a shoe shop and met up with the manager of the whole shebang first, and when I learned that the money behind the outfit was some posh bird with a rich daddy, I thought I was in for it. I was expecting some la-di-da woman in pearls and twinset to come over all lady bountiful on me and lecture me about morals and clean livin' and all the rest of it.'

Janet's grin grew suddenly wide. 'You could'a knocked me down with a feather when I finally met Monty, and realised she was living with the lead singer of the Lucky Cuckoos! Talk about your mind boggling! What a day that was. The big house, the garden, the staff. And *him* – in the flesh. Glen Bannister. What a hunk! I must have stood there like a guppy, with my mouth openin' and closing and nothing coming out.'

'You actually met her at her house? Evergreen?' Lyssa put in, a little surprised.

'Sure did. I took the bus, and walked down this country lane and there it was. A big country house with a swimming pool and everything. They were sitting out in the garden – this beautiful blonde girl and Glen Bannister, sitting at a table and drinking. Just like normal folk. The maid took me to them – a maid! I'd never seen a maid until then – not a real one, in one of those black outfits and white pinny. It was so funny. Like I said, I just stood there gaping at them, with my big-as-a-barrel belly, and then I just gasped and said, "You're Glen Bannister."' She gave a little gurgle of laughter.

Lyssa nodded, smiling widely herself now. 'I can just picture it. So what happened then?'

'Well, he looked back at me and said that he was, the last time he checked, then he got up and kissed the top of the blonde bird's head and said he'd leave us to it. He smiled at me as he passed by – it was a really nice smile too. He was wearing shorts and a white sleeveless vest. Bloody gorgeous he was! I watched him go until he was out of sight, then turned back, and saw this woman laughing at me. Oh, not in a nasty way – nothing snarky or anything like that. Just amused at me being star-struck, I suppose. And obviously fancying her fella. But not like she was worried about it or anything – more like . . . "Yeah, he's really something, ain't he?" and she gave me this knowing smile. Anyway, she came towards me, holding out her hand, and introduced herself. Just said, "Hello, I'm Monty," and then asked me to sit down. Offered me a drink – nothing alcoholic, like – and some biscuits. And we just started chatting.'

'That must have felt a bit surreal.'

'Huh?'

'I mean, it must have been weird and very strange.'

Janet laughed. 'You said it! Anyway, at first, I was still a bit wary like and asked her a lot of questions about what to expect. I told her straight off that I wasn't interested in giving my baby up to anybody, and she said good for you. Then she asked me if I had a permanent place to live, which I didn't, and asked if I had a regular doctor, which I also didn't. She made notes and told me she could help out with both of those things. Then she asked what kind of work I could do, and wanted to do, afterwards, to support myself and the baby. I told her I wasn't trained for nothing, but I was strong and not afraid of hard work. She asked if I didn't want to do more with my life than work as somebody's cleaner, or waitressing or whatever, and I said sure. Then she asked if I'd be interested in learning to type and whatnot and maybe become a secretary. I had to laugh at that. I said sure, but working-class girls like me stood about as much chance of being a secretary in an office as becoming an astronaut and flyin' to the moon. That made her laugh.'

Janet paused and glanced outside the window. From where Lyssa was sitting, her view was limited to a pretty flowering shrub growing outside on her nearest neighbour's wooden veranda, but she doubted that Janet was actually seeing the plant.

'She was a smashing girl, no matter what the papers said about her,' Janet said quietly. 'She treated me decent – like I was another human being. Know what I mean?'

'I think so,' Lyssa said softly.

'She didn't see me as some tart who'd got herself in the family way and was no use to anyone. She was dressed in this gorgeous summer frock straight out of Carnaby Street, and had diamonds on her fingers; funny, really, her life and mine must have been so different, and yet . . . somehow, she made me feel as if we were . . . Well, not friends, exactly, we'd only just met, but as if we could *become* friends, you know? In time.' She sighed. 'I remember feeling good about things. Myself. For the first time in ages.'

Lyssa felt a tightness in her throat and swallowed it back. 'It sounds as if it was a significant moment in your life.'

'Oh, it was. And not just that one lovely afternoon, neither. Like I said, I was a bit cynical about the whole thing. She had this reputation for being flaky and a dopehead and whatnot, so I wasn't getting my hopes up.'

'It sounded too good to be true?' Lyssa suggested.

'Exactly.' Janet nodded. 'But, turns out, she was as good as her word. She got the charity manager to find a small flat for me to live in, nothing fancy, but it was decent, and got me signed up with a gynacal . . . whatchamacallit doctor who made sure everything was all right with my Charlie, and found a midwife for me, and set up where I'd go to have him and all that. And later on, she set me up with a tech college where I could do this shorthand and typing course later in the year. She really came through for me,' Janet said wistfully. 'She was one of the few people in my life who ever did, now I come to think of it. I really dunno what would have happened to me, back then, if I hadn't met her. I still think about her sometimes, even to this day.'

'Her death must have been a real blow to you,' Lyssa said gently.

'Ain't that the truth! First Glen dying, then her, all in less than a year. Bloody awful it were. 'Course, by then I'd had my Charlie, and was near to finishing the secretarial course. Never did like typing much, if I'm honest, but it got me a job. Which was just as well,' she added darkly.

'Oh?'

'Yeah – once Monty was gone, so was the YMT, weren't it? That manager saw to that.'

Lyssa shifted a little on the chair. The mood in the pleasant lounge had definitely changed, and not for the better. 'The manager. You've mentioned him before.'

'Not him – her. Deborah Simmonds.'

The name rang a bell. 'Yes, of course. I came across her name during my research. She was Monty's friend and co-founder of the charity, wasn't she?'

'Co-founder, my foot!' Janet snorted. 'Monty set it all up and paid for everything. And if Deborah was a friend of hers, she had a funny way of showing it. Always bad-mouthing her behind her back.'

'Really?'

Janet scowled. 'Oh, she was all sweetness and light to Monty's face. It was all "Oh yes, Amelia, I can do that," and "I'll get on to that right away, Amelia" and sucking up to her. Made me sick to watch. But in the office, after Amelia left, she used to make fun of her. The Trust Fund Tart, she called her then. Or Daddy's Headache. Walking Trouble. And a lot worse.'

'Wow! Sounds as if their relationship was toxic. I wonder how they came to get together? I seem to remember reading that Deborah Simmonds was a fair bit older than Monty?'

'Yeah – the cow was in her forties, I suppose. She spoke a bit like Monty, you know, posh, and she lived in a nice area and had a nice car, so I suppose she was sort of upper crust-ish. Not like Monty was though – not a proper aristo, know what I mean? But I dare say they moved a little in the same circles.'

'Yes. Is that how she and Monty came together, do you think?'

'I dunno – it beats me why Monty chose her to run the show. I never trusted Deborah as far as I could throw her. To me she was an obvious phoney. But then' – she shrugged – 'I suppose she needed someone to help her do all the day-to-day routine stuff. Stands to reason someone like Monty wasn't going to waste her time in an office all day.'

Lyssa got the feeling that Monty had been placed on a pedestal all those years ago by the teenage Janet and, because of her death, had never had the chance to leave it since. It was a feeling that left her both sad and oddly comforted.

'What happened to the YMT after Monty died?' she asked next. 'My research stalled after that. I couldn't find any references to it anywhere. I assumed it just petered out?'

'It petered out pretty damn fast, if you ask me,' Janet said promptly. 'One minute, me and some other girls were being looked after – you know, flat, doctors, training, a little money helping to pay the bills, and the next – poof, all of it gone. The office closed, no more money, no more nothing.'

'And from what you say, you think that was Deborah's fault?' asked Lyssa.

'Well, that Deborah cow wasn't going to bust her gut to keep it going, was she? Too lazy for one thing. Besides, there'd be nothing in it for her, would there? Believe me, that one always had an eye out for the main chance. She only took the role on for what she could get out of it for herself. You know, trading on the fact that she was working for a lord's daughter, or whatever. Pathetic. But nasty with it. You ask me, she was the one who got her hands on whatever money was going.'

'You mean from the charity?' Lyssa squeaked, shocked.

'Sure – and anything else worth having. Probably sold all the office furniture too for all I know. Wouldn't put it past her.'

Lyssa thought about that for a moment. It was clear that Janet hated Deborah, so she needed to treat her statements with some caution. 'But surely Monty's family would have swooped in and reclaimed any and all assets?' she pointed out mildly. 'In my experience, the rich are always very good at making sure they get what's coming to them.'

At this, Janet laughed sardonically. 'Yeah – ain't they just?' She sounded both bitter and admiring in equal measure. 'And sure, maybe they did, for all I know,' she admitted candidly. 'But from what I remember, her family never had much to do with her. It was like, once she moved in with Glen, and got her name in the papers for being a party girl and all that other guff they printed about her, it was like she was giving off a bad smell. You know, too much for their hoity-toity little noses to cope with. And it wasn't as if the YMT was a big deal – not on their scale of things, I mean. Just this one little office, and the likes of Deborah Simmonds running the day-to-day stuff. Nothing major. I doubt it would have been worth the solicitor's fees to make a song and dance about it. No, you ask me, it was that cow Deborah Simmonds who somehow walked off with whatever it was that was going.'

'Any idea how much that could have been?' Lyssa asked curiously.

'Hell no. I was just one of those holding out their hand for charity, weren't I?' she said rancorously. 'But I can tell you this much – Monty meant business, and she was putting her own money where her mouth was. And she was helping a lot of girls by now. Couldn't have been cheap, and there always seemed to be plenty in the kitty. And another thing – I reckon I wasn't the only one who had Deborah Simmonds' true measure, neither.'

'Oh?' Lyssa's internal radar bleeped loudly. She'd always had an instinct for when something really meaty was about to be uncovered.

'Yeah. I remember, after the funeral – Monty's, I mean – I was standing outside the churchyard gates. I didn't go into the church or nothing like that,' she qualified hastily, 'it was all too big a deal. They wouldn't have let me in anyway, I suppose. What with the press, and Monty's family deigning to show up, and all the Lucky Cuckoos and the Bannisters and whatnot. A right circus it was. Fans of the band everywhere, even some coppers making sure it all went off smooth like. No, I just hung around on the outskirts and cried my eyes out. It felt like I was the only one there who really mourned her, you know? I dare say that sounds really big-headed, but that's what it felt like at the time. Her parents were all stiff upper lip and snooty sods. The boys in the band looked more relieved than anything. And as for the Bannisters – well, everyone knew they'd been suing Monty about Glen's Will and hassling her about it, for months. I doubt anybody there really cried for her.'

'Except you,' Lyssa pointed out softly.

Janet Connor swallowed hard. 'Yeah. Well, I might not have known her for as long as they did, but she changed my life, and that counts for a lot, don't it?' she said, sounding defensive. 'She was there for me when I was really desperate, so I suppose I felt guilty for not being there for her when she was the one who was feeling desperate. But I didn't know, did I? How could I?' Her voice rose a little as she looked at Lyssa appealingly.

Lyssa leaned forward and gently touched the top of her hand. Her knuckles felt hard and knobby with arthritis. So here was someone else who didn't think the accidental death verdict had been the right one. 'You think she committed suicide, don't you?'

Janet shrugged. 'I dunno. I don't like to think of it, but somehow . . . I just dunno. Maybe it was an accident,' she said, her voice utterly unconvinced.

'Did Deborah Simmonds accept the accidental verdict?' Lyssa asked, sensing the poor woman was near to tears.

'Her!' Janet snorted, her eyes flashing with anger. 'Of course she did. Or at least, pretended to. It was all, "Oh, poor Amelia, what a dreadful thing to happen. And on the day after her birthday too." As if that mattered. And, "I do think ponds should be fenced off or have some netting put over them or something. They can be so dangerous, can't they?" It made me sick listening to her.'

'I suppose she attended the funeral? As an official mourner?'

'Oh, try and keep her away! Dressed in black, like an old crow. I saw her, trying to hobnob with the Montroses. But they weren't having any of it,' she said, her face creasing in a satisfied smile. 'I suppose their kind can sniff out social climbers and the likes of Deborah Simmonds a mile off. You have to hand it to 'em. And, like I started to tell you before – I'm not the only one who was on to her, and what she was really like.'

'Yes – what about that?'

'Yeah. Well, like I said, after the funeral I was hanging around outside the churchyard, and I saw some young chap waylay her and they got into a right old ding-dong. Oh, not the noisy kind, the ones that draw everyone's attention. There was no shouting or pushin' and shovin'. No, they just had their heads close together and were sort of hissing quietly at each other, the way people do when they're furious but have to keep a lid on it. But I could tell Deborah was livid – she had a face on her like a thundercloud!' Janet laughed suddenly at the memory. 'I wish I'd been able to get close to them to hear what they were saying. That bloke looked ferocious, I mean, like he was ready to tear her head off.'

'Do you know who the man was?'

'No – not for sure. But I've always reckoned it was one of them. The Bannisters.'

Lyssa blinked at this. 'What makes you think that?'

'Because the man looked a lot like Glen, and he had a couple of brothers, didn't he? If I was a betting woman, I'd have laid odds on it being one of them.'

9

For the first half hour of the drive back to Oxford, Lyssa found herself, when waiting in traffic, going over all that Janet had said.

Was it possible that Monty's charity manager had somehow managed to get away with whatever had been left in the charity's accounts after Monty had died? She doubted it would be that easy to do nowadays, but back then? The charity wasn't a public one, she had learned that, but rather very much Monty's child, so presumably it had not been as liable to independent financial checks as the bigger and more famous and established charities of the day. And if Deborah Simmonds had had access to the accounts, then who was to say what she might have managed to divert into her own hands?

Especially since, after Monty's death, there must have been an awful lot of paperwork to go through. For a start, there were the dead woman's own tax papers and inheritance issues to be sorted out. Who inherited under her Will? And added to that, wouldn't the Bannisters' ongoing lawsuit to overturn their son Glen's Will have been thrown into confusion too, with Monty's death? And would Monty's inheritance from Glen even have been valid at that point? Lyssa had a vague feeling that there was some legal clause involved that said someone who inherited money had to live for a certain period of time after the death of the person who'd left them the legacy. Or was that a more modern thing?

As she sat waiting at the inevitable roadworks for the traffic lights to turn red, her head almost ached with the amount of research she would have to do on that issue alone. She'd have to get in touch with some of her friends who'd studied Jurisprudence at Oxford. They might be able to at least point her in the right direction.

Then there was the whole issue about the Lucky Cuckoos that must have muddied the waters surrounding Monty's finances. Had her funding of the band continued, even after their successes? Had the lovers, Glen and Monty, even bothered to set up some legal contracts concerning any possible repayment on her investment in the group? And now, given the whole issue about Monty having possibly – or even probably? – written some of their songs, had any acknowledgement of that been put in writing – and maybe conveniently lost? If it had been well known among the band that Monty had 'helped' Glen write the songs, Lyssa couldn't see any of the members of the Lucky Cuckoos being keen to let that stand unchallenged after her demise. Least of all Racey, who already had so many issues with her.

And what of Monty's family? According to Janet, it sounded as if they hadn't wanted anything to do with their scandalous daughter – but Lyssa found it very hard to believe they wouldn't at least put up a fight to make sure that Monty's estate got everything that was coming to it as far as Glen's considerable inheritance was concerned, as well as chase up the possibility of reimbursement for their daughter's initial financial backing of the band.

With so many people having so many fingers in so many pies, and all, no doubt, with their own agendas, the in-fighting must surely have been riotous. Easy, under those circumstances perhaps, for the charity manager to just quietly close down the YMT and slip away with the funds? For, if the charity had had so few staff, as Janet Connor had contested, what was to stop Deborah Simmonds from claiming anything she liked? She could say that Monty paid in a monthly amount to help support their unmarried mothers, and that she hadn't got around to filling the charity's coffers on that particular month when she died. With only a small office to rent and, presumably, Deborah Simmonds' employment to pay, the overheads couldn't have been that substantial. Which meant that there probably wouldn't have been any need for a complex accounting of the money. It might even have been part of Deborah's job to do the accounts for the charity. In which case, a clever woman could easily fiddle the books, given so much autonomy.

Or was Lyssa once again making too much of it? If she carried on like this, would she start seeing conspiracy theories everywhere? Lyssa met her reflection in the rear-view mirror and pulled a face at herself. First, she thought she was being followed by that car, now she was seeing fraud and larceny at every opportunity . . .

As she remembered her earlier unease at the same car being behind her for so long, her eyes automatically slid from her own gaze to the car waiting behind her. Or rather, the car that she could see waiting behind that. Wasn't it the same colour and make of car that she'd noticed before? It was a little hard to be sure, having to make it out through the windscreen and rear window of the intervening vehicle.

'Oh, get a grip, Lyssa!' she said out loud. Then grinned, as she had a sudden mental image of Jason, lounging on her sofa and eating grapes and drawling at her the old chestnut about just because she was being paranoid didn't mean . . .

'Oh, cut it out. Nobody's out to get me,' Lyssa told her reflection firmly, and just then the traffic light turned green, and she turned her attention back to her driving.

Jonas Bannister looked across his desk at his security chief, Ian Gorman, and sighed. 'So you're confident she's the real deal, then? This book thing isn't some sort of shakedown in disguise?'

'Yes, sir, her commission from the Grainger woman is genuine enough,' Gorman said in his usual, precise way. 'And she is very respected in her field.' He glanced down at the gadget in his hand and reeled off a list of her credits. 'All of them legitimate projects, some traditionally published, others privately published by the client who commissioned the book. The critics liked them too; she had good reviews from the academics (not surprisingly, given she's an Oxford woman) and also gets good reviews from readers on Amazon.'

'Well, bully for her,' Jonas griped. 'I was rather hoping it would all turn out to be a damp squib. Who the hell wants to read about a rock chick from the 1960s in this day and age anyway?' he asked, but Gorman remained diplomatically silent, considering – quite rightly – that the question had been purely rhetorical.

'So, tell me exactly what's she been up to so far, then?' Jonas demanded.

Again, Gorman consulted his smartphone. 'A lot of database searches, as you'd expect, and she's spoken to her client, Elizabeth Grainger, obviously. She's also interviewed the widow of the Lucky Cuckoos' guitarist, Ron Joiner, and she's currently on the way back from the south coast after talking to a woman named Janet Connor. Our man is keeping a close eye on her – and if she goes anywhere else, I'll be informed.'

'Who's this Connor woman?' Jonas asked suspiciously.

'We don't know yet, but we will soon,' Gorman reassured him. 'I have a man who can hack the Moore woman's emails. And if we need to, I can always find someone who can access her computer and all her notes and files. Even search her flat if need be.'

'I don't want to know about any of that!' Jonas snapped, looking alarmed. 'Just do what needs to be done, but don't bother me with the sordid details, please.' Then he sighed and shook his head. 'I just wish I knew what was behind it all.'

'You don't think this Grainger woman simply wants to do what she says she does?' Gorman asked mildly.

'What? Spend good money on having a biography published about a woman that history has had the good sense to forget about long ago? I doubt it.'

Ian Gorman allowed himself a small smile. 'Oh, I don't know. The 1960s and its music are still very popular today – and nostalgia is everywhere, or hadn't you noticed? The 50s and 60s and mid-century stuff is all the trend – everything is "retro" now. Furniture, fashion, you name it, it's all the rage. I can see there being a market for that kind of book all right. And the biographies of the really big names have already been done – so finding a fresh topic that hasn't been covered yet seems a legitimate project. And Amelia Montrose *was* a tragic and controversial figure – beautiful and a bit of an icon in her own right. There must still be a market out there for her story because the Grainger woman has already got a publisher interested. And not one of these self-publishing outfits either.'

Jonas merely grunted at this, in no mood to be mollified. 'You might be willing to give Elizabeth Grainger the benefit of the doubt, but I'm not. That family never did anything unless it had an ulterior motive. There'll be something in it for her, you mark my words.'

Gorman regarded his employer with genuine curiosity. 'You don't think you might be making this personal, sir? I mean, it's been sixty-odd years now since all that trouble. And your family *did* win the original lawsuit, didn't they? The money went to Glen Bannister's parents fair and square in the end. The judge did right by you, despite the Montroses having all the political pull. It wasn't as if you and your family lost out.'

'That's beside the point,' Jonas said wearily.

'Which is, sir?' Gorman prompted.

'Which is that aristocratic families like the Montroses get rich, and stay rich, by hook or by crook. They don't change – ever. Back in days of yore, they probably made their money by winning battles or indulging in land-grabs, or else the family beauty became the mistress of a king or whatever. And over the centuries, they've only become more and more used to being privileged and getting the biggest bite of the cherry. Believe me, their sense of entitlement is staggering. My father taught me that much. And not one of them – and that includes the Grainger woman – ever do anything unless there's something in it for them. I just wish I knew what it's all about this time, that's all.'

Gorman shrugged. He thought his employer was over-reacting but was not about to bite the hand that fed him. 'You want me to continue to monitor the situation, then?'

'Hell yes.'

'And keep Mrs Moore under observation?'

'Yes.'

'Even though all she appears to be doing is legitimately researching her next book?'

'Even so,' Jonas said. 'You may think I'm seeing shadows where there aren't any, but it's the things that you don't know about that can turn around and bite you in the backside. Elizabeth Grainger couldn't care tuppence about Glen's long-dead tart, so until I know what it is that she's actually up to, I won't be able to rest easy. And the best way of discovering that is by keeping track of the writer. What she knows, I want to know *before* she can pass it on to her employer.'

'Very good, sir,' Gorman said, rising from his chair. 'I'll see about the . . . er . . . investigations into Mrs Moore's activities.'

'Yes. And speaking of which, I suppose I'd better get in touch with her and agree to give her an interview. If nothing else, the direction of her questions might give me some kind of clue as to what this is really all about.'

But he didn't sound convinced.

And if the security chief secretly doubted his employer's chances of successfully getting the better of an Oxford graduate and seasoned interviewer, he was wise enough to keep very quiet about it.

After the ex-soldier had left, Jonas sighed and reached for his phone. Since the Moore woman was right now driving back to Oxford, he was hoping to get through to her voicemail and leave a message, rather than talk to her in person, which proved to be the case.

'Hello, this is Jonas Bannister. I've been giving it some thought, and I'd be happy to talk to you about Amelia Montrose and Uncle Glen. I'm just not sure that I'll have much to contribute to the biography,' he began, hoping he'd managed to induce some enthusiasm and helpfulness into his voice. 'I'd hate to waste your time. But if you'll contact my secretary here, she can arrange a time for us to meet.'

He hung up and sat scowling in his chair.

Was he worrying about nothing? Realistically, what were the chances that there could be any evidence left for the Moore woman to unearth after all these years that might bring to light just what his father had done so long ago?

Even if she really was as good at her job as Gorman had said she was, she couldn't conjure up proof out of thin air, could she?

Even so, he didn't like it. This niggling feeling that he wasn't safe – that his comfortable existence and way of life was in jeopardy – just wouldn't stop nagging away at him.

Not for the first time, he silently cursed his father's memory.

This Janet Connor, for instance – just who was *she*? Another groupie, perhaps, like Monty? A woman who'd hung about on the fringe of the Lucky Cuckoos and wanted to relive her glory days? Why should he be worried about people like that? And yet, a little voice at the back of his head insisted, it was people like that who just *might* have seen and heard things. Things that might have meant nothing to them at the time but might start to add up to a clever writer and researcher whose job it was to put all things into perspective.

With a tsk of annoyance at himself for allowing his anxiety to build up needlessly, he opened his laptop and forced himself to concentrate on his work. The here and now – that was what was important. That contract with the French consortium, for instance . . .

Once Lyssa arrived back at her flat, Bibbie gave her his usual disinterested stare from the sofa, before jumping down and deigning to walk across to her, his fluffy black tail raised in greeting. She knew why he was so glad to see her, of course – and walked straight to his bowl and sprinkled in a few morsels of his favourite dry-mix food. Typically, he sniffed them and turned away to wander off to where a patch of sun was shining on the carpet and claimed it for his own.

She then made herself a much-needed cup of coffee and played back the recording of Janet Connor's interview.

When she got to the part where she described seeing Deborah Simmonds and an unknown man arguing after Monty's funeral, she paused the recording and leaned back on the sofa. Had Janet been correct in thinking that it might have been one of Glen's brothers? And if so, which one?

She quickly consulted her notes. Glen had two brothers – one older than himself called Malcolm and one younger than himself called Robert.

She didn't have any photographs yet of either of them, but she was hopeful of finding some images of them somewhere. And if one of them resembled Glen more than the other, then she might be able to put a name to the man Deborah Simmonds had argued with.

But the odds were that both of Glen's brothers were now deceased. As, almost certainly, was Deborah Simmonds herself – unless she was one of the growing number of people who lived to be nearly 120!

She made a mental note to do a check and see if Deborah Simmonds had left behind her any children or grandchildren still living. Then she checked her voicemail and instantly shot upright on the couch as she heard Jonas Bannister's message.

Yes! Finally, an interview with a member of Glen's family. She quickly scrambled through her notes to find the phone number for Bannister's company and got through to his secretary. They then quickly agreed on a mutually convenient date on the day after tomorrow.

She hung up, feeling much happier. It was going to be interesting to hear his personal take on Amelia, as seen from the other side of the battlelines, so to speak. So far, all she had was Elizabeth's own point of view on things, which, almost inevitably, was bound to be biased.

She could only hope Jonas Bannister was going to prove fruitful, despite his worries that he'd be wasting her time. He wouldn't have been old enough to remember much about the band himself, but he must have heard plenty, growing up, from his father, Glen's younger brother.

Who knew, he might even have photographs of the Bannister family that he'd be willing to share?

In the meantime, she had to type up the Janet Connor notes. With a sigh, she turned to her laptop and created another file, clearly marking it 'J Connor Int/view' and began transcribing. She was still deep in the work when her phone rang nearly an hour later.

'Hello?' she answered it absently.

'Oh, so you're back from the wilds of Hayling Island then?' Freida's voice said perkily in her ear. 'Weren't you supposed to call me and let me know? Or did I just imagine that you'd agreed to keep us updated?'

Lyssa sighed theatrically. 'Hello, Freida. Yes, I'm back and I'm fine – I just forget to check in. Happy now?'

'Blissfully,' Freida said, and hung up.

Lyssa grinned at her now dead phone. 'Idiot,' she said fondly.

~

Once her notes had been typed up, she paced a bit, feeling restless. She knew why, of course. Justin Tillman was due to phone her to say whether he'd had any luck in finding the film footage of Monty's last night alive, and the fact that he hadn't yet done so was making her nervous. And for all she kept telling herself that it was silly to feel as if something had gone wrong, another part of her insisted that it had.

She'd noticed on Justin's Facebook page that he had posted a photograph of his daughter Chloe showing father and daughter celebrating what looked like her thirtieth birthday party.

Now Lyssa did a quick trawl of social media and discovered that Chloe Tillman hadn't moved far from the family home – only a matter of ten or so miles to Banbury, another large market town nearby.

But if the news from Justin was bad, and the film lead turned out to be a dead end, there were other avenues open to her when it came to finding out more about the night of Amelia's death. She scrolled through her notes until she came to the name of Derek Jameson. Jameson had been the investigating officer who'd handled Monty's case. He too was now deceased, her notes informed her, but his second wife, Alison, now his widow, had been much younger than himself and was still in the land of the living.

This might be a more hopeful and fruitful line of inquiry. She knew that a lot of retired police officers kept notes and files on the unsolved crimes that niggled away at them, but also liked to keep souvenirs from their most important cases; and surely Amelia Montrose's case must have been one of the highlights of his career? It had almost certainly been his most famous. The chances had to be good that he'd have kept some of the paperwork on it. And that might well include photographs taken on the night of the party – maybe even some stills from the cine film as well.

It shouldn't be too difficult to find Alison Jameson, and fingers crossed she'd be willing to check and see if her husband had kept anything relating to the Montrose case in his private papers. And wouldn't object to letting Lyssa peruse them, if so.

Just then her doorbell chimed and she went to answer the door.

'Hi,' Carter said, holding out a Tupperware container in front of him. 'I've made a pear tatin, and if I leave the leftovers in the fridge the gannet also known as Jason Howerd-Pitt will scoff the lot. I know pears are one of your favourites, so . . .' He wiggled the container at her playfully.

Lyssa beamed at him. 'You needn't ask twice,' she assured him, then, seeing a figure appear over Carter's shoulder, made a show of snatching it off him and hugging it protectively to her breast. 'And no shares-ies. It's all mine! *Mine*, I tell you.'

'What is?' Freida asked, standing on tiptoe and peering over Carter's shoulder. 'Ooooo, is that cake?'

'No, it's not,' Lyssa said, half turning around and pretending to mantle it under her arms.

'Liar,' Freida yelled. 'I can smell cake at one hundred metres, you know that. Come on, give!' She made to snatch it, and Lyssa ducked.

Downstairs in the hall, Neville Rickman paused outside his door, the key half in the lock. He heard Freida's playful shout echoing down from upstairs and smiled.

'No way,' he heard Lyssa teasing her. 'You wouldn't like it anyway. It's not cake, it's a tatin.'

'Who cares – just hand it over, girl, or I'll pulverise you,' Freida threatened.

'Ladies, ladies,' Carter's laughing voice cut in. 'There's plenty for both of you.'

'Good thing too,' Freida's grumbling voice responded. 'Or there might be another murder done. Lyssa's this time.'

Carter laughed. 'I've been told I'm a good cook, but I don't think my culinary efforts warrant homicide.'

'Oh, don't mind her,' Lyssa said. 'We've just got murder on the brain, I suppose. I tell you, I'm beginning to doubt more and more that Amelia's death was an accident, or suicide either, for that matter. Things just keep getting murkier and murkier on that front.'

'OK, that does it,' Carter said firmly. 'I'm not going anywhere now until you spill the beans.'

'And I'm not going anywhere until I get a piece of that cake,' Freida seconded.

Upstairs, Lyssa grinned, and threw open her door to let them in.

But down below, Neville Rickman stood frozen outside his own door. His face, which had at first looked startled at the turn of the conversation going on above him, began to slowly morph into one of anger.

And when he finally completed turning the key in his door and going inside, his expression was downright grim.

10

When Lyssa awoke the next morning, it was trying to rain, and the pearly grey light infusing her room instantly depressed her. She knew this feeling of old, and it meant potential trouble. She rolled over on to her side and stared at the empty space beside her for a while, and as if sensing her need, Bibbie jumped up and came to lie down beside her.

For a while she stroked him gently, but once he'd had enough of that (and every cat owner knows that moment!) she sighed, and forced herself to get up.

With the dim grey day already nibbling away at her psyche, she knew that if she wasn't careful, she was going to have one of her 'bad' days. She'd had plenty of them after Kyle had died, days when she couldn't even get out of bed, days when she could barely read a book, let alone write one. The passing year had winnowed them down to occasional occurrences now, but they hadn't passed completely.

Anything could be a harbinger for one – a restless night, filled with bad dreams. An anniversary – his birthday, hers, their wedding. Or sometimes, just a rainy day and an overwhelming sense of loneliness.

To make her blues even worse, Justin Tillman had failed to phone her by eight o'clock last night, so she'd called him instead but received no reply.

Now she reached for the phone and tried again. And this time it was picked up – but the voice which answered was young and female.

'Hello?'

Lyssa sat forward a little on the sofa. 'Oh, hello. Is this Justin Tillman's number?'

'Yes – that's my dad. He's not here right now.' Lyssa thought it was probably Chloe Tillman she was talking to but didn't want to freak her out by calling her by name. She was bound to ask how Lyssa knew it, and then she'd be drawn into a long explanation. Instead she said brightly, 'Oh, I see. I wonder when might be a good time to call back?'

There was a short silence on the line, and a sense of foreboding suddenly had the hairs on Lyssa's arms standing on end.

'That's hard to say. Dad's in the hospital right now.'

Lyssa felt her mouth go dry, and said quietly, 'It's nothing serious, I hope?'

Again, there was a short tense silence, and then, 'He's had a serious fall, I'm afraid. From the roof.'

'From the roof?' Lyssa echoed in surprise. She couldn't help it, and a moment later, she felt rather sick as a horrific thought hit. 'Oh, please don't tell me he was in the loft and fell from there?'

'What? No. He had been up in the loft earlier in the day, but then our next-door neighbour dropped in to ask Dad if he'd noticed that one of the tiles on the roof had come loose and Dad, being Dad, got the ladder out of the garage and went up to take a look.'

Lyssa felt a wave of relief wash over her at this blessed confirmation that she hadn't been inadvertently to blame for the Tillman family's trouble.

'Sorry, just who is this?' the voice, now sounding rather brittle, abruptly demanded.

'Oh yes, sorry – I'm a writer. I'm doing a biography of Amelia Montrose. I rang your father before because . . .'

'Oh yes, I can place you now,' Chloe Tillman interrupted, sounding a little less stressed. 'It's about the film Grandad took back in the 60s, right? Mum told me about it. She said he was chuffed that someone was still interested in something his father had done.'

Diplomatically, Lyssa decided not to mention that selling his story and film to the press for a nice fat profit might not have been her grandfather's finest hour. 'For a moment,' she said instead, 'when you said he'd fallen from the roof, my heart nearly stopped, because I thought he might have been in the loft when he fell.'

'I wish,' Chloe said bitterly, a catch in her voice now. 'He wouldn't be in the hospital if he had – or at least, it wouldn't be so bad.'

Hearing her distress even over the telephone line, Lyssa felt her heart start to pound sickeningly again. 'Oh no! Was he seriously hurt, then?'

'Yes, I'm afraid so. Broken leg and pelvis, concussion, all sorts. He's unconscious right now, and the doctors are waiting to see how bad the swelling in his skull is going to get. They'll know more if . . . I mean, when he wakes up.'

For a moment there was a dreadful silence as both women pretended not to notice her little slip.

Then Chloe rushed on. 'I just wish the silly sod had called a roofer instead. But he does stuff like that – he says that people nowadays charge the earth to do even the simplest things, and he can mix up a bit of cement and climb a ladder as well as the next man. And, to be fair, he really is quite good at doing repairs like that, and he's always extra careful about safety precautions. He has all the right gear when he's doing some welding – goggles and gloves and such. And when he's using his electric saw he has the guards in place and everything. And he's always careful when he goes up ladders, making sure they're secure. Which is why we can't understand how he came to fall.'

And once again the hairs on Lyssa's arms stood on end. Because what if it hadn't been an accident?

The moment she thought it, Lyssa told herself not to be silly. Of course it was an accident. The alternative was simply unthinkable. And absurd. And yet, suddenly, her hands had gone cold.

'I'm so sorry. I hope you get good news from the doctors soon,' she said, realising how feeble the words sounded. But really, what could you say to a stranger over the telephone that might make them feel better?

'Yes, Mum's still at the hospital, and I've taken some time off work. I've just popped back here to fetch Dad some extra things – slippers and shaving gear and all that. He'll be needing it soon,' she said firmly. As if, by saying it, she could make it so. But Lyssa knew she must be wondering if her father would ever need his shaving things again, and her heart went out to her.

'I'm sorry – I totally forgot about why you called! About Grandad's film . . .' Chloe began.

'Oh no, don't even think about that right now,' Lyssa interrupted her, aghast. 'You have much more important things to think about than . . .'

'That's the problem, to be honest,' Chloe said quickly, her voice a little thick with the tears she was holding back. 'Right now, I'm thinking about them too much, so I'll be glad of the distraction. Let's see . . . Mum said he'd been up in the loft and had brought a cardboard box down. I think it's probably in his man cave. Or as me and Mum call it, the cubby hole in the garage! I'll check it out when I come back from the hospital and see if I can find what you're looking for.'

'Oh, you needn't . . .'

'No, no, like I said, it'll give me something practical I can do. And going through old film canisters is as good a distraction as any. What can you tell me about the date and the subject?'

Lyssa quickly passed over Monty's name and the date of the party, and feeling guilty and still protesting that Chloe didn't need to do it if she didn't feel up to it, she finally ended the call.

For a moment she sat very still on the sofa, feeling totally wrong-footed and uneasy. Then, realising that if she stayed indoors now, she'd just go around and around in circles, fretting about the Tillmans and probably going down a rabbit hole of pointless speculation, she stood up and told herself to get a grip.

She was in danger of seriously losing it if she was seeing conspiracy theories about a poor man falling off his roof whilst attempting to fix a tile!

Determined to nip this bout of blues in the bud before it could get properly started, she went to the closet containing her outdoor coats, boots, hats and bulky clothing like that, to don her running gear.

As she further opened the already ajar door, Bibbie raised his head and glared at her for the disturbance. The floor of the closet, where the odd scarf, exercise towel or bulky dressing gown occasionally fell, provided him with a comfy bed, and was one of his favourite spots for a snooze.

'Sorry, Bibs,' she said, and the cat got up and yawned vigorously, then stuck out his front paws in a sumptuous stretch. As he did so, one of his claws over-reached the towel he was lying on and hooked on to the tip of something that had slipped between the slot of the back wall of the closet and one of the sides.

She saw the small flash of a white square before her pet shook it free and, curious, she reached down and picked it up.

The printing on it was slightly faded, but as she turned it over and read it, she realised it was the receipt from a storage facility nearby, and she frowned. She knew she hadn't ever rented out extra space . . .

And then her breath caught, as she realised Kyle must have done so. She rubbed the paper in her hand, knowing that he'd once held it too, and felt a familiar ache of loss start up inside her. To distract herself, she checked the dates, and realised he'd paid for it just a few months before his death, which meant that the three-year lease was still current.

Funny, but she couldn't remember him ever telling her about it. Maybe he'd forgotten to? The closet was where he'd kept his bulky clothes too, so it had probably fallen out of one of his coat pockets and had wafted down to almost disappear into the crack between the wooden slots, until her cat had accidentally rescued it.

She sighed and slipped the piece of paper on to the high shelf above her head. Now that she knew about it, she would have to find the place and see what was inside – but she could only imagine it would be stuff from his work. It would be the ideal place for him to store his bulky and heavy fitness gadgets and equipment or keep the latest new workout machines that his clients were always demanding.

But that would have to wait for a while. She knew that finding and dealing with whatever remnants of Kyle's old life she found there would make her miss him so much it would leave her feeling sad and depressed for days.

And right now she was too busy and couldn't afford to be distracted. Once *Wild Thing* was written and ready to be published, she could see about disposing of whatever it was and relinquishing the unit.

That decision made, she changed into her running outfit, went through her usual warm-up routine and padded listlessly outside.

On the pavement, she donned her earbuds and called up the Lucky Cuckoos playlist she'd made earlier, and to the sound of their tracks, forced herself into a gentle trot, trusting in the music and the exercise to chase the 'black dog' of depression away.

An hour later, and telling herself that she felt better, she was back home and making some scrambled eggs and toast, instead of her usual breakfast of a cup of coffee. She made herself eat it all, for 'doing something' always helped, and after the run the extra calories wouldn't hurt.

She'd just finished and was wiping her plate, when the sound of her doorbell made her jump a little. She wasn't expecting any of her friends to be dropping in at this hour, as they'd all be at work. And cold callers to the flat were rare.

Aware of feeling just a little uneasy – and angry at herself for feeling that way – she approached the door. Although she was beginning to suspect that there was more to Amelia Montrose's death than at first appeared, she mustn't let herself get spooked by it. After all, anything bad that had happened, had happened sixty years ago. Even if the worst-case scenario turned out to be true, and Monty was murdered, that could hardly affect *her*, here and now, could it?

If she didn't get a real grip on herself, she'd be jumping at shadows next. Nevertheless, as she reached the door, instead of opening it in the normal manner, she found herself calling through it first.

'Hello? Yes?'

Even as she did so, she was wondering what it was that she was really afraid of. Did she truly suspect that the driver of the car that had supposedly followed her yesterday had turned up on her doorstep to warn her off and intimidate her, like they always did on television programmes? Or that it was somebody claiming to be from British Gas in order to trick their way in, so that they could rob her? (Which would have been a bit of a non-starter, since the flats didn't have gas!)

What she got was a rather cross female voice, asking, 'I'm looking for Alyssa Moore. She's writing a book about my father.'

At this, Lyssa both relaxed and couldn't help but give a small, rueful grin. In the crime thrillers she watched at the cinema, wasn't the heroine invariably lured into a trap by letting her curiosity get the better of her? Or meeting strangers alone in out-of-the-way places, or falling for lines that were obviously phoney to everyone else?

Well, if that was so, she supposed she must be something of a living cliché, because she opened the door determinedly (instead of sensibly hiding somewhere or climbing out of a window) and regarded the woman standing there with a jaundiced eye. 'Hello, yes, I'm Lyssa Moore.'

Her visitor was well into her fifties, with a slightly dumpy figure and hair that was clearly dyed platinum blonde. She was wearing over-large glasses and dressed in a trouser suit of moss green that made quite a fashion statement.

'Ah, I hoped I'd got the right address,' the woman said, looking self-satisfied. 'You spoke to my mother, who told me all about you, and as I had to be in Wallingford today, I thought I might as well detour here first and save you the bother of coming to me.'

So far, Lyssa was standing firmly square in the middle of the door and had no intention, yet, of letting her in. 'Your mother?'

'Yes – Monica Farley, formerly Joiner. My father was a famous rock and roll musician in the 60s. You approached her about the book you're writing about the Lucky Cuckoos, his band?'

'Oh, you must be Jennifer,' Lyssa said, satisfied as to her bone fides, and finally stepping to one side to let her in.

'That's right,' her visitor said, taking in what she could see of the flat in one sweep of her grey eyes. 'Nice view,' she commented.

'Thanks,' Lyssa said, feeling just a little off-balance and unprepared. Whenever she was doing an interview, she preferred to have done all her homework first and have a mental list of questions she wanted to ask. Having an opportunity for work thrust upon her like this out of the blue was a new one for her, and she wasn't sure that she liked it.

And was she overthinking things, or wasn't this rather an aggressive move on Jennifer Joiner's part? Or had she just – almost literally – got out of bed on the wrong side this morning, and was still feeling grumpy?

'Would you like tea or coffee?' she asked, forcing herself to be pleasant.

'Either's fine, thanks, but I prefer coffee,' her visitor said diffidently, trailing after her towards the kitchen area, but pausing by the balcony to look outside. 'That the Thames?'

'The Isis,' Lyssa corrected with a smile. 'This is Oxford – apparently we can't call it the same as everyone else.'

Jennifer Joiner looked at her blankly, and Lyssa made a mental note to be very literal from now on. 'It's very kind of you to seek me out,' she said, not really meaning it, 'but I would have been happy to come to you. Your mother was very helpful,' she added sweetly, afraid she might be letting her feelings of antagonism show.

'Hmmm,' Jennifer said sceptically.

Lyssa, a mental image of Jennifer's mother slumbering on her sofa after one too many Pimm's, hastily concentrated on making the coffee as her visitor liked it – black with no sugar – and then ushered her towards her most comfortable armchair.

Jennifer sat down in it and then watched, flat-eyed, as Lyssa gathered her accoutrements around her – notebook, pen and recorder.

'Do you mind if I record this?' Lyssa asked, and for the first time in a long time wondered if her subject would object. But after a long thoughtful glance at the gadget, Jennifer merely shrugged.

'I don't mind, so long as you don't use it for any other purpose than your work,' she said, with a little sniff.

Lyssa assured her she wouldn't, but at the same time couldn't help but wonder what other use Jennifer thought she might have for it. Incorporate it into a modern 'audio artwork' for the Tate Modern perhaps? Play it back at night instead of whale music to help her sleep?

Aware that her earlier depression was in danger of turning her downright snarky, she forced a smile and switched on the recorder.

'Like I said, your mother was very helpful,' she began, trying to summon up some professionalism. 'She told me all about how she met your father, and being friends with his sister, and how she used to go around to Racey's house and was friendly with his mum and dad. She must have talked about him a lot, when you were growing up?'

'Not enough,' Jennifer said flatly. 'I was barely ten years old when he died. He always made me feel like I was special. Not like Mum. Of course, I have a fair few memories of him, but not as many as I'd like. He was taken away too soon – it wasn't fair. And it's a pity the band had broken up by the time I was old enough to understand their importance. If he'd lived until I was older, I could have shared more of that part of his life with him. I'd have been happy to talk to him for hours about his glory days. Very few people can say they touched other people's lives like he did. Just knowing he was my dad made me feel special too.'

Lyssa nodded. 'It must have been quite something to have had such a glamorous figure for a parent,' she began cautiously. Perhaps flattery might improve matters? She hadn't totally got the measure of her subject yet, but apart from the fact that Jennifer didn't seem to have much of a sense of humour, Lyssa was now sure that she could detect some sort of latent hostility hovering somewhere under this woman's surface manner, and she couldn't quite figure out its source.

'Oh yes – I had posters of him and the band up in my bedroom, and photographs of him in costume, performing on *Top of the Pops*. I think it was Alan Freeman who introduced them that time. My mother couldn't remember. Which is typical. They performed on all the shows, you know – *Juke Box Jury* with their first ever hit, and something called *Thank Your Lucky Stars*. All my friends wanted to meet him,' she added with the first hint of a smile. 'You know what teenagers are like.'

Lyssa heard a faint warning bell pinging away somewhere in the back of her mind. It was something she'd developed over the years, and it only happened whenever she sensed that something she was being told couldn't be quite right.

Rapidly, she did a mental trawl of what it could be. She remembered Racey Joiner had died in 1980, so presumably, if she'd been ten years old at the time, Jennifer had been born sometime in 1970. The Lucky Cuckoos had limped along for a few years after Glen's death in December 1965, but surely they would have been long forgotten by the time this woman had become a teenager? The music scene of the 1980s was vastly different from that of her father's era – all Duran Duran and the New Romantics, wasn't it?

She doubted that any of this woman's friends would ever have heard of the Lucky Cuckoos, let alone been impressed by their out-of-date sound.

OK, so maybe the fact that she'd had a dad who'd been a rock musician would have given her some kudos, but even so.

'You sound as if you admired him very much,' she remarked gently.

'Oh yes. I have gathered as many clips of the band playing as I can find. There aren't that many, sadly. Television programmes back then were very lax about keeping their recordings. Some got recorded over just to save money, even!' she said scornfully. 'Others were just chucked out.' She tossed her head angrily. 'Can you imagine the short-sightedness of it?'

'Yes, I'd heard that,' Lyssa said mildly. 'Didn't they lose whole episodes of really iconic things. Like *The Goon Show* and *Steptoe and Son*, was it, and things like that?'

Jennifer shrugged, clearly not caring that examples of Peter Sellers or Spike Milligan's comedic genius and that of their fellow Goons had been lost to posterity.

'I'd be very grateful if you could let me have digital copies of what you have,' she said, keeping her eyes firmly on the prize. 'Describing their performances and featuring some still photographs from them would make a good focal point for some of the chapters in the book,' she added. She was now completely convinced that this rather uptight woman would leap at the chance to have her father's achievements lauded to a whole new generation.

And she was not wrong.

'I can do that,' Jennifer agreed eagerly, then added sharply, 'but I want to read your manuscript before it goes to print.'

Lyssa felt herself stiffen at this instantly and told herself to calm down. 'Oh, I'm afraid that would have to depend on my client,' she said, as calmly as she could manage. 'The focus of my biography, *Wild Thing*, isn't the Lucky Cuckoos, as your mother must have told you, but rather Amelia Montrose.'

Instantly, Jennifer's face froze and became a shade paler. 'Her! Why her? She was nothing,' she hissed.

Lyssa shifted uncomfortably on the sofa. She had not expected such a venomous response, and she suddenly became aware that she was alone, in her flat, with a woman of very uncertain temperament. What was more, she had to wonder why Monica hadn't told her daughter that the proposed biography was about Amelia and not the band. Had she just not thought to mention it – or had she deliberately held back that information?

Now she came to think of it, hadn't Monica seemed to become rather indifferent when mentioning her daughter?

Aware that Jennifer was now glaring at her, waiting for an explanation, Lyssa snapped her attention back to the here and now. 'My client is a relative of hers,' she began to explain, careful to keep her own tone neutral and calm. The last thing she wanted was to escalate the tension she could now feel emanating from her unexpected visitor. 'She feels that the press at the time gave her a very hard time, and that the subsequent image of her has always been very one-sided and biased. She thinks . . .'

But Lyssa didn't get the chance to finish. Jennifer was already rising to her feet and snatching up her handbag and slinging it angrily over her shoulder.

'I have no interest in a book that sets about glorifying the likes of her,' she snapped and headed for the door.

Lyssa shot up and overtook her, managing to get to the door first and open it for her. 'I'm so sorry you weren't aware of the nature of my book,' she said quickly. 'I assumed your mother would have . . .'

'My mother is a disgrace,' Jennifer said stiffly, pausing at the now open door to stare at Lyssa balefully. 'She drinks, and she remarried someone so mediocre that my poor father must be turning in his grave. Worse, she feels no loyalty towards him, which is why I've taken over managing his legacy.'

'I didn't mean to upset you,' Lyssa tried again, but the older woman had already brushed past her and stepped out into the hall.

There, she suddenly spun around and levelled a fulminating glare at Lyssa. 'I warn you, if you publish anything libellous about my father, I'll sue you, your client and your publisher.'

And with that parting shot, and with her colour high, she marched off down the hall and headed for the stairs.

Lyssa turned back into her flat, shut the door behind her and leaned against it, her heart thumping in her chest.

'Phew!' she said and tried to see the funny side of it.

In her career, she'd had a few humdingers of an interview with various people, and emotions could sometimes get the better of them. This was not surprising when people were talking to her about the death of someone they'd loved, for instance. And one of her clients, who'd wanted her to write the memoir of her husband who'd died in the Falklands, had been so upset, she'd cried at practically every session. So, this latest episode wasn't that bad, not on the scale of things.

Nevertheless, there had been something . . . unbalanced . . . in Jennifer Joiner's manner that left her feeling unnerved. Talk about a woman with a Daddy fixation ramped up to the max!

Still trying to shake off her unsteadiness, she returned slowly to the sofa, paused the recording and listened back to it. There were one or two comments in there that she'd have liked to have included. The image of a doting teenage daughter surrounded by posters of her recently deceased rock-star father was heartbreakingly poignant, for instance, and would be bound to resonate with her readers. But she would never dream of including them without Jennifer's permission, naturally. And somehow, she didn't think that would be forthcoming now.

She sighed heavily. Given that someone had just threatened possible legal action against the book, she supposed she'd better inform Elizabeth of the latest developments. With another sigh, she set about doing just that. She only hoped that her client wouldn't question her competence or professionalism and blame her for the way things had turned out.

Elizabeth was scanning the mock-ups of an interior that she was designing for a fashion shop in Marlow when her mobile rang. She didn't often answer phone calls when working, but recognising Alyssa Moore's number, she hit the green button at once and put the phone to her ear.

'Lyssa! How are things going?' she asked brightly.

'Funny you should ask me that,' Lyssa replied with a wry grin. 'I've run into a bit of a drama, as it happens.'

Elizabeth leaned back in her chair, her eyes widening slightly as Lyssa related her run-in with Jennifer Joiner.

'Good grief!' she said with a laugh, when the writer had finished her tale of woe. 'It all sounds rather bizarre. And as for letting her see the manuscript and giving her approval before publication, she must be out of her mind!'

'That's what I thought,' Lyssa said dryly. 'I was feeling wrong-footed right from the start by the way she just turned up, and it all went quickly downhill from there. I tried to turn it around, and it all seemed to be going well enough, I suppose, until she learned that the book wasn't about her father's band, so much as about Amelia. And it was as if a switch just flipped in her head.'

'Ah.' Elizabeth nodded sagely. 'I suppose that makes some sort of sense, at least. I read your account of the interview with her mother last night, and if even half of what she said about Monty and her toxic relationship with Racey Joiner is right, no wonder Racey's daughter saw red. She must have grown up thinking of poor Monty as the wicked witch of the west, trying to rob her father of his rightful place in the band.'

'Yes, I agree,' Lyssa said. 'I was a little surprised by her vehemence, even so. It was really over the top.'

'She sounds to me like she's got some kind of father fixation.'

Over the line, she heard the writer sigh softly. 'Maybe. I'm just worried that, with her being so hostile to us, we might be losing a much-needed source of information.'

Elizabeth scowled, as this hadn't yet occurred to her. 'Damn – you're right. What do you suggest?'

'I thought I'd better phone Monica,' Lyssa said. 'When I initially talked to her, I got the feeling that she was trying to tell me something about her daughter. I think I know now what it was.'

'That she's bonkers, you mean?' Elizabeth drawled.

She heard Lyssa laugh slightly. 'No – not quite that. But I do think I need to do some damage limitation. And talking to Monica, before Jennifer has the chance to poison her against us, is our best shot. The last thing we need is for Monica to dry up on us as well.'

'Good idea,' Elizabeth agreed, staring thoughtfully at a colour chart. 'And don't forget to ask her if she has anything of Racey's that we can use – old letters, journals, that type of thing, that can bolster our case that Monty wrote the lyrics for those songs. On the record label, it only credits Glen as being the songwriter. Racey's daughter might *think* she's carrying the torch forward for her father and has her hands on all the keepsakes and what have you, but in my experience, the wife knows where all the bodies are buried. If Racey complained to anyone about Monty, it will have been to her.'

'Well, if it turns out that you're right about Monty contributing to the songwriting, I doubt Racey would have admitted as much – even to Monica,' Lyssa objected. 'He wouldn't have wanted to say anything good about her.'

'Oh, I doubt he would have said anything complimentary,' Elizabeth agreed with a laugh. 'But he might have written something about her "interfering" or "bothering Glen with her stupid ideas", or "trying to force her poetry on him", or whatever. Don't you think?'

'Perhaps,' Lyssa said doubtfully. 'Anyway, I'd better get on and phone Monica. Keep your fingers crossed for me.'

'You bet,' Elizabeth said. 'And good luck.'

She shut off the phone and put it down on her desk, her face thoughtful.

As she'd hoped, Lyssa Moore was beginning to stir things up, and who knew what was going to float to the surface as a result?

~

Lyssa usually preferred to talk to people face to face, but in this instance, she felt she had no choice. Taking a deep breath, she dialled Monica's phone, hoping that she wasn't still in bed. It was now gone ten o'clock, but she had no idea what the older woman's sleeping habits were. The last thing she wanted was to rouse her from sleep and start things off on the wrong foot.

But after only two rings, Monica answered, sounding chipper and alert.

'Hello? If you're about to spout nonsense that my computer is faulty and I need to talk to your IT expert, you're out of luck. I'm a silver surfer! You don't scam me.'

Lyssa couldn't help but grin. 'Hello, Monica – it's Lyssa Moore. We spoke the other day about the biography I'm writing?'

'Ah, the lovely Lyssa. Of course, I remember you, sweetheart. What's up?'

'I've just had a visit from your daughter, Jennifer.' And now that she thought about it, Lyssa mused, just how had the woman found her address? Not that it was that hard to do nowadays, she supposed. Even so, the thought of Jennifer Joiner tracking her down left her feeling distinctly uncomfortable.

There was a deafening silence on the other end of the line for a few heartbeats, and then a slight sigh. 'Oh dear. I hope she wasn't too rude? Jen can be . . . somewhat abrupt sometimes. But she doesn't mean anything by it, it's just her way.'

'Oh no, nothing like that,' Lyssa fibbed. 'Only I think I might have inadvertently upset her.'

To her relief, there came a dry laugh down the line. 'Oh, that's easily done. I shouldn't let it worry you.'

'I'm glad to hear you say that,' Lyssa confessed. 'I'm afraid she was quite upset to hear that it was Monty that I was writing about, and not the Lucky Cuckoos, as such. I almost got the impression that she seemed to take it for granted that the book was specifically all about her father?'

'Oh yes, she probably *would* think that, I'm afraid,' her mother said, trying to sound offhand and unconcerned, but Lyssa was fairly sure that was just a front. Over the years, she'd become very sensitive to nuances and tones of voice, and she was certain that she could hear a quaver in Monica's voice that meant Monica wasn't as unworried about it as she was trying to sound. 'Jen has a bit of a bee in her bonnet about her father, that's all. I think losing him at such a young age really affected her. Now she's very protective of him, and his memory.'

'I'm sure that's only natural,' Lyssa said soothingly. 'I just wanted to let you know that we'd talked and that I don't think she's going to be participating in the book.'

'I'm sorry to hear that, but not really surprised,' Monica said, her effervescence deserting her, and now sounding rather flat.

Mindful of Elizabeth's desire to learn more about Monty's potential songwriting contributions, Lyssa hesitated for a moment about how best to bring the subject up, then decided to simply take a punt. Instinct told her there would be little point trying to beat about the bush with Monica. 'Jennifer gave me the impression that she was in possession of most of her father's memorabilia and papers, but I was wondering if you had any letters from Racey that I might look at?'

'I doubt it, sweetheart,' Monica said, sounding genuinely regretful. 'I gave them all to Jen long ago. She seemed to need them,' she added defensively.

Lyssa couldn't help but sigh. 'I don't suppose he kept a journal by any chance?'

At this, Monica let out a small yelp of a laugh. 'Racey? Keep a diary? Not him – he was too busy living life and having a good time. Or being miserable. Either way, he wasn't much for writing anything down – he didn't have the patience for it for a start. And writing wasn't his thing.'

Lyssa, seeing the opening, went for it. 'Oh, so he never helped Glen with the songwriting, then?'

'No – oh, he would play guitar riffs, but even then, it was up to Glen to actually write the music down. But to be honest, no matter what Racey said, I don't think many of his music riffs made it into the songs either. That was mostly Glen – he was the one with the real ear for tunes.'

'And words, presumably,' Lyssa added, very nonchalantly.

'Yeah, I suppose so,' Monica said, not sounding so certain now. 'Funny, but I got the impression that though he could sing well enough, Glen wasn't particularly erudite, if you know what I mean?'

Lyssa nodded to herself. Although it was hardly confirmation, it did go some way to bolstering Elizabeth's contention that Monty might well have been the person who'd added the words to Glen Bannister's catchy tunes.

'I don't suppose you have anything of Racey's like sheet music, or Glen's notes on the songs or anything like that?' she asked, without much hope.

'Sorry, no.'

'Yes – I was afraid you might say that,' Lyssa said.

Something of her deflation must have sounded in her voice, for Monica said next, 'Was there anything specific you were after? I might be able to help.'

At this, Lyssa felt herself give a mental shrug. Why not just ask her outright what she wanted to know? She had little to lose at this point. 'I was just wondering if you had anything from Racey, or one of the other members of the band for that matter, that indicated that Monty might have helped Glen out with the lyrics on some of their songs?'

'Not that I can think of,' Monica said, after a moment's thought, clearly not at all startled by the idea that Monty might have done so. Which was another, minor, plus-point for Elizabeth's theory. 'But if anyone would have known anything about that, then it would have been Luke Raines.'

'The manager?'

'Yeah – he and Monty were tight, don't forget,' Monica said. 'And he had his finger on the pulse of everything the band did. He died yonks ago now, of course, but I'm sure he had a daughter . . . or maybe it wasn't a daughter. There was something sad I seem to remember about him . . . I might be wrong, so you'll have to check up on it, but I have a feeling he raised someone as his daughter after her parents died. His brother's kid maybe? Or was it the sister who died? I'm not sure. What was her name now . . .' Over the line came a gentle sigh. 'I remember thinking how horrible it must be to lose your parents like that,' Monica mused. 'I was only a teenager myself at the time, of course, so it struck a chord . . . Caroline! Or Carol? Or Karen? Something along those lines. If you can find her, she might be able to help you out.'

Lyssa smiled. 'Bless you, Monica, I'll do that.' Of course, the orphaned girl might not have kept any of Luke's papers, she mused, warning herself not to get too excited just yet. But negative thinking never helped anyone – least of all a biographer!

'And Lyssa – don't worry about Jen, yeah?' Monica said.

And something sad and wistful – and maybe just a little bit fearful – in her voice, tugged at Lyssa's heartstrings, making her respond warmly. 'Oh no, it's fine Monica, really. I was just sorry we parted on rather bad terms. I didn't mean to upset her.'

And with that, the two women said their somewhat muted goodbyes.

~

Lyssa spent the rest of the day researching the most pressing items on her to-do list (she mustn't forget about setting up a session with Jason's Aunt Edna!) and went to bed, if not totally free of the vague depression that had been with her all day, then at least not totally deflated.

After all, tomorrow she was due to talk to Jonas Bannister, and who knew what he might be able to contribute. His father had been one of those actively engaged with Monty and Glen during the Lucky Cuckoos' heyday and he must surely have told his son plenty of stories about them both.

11

Lyssa took the train to Gloucester, telling herself that it was only because she'd done a lot of driving recently, and she really didn't like it very much, and that it had nothing at all to do with her fear that she might just see the same nondescript car following her again.

But she knew she was lying to herself.

Ever since she'd heard about Justin Tillman's fall, she had been unable to shake off the feeling that everything was connected somehow. And no matter how hard she tried to convince herself otherwise, a little voice in the back of her head kept insisting that something dangerous was happening to her. Or around her. Or both.

The taxi driver knew the way to Jonas Bannister's company, which was in the middle of the city in a rather grand-looking Cotswold-stone building. Since she'd been half expecting that his offices would be situated on the outskirts in some sort of anonymous industrial complex, she was pleasantly surprised when she arrived, and hoped that being in a new city and in such interesting surroundings would help her shake off her bout of the jitters.

Up in his office, Ian Gorman was informed that Mrs Moore had arrived for her appointment, thanked the receptionist politely and left his desk. He'd asked to be notified the moment of her arrival, and now he was careful to take the back stairs, so that there was no chance he might inadvertently cross paths with her.

Once downstairs, he walked to where his car was parked. Inside it, two men were waiting, one behind the wheel whilst the other was sitting in the back. Ian joined the man in the back as, without prompting, the driver pulled away and headed out of town. There was no need for Ian to give him directions – he already knew they were heading to Oxford.

Jonas' security chief glanced at his fellow passenger. 'You have all that you need?' he asked crisply.

'Yes, boss.'

'You know the brief?'

'Yes, boss.'

'It should be a simple enough job,' Ian said, more to himself than his companion. 'There's nothing really fancy involved. Just get in, do the business and get out again and make sure that you're not seen.'

'No worries and I've got all that I need right here,' the other man assured him, patting a small flat briefcase that was set across his lap. He was dressed in a business suit and looked rather young. There was nothing about him that would make any casual observer look twice.

Ian nodded and glanced at his watch. Right about now, the Moore woman should be entering Jonas' office, and his employer was all set to keep her talking for as long as he could.

Which meant that they would have plenty of time.

Lyssa took the comfortable-looking seat opposite Jonas Bannister's large desk and got out her notebook and recorder. She went through the usual routine of asking him if he minded being recorded, and after an initial hesitation, he said that he didn't.

Although he was middle-aged and only Glen Bannister's nephew, Lyssa thought that she could see a distinct family resemblance. But then, Lyssa had spent so much time recently looking at images of Glen and Monty – 'the golden couple' – that they had become almost imprinted on her mind.

'Thank you for agreeing to talk to me, Mr Bannister. I appreciate you taking the time.' She glanced around the office. 'You must be very proud of what you do here. Green energy, trying to help save the planet and all that. Talking about long-dead people from a bygone era must seem rather unimportant.'

She was soft-soaping him a little, but it never hurt to put your subject at ease. Besides, she meant what she said; their poor planet needed all the help everyone could give it.

Jonas waved a hand in a dismissive gesture and gave her a brief smile. 'Not at all. I know my father and grandparents were very proud of Glen and what he achieved. It seems the least I can do is to participate in any book that includes him and the musical legacy he left behind.'

'Your father was Glen's younger brother, am I right?' Lyssa asked. Although she already knew that he was, and had memorised all the relevant facts that she might need earlier this morning, she had often found that it helped put people at their ease if you appealed for their help right from the start. It served to break down any psychological barriers that might be up and paved the way towards setting up a sense of mutual cooperation between them.

'Yes, that's right. My father was only twenty-one when Uncle Glen died,' Jonas agreed.

'Glen dying so unexpectedly as he did must have been a massive shock to his family. His mother and father especially?'

'Oh yes, it was. Dad said he could remember Nan crying for days on end. It didn't help that they had the press camped on their doorstep either. He couldn't go to work without someone snapping his picture. Luckily it didn't last all that long though. After Uncle Glen's funeral they eventually found someone else to pester.'

Mindful of his security chief's instructions to make the interview a long one, Jonas settled back in his chair, content to talk as much as the woman wanted. He'd just have to be careful not to let anything truly important slip, that was all.

'Yes – even reading the newspaper articles from the distance of all these years, I could still get a sense of how frenzied it must all have been and felt. But the press seemed to reserve most of their vitriol for Amelia Montrose.'

'Yes, I suppose they did,' Jonas conceded. 'She was probably too much of a good thing for them to pass up. Beautiful, wild, grieving, a lot of people were fascinated by her, Dad said. And you know human nature – it seems if you have even the least bit of success, everybody can't wait to tear you down. I suppose she was a sitting duck.'

'And the unpleasantness about your uncle's Will couldn't have helped,' she slipped in gently. She'd known all along this would be a sore point, and she felt a little tense as she waited to see how he'd react to the implied criticism of his family.

But Jonas merely shrugged and spread his hands. 'Yes – it all got rather bitter and legally technical. My father said that he could remember himself, Grandad, Nan and my uncle Malcolm all sitting in the front room with these men in suits, talking about courts and injunctions and fees and things. It must have been bewildering for everyone. They were just ordinary working-class people before Glen made it big, living in a housing estate, and going through the same routine every day. Eat, sleep, work, repeat and all that. Up until then, they'd never had any reason to have anything to do with weighty legal matters and handling the press and what have you.'

'No, I can imagine it must have been very hard for them. Who was it, do you know, who decided to challenge your uncle's Will in the court?'

'Oh, Grandad to begin with, but Nan agreed with him. Dad always said that it just didn't seem right, you see, for Glen's money to go away from his family – his own flesh and blood – to some woman he'd just been shacked up with for a few years. Besides, they all needed it, you see, whereas Amelia Montrose was filthy rich already. Her dad owned half a county or something, and she'd been brought up in this big stately home and spoke as if she had a plum in her mouth and drove a flash sports car and all that. Whereas they had nothing.'

His tone seemed mild enough, and didn't appear to hold any sense of injustice, but then this man hadn't been born when all this was happening, so there was no reason why it should have affected him overly much.

Or had the fury and the bitterness of the earlier generation been passed down?

'By the time you were born and had grown up enough to understand about the things that had happened, it must have seemed to you to be all rather irrelevant, I imagine?' she asked artlessly.

'Not really,' Jonas contradicted her, after a moment's thought. 'You have to remember that I'd grown up with the legend of it, if you see what I mean. My grandparents lived to a good age and talked about it a lot, and my dad made no secret of what had gone on. He remembered how gutted he was when Glen died, and often spoke of him,' Jonas said sadly. 'His big brother was a bit of an idol of his, I suppose.'

'A bit of hero-worship going on?'

'Yes – maybe. My dad was a handsome man in his own right, but there's no doubt that Uncle Glen had been really striking, and what's more, the one with all the talent. He was the one who became famous and had all the young girls screaming at him on stage. He made the money that allowed them all to get free of the slums and the humdrum existence of holding down dreary jobs; jobs that paid enough to cover the rent and buy food and clothes, but none of the little luxuries and extras that made life worth living.'

'No wonder your dad looked up to him.'

Jonas nodded. 'Yes. He often talked, for instance, of the day when Glen bought Nan and Grandad the nice house in the suburbs. How chuffed they were to have an indoor loo, and not one out in the back passage next to the coal hole, which froze over in winter! He bought a car for my dad too, and one for Uncle Malcolm. I remember seeing a photo of my dad with this car – a Riley, I think it was. His first car – he looked as proud as a peacock, posing in front of it. As well he might – none of the kids he'd grown up with on the estate or gone to school with could afford a car. They had to still get around on bikes or take the bus.'

'He sounds like a great big brother to have had. I don't suppose you have any family photographs of all the brothers together?' she asked casually, wondering if Janet Connor might be able, after all this time, to pick out the man she'd seen arguing with Deborah Simmonds on the day of Monty's funeral.

'I probably have – somewhere,' Jonas admitted, but without much enthusiasm.

'I'd be grateful if you could let me have a copy of any old family photos you'd be willing to share with the world.'

Jonas shuffled, looking uncomfortable, and Lyssa quickly backed off.

'You were saying how much Glen did for the family? Do you know if he gave much to charity?' she asked, thinking of one in particular. 'The YMT, for instance?'

'He probably did,' Jonas said vaguely. 'My dad always said Glen was the best. He might have become a big pop star, but he never forgot his roots. And he was generous to a fault.'

'And yet he left his estate to Amelia?' Lyssa put in. 'He must have loved her very much.'

Jonas shrugged. 'I suppose he must have. Either that, or by then the drugs and drink had addled his mind a bit.'

'Was he really into the drug culture though?' Lyssa wondered aloud. 'From what some people have been saying who knew him back then, he wasn't as heavily into it as some of his contemporaries.'

Again, Jonas merely shrugged. 'Who knows? The very fact that he died of a drugs overdose proves that he dabbled, at least. I think that's what upset Nan the most – that he died so young. Dad said she went around for months and months saying that it should never have happened. He had his whole life ahead of him, and all that. And she blamed her – Amelia Montrose – for it. I know that much.'

Lyssa nodded. 'Did your father think she was to blame too?'

'Oh yeah. I mean, she must have encouraged Glen, mustn't she? She was a bit of a rebel long before she met him, so it stands to reason, doesn't it? She was expelled from her posh boarding school for drinking and driving and all that. She was already smoking cannabis when she first heard the Lucky Cuckoos playing in that pub, I know that much, because Dad said he could remember Glen talking about it. He was at Monty's Mansion one day, and Glen offered him a spliff. Dad said he was a bit shocked, but also excited, and smoked it because he would have felt naïve and square if he hadn't.'

Jonas paused, then smiled dryly. 'He actually used that word, "square". It sounds so pathetically outdated now, doesn't it? In fact, looking back, it all seems rather sad and squalid. Two brothers smoking weed and neither one of them having any idea what the future held.'

'I'm sorry if talking about it is bringing back bad memories for you,' she apologised.

'Oh, I don't mind,' Jonas said, meaning it, his eyes drifting to the clock, then back to the woman seated in front of him. He hadn't expected her to be so lovely to look at, but he couldn't let all that long black hair or shapely long legs distract him from the fact that she could cause him some serious trouble.

'I can probably talk about the past until you're fed up with hearing it,' he said, a queer sort of smile flitting across his face.

Catching it, Lyssa, for some reason, felt a slight chill creep down her back and told herself not to be silly. She needed to concentrate on learning all that she could from him – especially as he seemed to be so amenable.

'For all that, your grandparents still accepted Monty's invitation to her birthday party, didn't they?' she asked, again careful to keep her voice neutral and light. 'They were even staying the night at her house, along with their youngest child.'

'Aunt Emily? Yes, that's right. I'd forgotten about that. Poor Aunt Em – she must have been only, what, eleven years old at the time,' Jonas mused.

Lyssa nodded. 'Yes, that's right. By why "poor" Aunt Em?' she asked, getting distracted somewhat.

'Oh, I didn't mean anything by that,' Jonas said with a light laugh. 'There's nothing particularly tragic about her. Granted, she's not all that well, and is living in a nursing home. It's just that I've always thought of her that way.'

'Any specific reason?' Lyssa persisted.

'No. Well, yes, I suppose. It's just that she was always one of those people with a single over-riding passion in their lives, that blotted out everything else. In Aunt Em's case it was the desire to be an artist. My dad said that even as a very small girl she was always drawing with crayons and painting, getting mess everywhere. Drove Nan mad. Pictures and pictures of cats and trees and houses stuck up around the house everywhere! She was desperate to be a painter and had already won one or two kids' art prizes that the newspapers and comics ran – you know the sort of thing. Win a set of paints and a "proper" artist's sketchbook for the best painting of a cat or something.'

'Did she achieve her ambition?'

'Oh yes. Well, no,' Jonas said, confusingly. Then he smiled at himself. 'I mean, yes, she became an artist all right and has been one all her life. But she never made it big. Not really big. Several galleries over the years have displayed and sold her work regularly, and she's had one or two very modest critical successes with some of her more inventive canvasses, but mostly she was just popular with the middle-of-the-roaders. You know, those people who buy pictures because they like them, and think they'll look nice in the spare room or go with their current décor, or what have you. But she was never feted by her fellow artists, never invited to join the Royal Academy or the things that really mattered to her. I think that must be more soul-destroying than total failure, don't you?'

Lyssa sighed. 'You mean, better to be a talentless no-hoper, than to have just enough talent to succeed, but not so much that you could ever achieve greatness? Yes, I think I agree with you there.'

'Hence, poor Aunt Em.' Jonas nodded. 'She never married, you know. Didn't have time for a husband and kids. Still, I suppose she must have felt it was all worth it. Following her dream and all that; and to be fair, she did enjoy painting so much, so who knows? Perhaps she was the lucky one! At least she was able to go to art college after all. Even as a little kid, Dad said, she'd been desperate to go. And by the time she was old enough, the courts had already decided that Uncle Glen's money should come to us anyway, so Grandad and Nan could afford to send her.'

'Did your grandad and nan ever talk to you about that night – the night Monty died?' Lyssa asked, firmly drawing the conversation back to where she wanted it. 'It must have been something they could never forget.'

Jonas nodded. 'Sure – they talked about it a bit. But not much. I think they found the whole thing a total nightmare. To begin with, they'd only gone in the first place to try and see if they could get Monty to do the decent thing and just hand over Glen's legacy without having to keep on dragging it through the courts. Then when she was found dead, the police came and questioned them, and all the other guests, and until the inquest brought in a verdict of accidental death nobody really knew if she might have committed suicide after all.'

He paused and shook his head slightly. 'That upset Nan very much, I know – the thought that all her friends and neighbours were talking about her behind her back, speculating that the court case might have driven Monty to it, and that they might be blaming her and Grandad for putting extra pressure on Amelia. Public opinion at that point seemed to divide somewhat, Dad said. Whilst Monty was alive and Glen was dead, she was the scarlet woman, and all that guff. But after she drowned, she became more of a tragic figure. I don't know – perhaps the Great British Public wanted to think that the wild child had redeemed herself somehow, by committing suicide for the sake of love. Or perhaps it was just the pathos that surrounded the death of a young, beautiful girl who should have had her life ahead of her. Who can say? But others still held fast and true to the idea that she'd brought it all upon herself with her lifestyle, and flaunting society's rules. Either way, Dad said they had a rough time of it for quite a while right after she died.'

'It must have been very unpleasant for them,' Lyssa agreed quietly.

'And of course, it set the bloody press off all over again,' Jonas added. 'Pestering them, following them, jumping out of the bushes and shouting out questions over the neighbours' hedges. Dad said it drove them mad. And it didn't help that things dragged on a bit and that it took ages for Glen's money to finally be handed over.'

He stopped speaking abruptly, realising that he shouldn't have said that last bit, and hastily sought for something else to say to distract her. 'At least the police ascertained pretty quickly that Grandad and Nan stayed inside the house during the whole of the party. Those guests that had wandered outside into the gardens at any point were really put through it, though. Dad said he was glad he had kept well away from it all. He was just lucky he'd been at the pub with his mates back in their hometown at the time and could prove it.'

Once again, Lyssa saw his eyes slide away from her and consult the clock on the wall. She hoped he wasn't beginning to weary of all this talking – she still had so much to ask him about.

'Would you like a cup of tea?' he offered pleasantly.

And relieved to have an excuse to prolong the interview, Lyssa happily agreed.

Jonas smiled and reached for his intercom.

12

In Osney Mead, Ian Gorman glanced up at the elegant, white block of flats and checked his watch. His men had been inside for nearly twenty minutes, but he wasn't concerned. He knew that to do a thorough job took time.

He'd never been to Oxford before, and the beauty of the university city wasn't lost on him, but what he liked about it most of all was that this pleasant, leafy suburb was set in a quiet backwater, overlooking the river, and foot traffic was light. It was a sunshine-and-cloudy day, and right now the clouds had covered the sun, and hardly anybody was in sight.

He'd had his man park the car with the front door of the small block of flats in plain sight, and nobody had yet gone in or come out of the building – save for his men. This did not surprise him, since he imagined that the majority of the people who lived here were well-off professionals who were out at work all day, busy earning the mortgage payments. In fact, he was willing to bet that there was a good chance that his two men were currently the only inhabitants of the building.

He'd have lost that bet, however, for there *was* someone else in the building, and right now, he was standing a little to one side of the blinds covering his main window, and was watching Ian's car with cool, assessing eyes.

Neville Rickman lowered the small but powerful pair of binoculars from his eyes and jotted down the number plate of the car, as well as its make, colour and any other details that stood out. He was sure there was someone sitting in the back of the car, but he'd yet to get a good look at him.

He moved swiftly from his post by the window and moved to his front door. His ears had just detected a slight sound from the hall outside, and now he pressed his head to the wood, then slowly, carefully, inched the door open.

He was just in time to see two men slip out of the building's entrance, and he raced back to his position by the window and snatched up a camera with a telephoto lens attached to it. He drew a couple of the blinds apart and snapped away.

As he suspected, the two men made their way straight to the parked car, one getting behind the wheel, the other slipping smoothly into the back. When each man turned to open the door and get in, Neville got a good picture of their faces.

The car pulled smoothly away and disappeared.

Neville nodded grimly. Yes. It was as he'd thought. Someone else was taking an interest in Lyssa Moore and – unless he missed his guess – had just been in her flat.

~

On the train home, Lyssa was feeling quite pleased with how things had gone. She resisted the urge to listen back to the recording with Jonas Bannister, knowing that she'd have to transcribe it all in detail later, but instead reviewed what she needed to do next.

In the searches she'd done yesterday, she'd managed to get the contact details for Alison Jameson, the widow of the police officer who'd handled Monty's case. She'd been lucky enough to find Mrs Jameson at her first attempt at phoning her, and she was happy to cooperate with the book as it meant that her husband's name would live on, in some small way. She lived up in Scotland, however, so they'd agreed that a Zoom call was in order.

Alison had been sure that she'd find something of interest in her husband's 'archives' which she'd consigned to the attic years ago, and once she'd managed to lure a handy nephew over to help her get the boxes down, she would arrange the call. Again, with the help of the long-suffering nephew, who 'knew all about that sort of thing' as she 'didn't do computers and stuff'.

So Lyssa would have to check to see if Alison had left any messages, although it was probably far too early for that yet.

Lyssa had struck lucky again in that she had managed to find a direct descendent of Deborah Simmonds, Monty's charity co-worker – a great-grandson named Jack Flynn. Alas, her luck ran out at that point, for she hadn't yet got him to answer his phone; however, she'd messaged and texted him, and although she'd had no response so far, she was not about to give up. She'd just have to keep ringing and texting him and hope that pester-power would eventually get him to respond.

Of course, once he did, she knew that it might prove to be a somewhat tricky conversation, for she couldn't expect him to be very happy if he twigged, by her line of questioning, that she suspected his relative of pinching charity funds! Which meant that she'd have to choose her words very carefully and be very subtle.

She was still debating whether it would be better to try and arrange to speak to Jack Flynn in person (which meant that she could gauge his body language) or play it light and breezy over a 'chatty' phone call when she boarded the double-decker bus at the train station. Swiping her phone over the pay point, she decided to cross that bridge when she came to it and went upstairs for a seat with a view.

Making a mental note to pass on these troubling developments to Elizabeth when next they spoke, she forced herself to settle down. Speculation was very exciting and all that, but it was steady, hard graft that got the job done. Right now, she needed to focus on her research.

In Osney, she got off at her nearest stop and walked home, feeling pleasantly weary. She again ignored the stairs (she was going to have to watch that – it could become a habit!) and took the lift to her flat. Once inside, she kicked off her shoes luxuriously and then slung her tote bag with a sigh of relief on to the sofa. Thus unburdened and liberated, she made her way automatically to the kitchen area and switched on the ever waiting and obliging coffee machine.

She was just returning to the sofa with her now full coffee mug in hand when she froze in place.

She stared hard at the photograph of Kyle.

Which wasn't quite where it should have been.

'Are you sure you didn't move it when you were dusting or something and just didn't notice?' Freida asked her anxiously, three quarters of an hour later.

Being her own boss, Freida could take off from her office whenever she wanted to, and after getting Lyssa's strained phone call, hadn't hesitated to head right over.

'No,' Lyssa told her now flatly. 'I always keep his photograph in exactly the same place – you know that. It's where the light catches it best – not too near the front where I might accidentally snag it with my elbow when moving past, and not right up against the back of the wall either, where the shadow of the vase might obscure it. I'm telling you – it's definitely been moved. And Bibbie doesn't jump up here, he knows it's off-limits, and he's always been good about it. It's as if he knows the things on here are precious to me.'

Freida glanced at her friend, not liking how pale and strained she looked. 'OK,' she said, inclined to take her at her word, for she knew how obsessive Lyssa tended to be over things relating to Kyle. Which was perhaps not so surprising, under the circumstances.

Kyle had been one of those fit, athletic young men that you thought would live forever – always careful about what he ate, he'd hardly been to the doctor a day in his life. Freida had always found him to be rather aloof in many ways – the kind of man who didn't like you to get close to him. She often wondered if he had an inferiority complex or something, and was thus constantly afraid that people might start thinking he was a fraud; that although he was physically big and strong, and had built up a good business for himself, he was somehow inadequate. She often dropped it into their conversations that everyone suffered from anxieties and worries, and nobody was perfect. But she continued to feel that he was guarded about what he said and did, except, she presumed, with Lyssa.

And then, one day, he'd simply dropped dead on the street on his way to do a fitness programme with one of his private clients. People had rushed to his aid, a passerby who knew CPR had even worked on him, and an ambulance had arrived in short time. But he was dead on arrival at the hospital, and a subsequent post-mortem had found a hitherto unsuspected heart condition – and that was that.

He might have gone at any time, they'd explained sadly. Which didn't alter the simple fact that he was gone now, and without any warning whatsoever.

Lyssa had been initially numb with shock, then distraught and grief-stricken, and then had gone around in a daze for months.

Even now, Freida knew, her friend was not yet quite back on an even keel.

Lyssa cocked her head a little to one side and gave her friend a dry smile. 'I know what you're thinking,' she chided softly. 'You think I've finally lost the plot. But that's not the only thing. Once I noticed Kyle's picture was out of place, I've now done a complete tour of all the rooms in the flat. And it's not the only thing that's not quite right.'

Freida put up a finger. 'Just a sec – I want to see if the boys are in.' So saying, she got up and went out, quickly returning with Carter and Jason. Carter looked concerned, Jason intrigued.

'What's all this?' Jason demanded, looking around ostentatiously. 'Have you been burgled? We only just got back ten minutes ago, but we didn't see anyone suspicious lurking about, did we?' He looked at the American for confirmation.

'Nothing's actually been taken,' Lyssa corrected him, before Carter could back him up. 'All my jewellery is still in the box. The television's still here, so is my laptop. I'd have gone spare if that had disappeared. But things aren't right. My notebooks aren't in order for one thing. And before you say it' – she held up a hand – 'I'm not untidy like you, Jason, and I need to keep my notes in numerical order when I'm doing research, so that I can find things in a hurry. I always number them and keep them from the latest to the earliest. And two have been transposed in the pile.'

She saw Carter nod in understanding. As a perpetual student, he too was fussy about keeping his research things neat and tidy, but Jason looked a bit sceptical and glanced at Freida, who was still watching her friend with a small scowl on her face.

'So, you think – what? Somebody's searched the place, rather than stolen anything?' Freida asked.

At this, Lyssa realised how absurd it sounded. She shrugged helplessly. 'I know, I know! It's crazy, right? I mean . . .'

But she didn't get to finish the sentence as the doorbell sounded. With a sigh of impatience at the unwanted interruption, she walked quickly to the door and opened it, then took a swift breath as Neville Rickman smiled back at her.

'Hello, I hope I'm not intruding?' he asked.

Since she was so tall, not many people could peer over her shoulder, but Neville was one of those who could – and did so now.

'I can always come back later,' he said, beginning to back away as he spotted the trio already there.

'No, no, come in,' Freida called out quickly, flashing him a smile.

Freida's speculative gaze went to Lyssa, then to her caller, then back once more to Lyssa.

'I just thought I'd let you know, someone's been prowling around inside the building,' Neville said, his quick eyes not missing the startled looks everyone began shooting at everyone else. 'I got back early from a meeting, and as I came in I thought I heard someone coming down the stairs. I thought it was probably you, as you're the only one who works from home, but when I made a noise, the footsteps suddenly stopped. It immediately struck me as furtive somehow.'

He slowly moved forward, and Lyssa stood aside to let him pass.

'Well, naturally, that pricked my curiosity,' he continued, 'so I walked to the bottom of the stairs, and the footsteps actually retreated back upwards. And that *really* rang alarm bells. So then I made a big deal of walking to my door and opening it, going inside and then shutting it loudly. But then I waited for a bit, and sneakily opened it. But by then, it had occurred to me that I might have been over-reacting, and it was probably just someone who didn't want to be seen after visiting one of our neighbours for a bit of, er . . .'

'Nooky? Forbidden passion? Illicit love in the afternoon whilst one's nearest and dearest is away toiling at the mill?' Jason drawled. 'How delightfully tacky. I bet it was that sour-faced woman in flat 8. She looks the sort to have a secret toy boy.'

'Shut up, Jason,' Carter said mildly, watching Neville closely. 'Don't tell me you had an attack of very British conscience, and closed your door again and didn't look?' he demanded.

Neville smiled. 'Perhaps I'm not much of a gentleman,' he conceded with a rueful grin, 'but I have to admit that I looked all right. And saw two men come down and very quietly make their way out the front door.'

'Wow – *two*!' Jason said, impressed. 'Definitely the woman in flat 8.'

Everyone ignored him.

'Had you seen either of them hanging around here before?' Carter asked.

'No – and there wasn't anything obviously suspicious about them,' Neville said. 'Apart from the fact that they'd gone out of their way not to be seen.'

'What – they weren't dressed in black-and-white striped shirts, wearing black eye masks and carrying a bag marked "Swag" over their backs?' Jason asked, but even he didn't sound particularly jocular now.

'I'm afraid not,' Neville said. 'They were dressed in suits and ties, and one looked barely out of his teens. But I didn't like the look of them even so, so I thought I'd just go around and drop a note through everyone's door' – at this point he waved his hand, which did, indeed, hold a sheaf of white notepaper – 'and ask them to check that nothing's been taken. But I heard voices from inside here, so . . .'

He shrugged, then looked from Lyssa to the others and back to Lyssa. 'Is everything all right?' he asked quietly.

'No, it isn't,' Freida put in, before Lyssa could respond. 'We're pretty sure someone's been in here.'

Neville took an automatic step towards Lyssa, then stopped himself. 'You should call the police,' he said immediately. 'And change your locks. Do you have an alarm system fitted?'

'No,' Lyssa admitted. She'd always thought of her home as being in a safe neighbourhood and, being surrounded by other flats, she'd always felt reassured to have other human beings close by – just in case. Now though, she was beginning to feel as if she might have been rather naïve.

'We haven't got one either,' Carter confessed, seeing her expression. 'Perhaps we should get one too. Lyss, I can arrange it, if you like?'

Lyssa nodded reluctantly. Although she didn't much like the idea of living in a fortress – and she was sure to forget the alarm code or not set it properly or what have you. How embarrassing it would be if it went off, making an awful racket, and she couldn't figure out how to shut it off! This was the sort of thing Kyle would have seen to and taken on . . .

She mentally pushed the thought aside. 'Yes, I suppose it's for the best.' She sighed. She didn't like the thought of having to do it, but it was better than feeling like this. Invaded. Frightened. Unsafe in her own home.

'Good idea,' Neville said. 'I can recommend a really good system – and a security company as well if you like.'

'Does your flat have a burglar alarm?' Lyssa asked, curious.

Neville gave a brief, rather hard sort of a smile and a firm nod. 'Oh yes. And a proper bolt and chain on the door.' So saying he turned and looked at her own front door, which was still standing slightly ajar behind him. 'I see you don't have one of those either. I think it would be just as well if you did. Sometimes burglary gangs "canvass" a place before actually doing it over, and that might be what's going on here. The last thing you want is to be at home when they come sneaking in, and not having any means of physically barring your door.'

Lyssa nodded. 'OK. Thanks.'

Neville nodded, then glanced at Carter. 'I'll text you the name of the company and some recommendations as to what options are best for here?'

The two men exchanged nods and knowing looks.

Lyssa walked Neville to the door and thanked him, then watched him walk away down the corridor. When she came back into the room, she stood looking at her friends, miserably. 'You'd better go and check your own place is OK, guys,' she told Carter and Jason. 'Make sure they haven't been through your stuff as well.'

They agreed, and Lyssa and Freida watched them hustle off. Then Lyssa jumped a little when Freida gently placed a hand on her shoulder. 'Do you really think everyone in the building has been targeted?' she asked her anxiously.

But Lyssa could only shrug.

And wondered just what it was that Neville Rickman did for a living that required him to keep his home locked up like a bank vault and have the specs of security systems at his fingertips.

In High Wycombe, a naked Elizabeth Grainger stretched luxuriously on her bed and then rolled over to kiss the shoulder of the man lying beside her. 'That was nice,' she said simply. 'Especially as I wasn't expecting you.'

Her lover grinned at her. 'You know how it is. I have to keep you on your toes. Make sure I don't have any rivals that I don't know about.'

'Hah! As if! Want a drink?'

'Can't – I'm driving. I have to be back at the studios in a couple of hours.'

'What are you filming?'

'Something for Netflix.'

Elizabeth reached into the top drawer of her bedside cabinet and lit a cigarette. Seeing this activity, the man made a face and got out of bed and walked naked to the window, which he threw open, letting in the fresh air. Elizabeth watched him, half amused, half annoyed. She was not about to quit smoking for anyone, but she was in no mood for an argument about it.

'So, it's definitely on, then?' she said instead, watching the glowing tip of the cigarette end with a thoughtful gaze.

'Yes, it's on,' her lover said. 'But I'll have to make the pitch by the end of the month.'

'That doesn't give me much time,' Elizabeth objected. 'Can't you string it out a bit?'

'Not really. They might go with another proposal if I do.'

'No – don't let them do that,' Elizabeth said quickly. 'I'll just have to hope for the best. It was always a bit of a punt anyway.'

Her lover turned from his contemplation of her tiny garden and the view across High Wycombe's wooded valley. He smiled lazily at her. 'Well, if things don't turn out, at least you'll have got a book out of it.'

Elizabeth stuck her tongue out at him and threw a pillow his way, which he caught easily. 'Put that bloody cigarette out and I'll come back to bed,' he told her.

Elizabeth cheekily took another drag on it, then smiled and put it out in an already overflowing ashtray. She wriggled her fingers at him, beckoning him closer. It was easy to be nice to him, especially when he'd been so good to her.

Freida had returned to work, but within the hour Carter and Jason were back in Lyssa's flat, with both of them reassuring her that nothing had been taken, and Carter, at least, sure that none of his things had been trifled with. Jason, who was much messier than his better half, said he didn't think anything of his had been touched either, but couldn't swear to it.

'So just what the heck is going on?' Carter asked gently, sitting on the sofa and watching her with troubled eyes. 'Do you really think it has something to do with the book you're writing?'

Lyssa paced up and down, shaking her head. From his favourite perch on top of Lyssa's work desk, Bibbie watched her prowling, with his ears back and his own tail twitching, clearly picking up on her stress. 'I don't know. I can't see how it can have – I mean, not really. OK, we've sort of toyed with the idea that maybe Amelia Montrose was murdered, but that's just pure speculation. And even if she was, why would anyone be worried about it all these years later? No, it's probably just as Neville said – we've had a couple of chancers scoping us out, and we'll just have to be on the alert until we get the alarms and stuff fitted.'

She paused, then said slowly, 'Unless . . . but no, it doesn't make sense.' She shook her head fretfully.

'Come on, chicken, cough it up,' Carter said dryly. 'What doesn't make sense?'

Briefly, she filled them in on the Tillman family – starting with the grandfather who'd taken the original film, down to Justin Tillman, who was trying to cash in. 'But I can't see any good reason why he might send someone to check me out – it's not as if *I* have anything *he* wants. It's the other way around.'

'You're right,' Carter conceded. 'Doesn't sound likely he'll have had anything to do with it.'

Jason, perhaps to make up for his joking attitude earlier, said suddenly, 'You know, if you're really worried, I have this mate who's great with IT and stuff. He can check out your laptop for you – make sure nobody's accessed it or is hacking into your emails or what have you.'

'Isn't that taking things a bit far?' Lyssa asked.

'I don't know. Is it?' Jason asked, his expression, for once, deadly serious.

Lyssa blinked, then felt her shoulders slump. 'All right. As my gran always said – better safe than sorry.'

'My gran too,' Carter said.

'My granny's advice was to always bite down on the metal to make sure it was gold before buying,' Jason said sardonically.

Lyssa couldn't help but laugh. 'I think I'd have liked your granny.'

'You'd be the only one, then. Nobody else could stick the old bat.'

13

When they'd gone, Lyssa continued to roam around, feeling as restless as Bibbie on Bonfire Night. She knew someone had been here, touching her things, and everything felt contaminated. Her very skin seemed to itch. Telling herself to stop moping and actually do something about it, she went into the cupboard under the kitchen sink and got out all her various cleaning fluids and rags and proceeded to vigorously clean the apartment from top to bottom.

When she'd finished, she was slightly sticky and exhausted, but felt a little better in herself. She took a long shower, climbed into her favourite pyjamas, pulled on her oldest and most comfortable dressing gown and slumped on to her favourite chair. Instantly, Bibbie jumped up and settled on her lap.

She knew she should type up her notes on the Jonas Bannister interview whilst it was still fresh in her mind, but she just didn't have the energy – or the will – to do it right now.

Instead, she reached for her phone and checked it for messages. There was just one – a stark, short text from Chloe telling her that her father was in a coma. And instantly she was aware of feeling afraid. For she couldn't help but wonder if she was somehow responsible for what had happened to him. What if her quest to find out the truth about what had happened to Monty all those years ago was somehow harming people in the here and now?

Angry with herself, Lyssa shook her head. Now she really was in danger of falling down the rabbit hole! She had to get a grip on herself and stay focused on her work and not indulge in sheer flights of fancy.

Feeling grumpy and unsettled in equal measure, she crossly stabbed out the number for Jack Flynn, expecting to get the usual voicemail message. So she was totally wrong-footed when it was actually answered.

'Yeah? This is Jack.'

'Oh – Mr Flynn, I'm glad to have finally connected with you,' she heard herself mumble. 'This is Alyssa Moore. You might have got my voicemail messages and texts?' she added, trying to sound more professional.

'Uh? Probably not – I've been really busy lately,' said the voice, which sounded young and just slightly belligerent. 'Whaddaya want?'

'I understand you're a relative of Deborah Simmonds?' Lyssa began.

'Who?' the voice shot back uncompromisingly, and Lyssa felt her heart sink. This did not bode well.

'Deborah Simmonds – she'd have been your great-grandmother? On your mother's side of the family.'

'Yeah? If you say so.'

Lyssa sighed, all hope now gone, and only going through the motions. 'I'm writing a book about Amelia Montrose. She and your great-grandmother worked closely together, and I was hoping to gather information on her – your relative, I mean. I take it you never knew her?'

'A book?' The voice sounded sharper now. 'What sort of book?'

'It's a biography of Amelia Montrose. She was associated with the Lucky Cuckoos, a pop group in the 1960s.' She didn't bother to ask if he'd heard of them – she doubted the youth on the other end of the line had even heard of U2. 'Deborah Simmonds helped her run a charity. I was hoping that there might be some family papers or photographs I could use and incorporate in the book.'

'What, for cash in hand, like?'

Lyssa closed her eyes at the inevitability of that question, but remembered Elizabeth's willingness to pay for good material, if necessary. But she'd have to be careful. She was beginning to suspect that Jack Flynn might be very adept at relieving people of their money.

'That would depend,' she said, careful to keep her voice neutral. 'If you have any paperwork relating to the charity they ran – it was called the Young Mothers' Trust, or YMT for short – then there might be something that we can work out.'

'My mum died last month – there's still some stuff in her house to clear out. I can take a look if you like,' he offered.

'Oh, I'm so sorry to hear about your mother,' Lyssa said, immediately feeling guilty. Here she was, allowing her recent upsets to put her in a bad mood and feel antagonistic towards someone she'd never met, and all the time he'd been grieving. 'We don't have to do this now, if you like, I can always . . .'

'Nah, it's fine. The council's been banging on at me to clear the place out, so I need to get it done anyway. I'll go over now and pick up any papers and photos and stuff and look through it. What was that name you wanted? YMTA?'

Slowly Lyssa repeated the name of the charity. 'Also, any photographs you might have of Deborah, please.'

'Dunno that I'd recognise her,' Jack Flynn pointed out. 'But Mum was a stickler for writing things down, so she might well have written the names of the people on the back. It's the sort of thing wrinklies like to do, innit?'

'She sounds like she was a well-organised woman,' Lyssa said approvingly.

'Yeah – s'pose she was. She was a bit of a pack rat too. Her house is full of old tat and stuff.' He sighed, no doubt at the thought of all the work involved in clearing it out.

'Well, please let me know what you find.'

'Yeah, I will,' he said, and sounded as if he meant it. As he no doubt did, if he could smell a profit.

Lyssa rang off and tossed the phone on to the sofa. Somehow, her chat with Mr Flynn had failed to lift her mood!

Instinctively, she reached down to caress the soft silky head of her cat, who had long since fallen asleep. Great. Now she wouldn't be able to get up until he woke and climbed back off her lap.

Downstairs in his flat, Neville reviewed the conversation he'd had with Lyssa Moore and her friends. He was confident that the lies he'd told her had been accepted and had been taken at face value, which was good. It meant that she trusted him.

What was not so good was the escalation that her home invasion indicated. He reached for his phone and speed-dialled a number.

'It's me,' he said. 'We need to meet. I don't like the way things are going.'

In Nuneaton, Jack Flynn left his bedsit and headed out of the door, slinging an empty backpack over one shoulder. He'd only been out of his last stint in prison for two weeks and hadn't yet got his own set of wheels, which was annoying, but a few raids on some building sites would soon sort that out. Besides, he was reconnecting with some old members of his gang, and they had their eye on a warehouse or two, so he should soon be flush.

Of course, he'd have to have eyes in the back of his head, and trust no one. Nowadays narks were everywhere, and it only needed someone with a grudge against him to rat him out to his parole officer, and he'd be back inside. Associating with known criminals was a definite no-no.

So, the idea of making some perfectly legit cash in the meantime, just to tide him over, was sweet.

He rode the bus to the housing estate where his mum had lived her whole life, and let himself into the tiny, mid-terrace council house after carefully glancing around to make sure that he wasn't being observed. That was partly out of pure habit, but partly because they were a nosy bunch of losers around here.

He was confident, at least, that none of the local talent would have bothered breaking in here – his mum had been as poor as a church mouse and everyone knew it.

Inside the tiny sitting room, he gazed around with a mixture of sadness and contempt. He had three sisters, and all of 'em had been the apple of her eye. Unlike himself. In return, they'd given her all this dross at Christmas time and on her birthday – little china ornaments, tiny wooden carved animals, tea cosies and twee prints. None of it worth even scrap value, he thought in disgust.

Ignoring the room, he bounded up the stairs and stood on the landing, eyeing the loft door in the ceiling. By climbing precariously up on the bannisters, he was able to stretch out and put his finger through the little metal ring and detach the hatch. This he then tossed on to the floor and swung himself up, pulling himself through the opening.

He'd always been a little runt, but his skinny body had a certain wiry strength which had served him well growing up and meant that he could wriggle his way through smaller windows than most of his rivals in his line of business could manage. And carrying a flick-knife and earning a reputation for knowing how to use it properly when he was out and about had kept him safe from roving scavengers over the years.

Once in the attic, he turned on the dim overhead light and looked around in dismay. Wonky kitchen chairs with broken legs, vacuum cleaners that would never suck again and a box of toys and stuffed bears, busily moulting. Why his old mum hadn't just chucked the lot on the skip, he didn't know. It stank of old memories and damp woodwork. No doubt there was a bloody leak in the roof somewhere.

Well, that was the council's problem.

He walked over to a pile of big cardboard boxes that had once housed blankets and worn sheets, and saw familiar writing on the side, listing their new contents. Good old Mum!

He pulled the boxes about until he found the name of his grandmother – Alice – written prominently in black felt tip pen. The woman on the phone had been on about a Deborah Simmonds, so Alice must have been Deborah's daughter. And his mum, silly sentimental twit that she was, had kept all her mum's old stuff up here all these years. If there was any of this Deborah woman's stuff going, it would be in here, he reckoned. He was pretty sure his nan had been a pack rat too.

Why the hell the women in the family bothered to hold on to dead people's junk he didn't know, but it was funny to think that it might turn out to be a nice bit of luck for him that they had.

Dragging the box to the open entrance of the hatch, he lay flat on his stomach and shifted the box awkwardly over the hole, lowering his arms down as far as they'd go before dropping the box. It hit the landing with a cloud of dust, but luckily didn't break apart. Coughing and cursing in the suddenly dry and dusty air, he dropped back down on to the landing himself, and then knelt beside the box, opening it up.

There were some clothes and stuff on the top, and a scrapbook or two, which he carefully set aside. That might interest the writer woman who'd called him. There were some pewter coffee pots that might have some scrap value, and these he also put aside. The rest of the box was full of crap, but at the very bottom were stacked some leather-bound tomes which, when he opened them up, showed yellowing pages.

Which meant they must be old. They were full of handwritten stuff, and one tome looked like some sort of set of accounts – again handwritten in fading blue ink, listing columns of numbers with letters at the top. L/S/D. That made him guffaw for a bit, imagining his old nan high on psychedelics. But somewhere in the murky and distant past, he was sure his mum had said something about 'old' money – pounds, shillings and pence, and how, for some reason, they had been known by these letters.

Feeling optimistic that he might now have something to bargain with when he called this Moore woman back later, he opened the rucksack and shoved everything inside that he thought might contain paydirt. He'd take it back to his place and look through it more carefully tonight. Fingers crossed, he'd find something the woman on the telephone had mentioned and sell it for whatever he could get. And the scrapbook was bound to have photos and stuff – and who knew, there might even be something in there about that pop groupie the writer had been banging on about.

He couldn't for the life of him figure out why people bothered to read books when there was the internet, but if there was money in it, he was bloody well going to get his share.

The pewter he'd drop off at some junk shop on the way back. With any luck, it would cover the cost of a few takeaways.

Lyssa, now free of Bibbie, who was stuffing his face with left-over salmon, still felt unable to cope with the chore of transcribing the Jonas Bannister recordings, so hit the internet instead. She'd already started on trying to track down what had happened to Luke Raines after the Lucky Cuckoos had disbanded, and found he'd gone on to manage several bands in the 1970s – some that had had more success than others.

But come the 1980s he must have felt he was too far out of the loop to stay in the music business, and he'd retired to the south coast, in a small landlocked town in Dorset. There she'd found an obituary for him in the local paper. Which led her to the useful information that he'd been survived by his 'beloved niece, Caroline, who still lived in the family home'.

Unfortunately, Monica's vague recollection that Caroline was orphaned young and had been raised by Luke had proved to be only too true, and when she'd begun a search for all of Luke's siblings, she'd found that those of his youngest sister had been lost in a records fire in their hometown. Which meant she still had no idea of Caroline's surname – for if she was indeed the child of Luke's sister, then the sister would have married and taken on her husband's name. Which meant she'd have to do things the hard – and long – way.

Several ancestry search engines helped her to eventually come up with a few possibilities and she noted them down. The first two possible Carolines ended – literally – in a dead end, when she searched the registry of death databases. But three were still in the land of the living.

The first one had a Facebook page, but a quick scan convinced Lyssa that she was not the Caroline she wanted. Although she wasn't expecting Luke Raines' niece to still be posting much about her dead uncle or her connection to the Lucky Cuckoos, she was sure that there'd be something – but after an hour of trawling back in her timeline, there was nothing.

The second Caroline had emigrated to the US when Luke Raines would still have been alive and, since the one she wanted had still been living with her uncle at the time of his death, could not be the right person.

The third Caroline had no social media profile at all – which was perhaps not so surprising. Not everyone was a silver surfer. She was the one who'd married a farmer from the same area of Dorset as the one her uncle had retired to, so she looked to be the most promising. But a hunt through the land registry showed that the farm had been sold for a huge amount of money in 2002 to a property developer, and there the trail ended.

But not one to be defeated, Lyssa made a list of farming society websites and began to trawl. Farmers, she knew, had a high suicide rate, and consequently there were a lot of clubs and help sites set up to help them stay in contact with their contemporaries.

Drafting a message for anyone with any information about a Mrs Caroline Dixon-Hayes to contact her, she posted on all of them and finally turned off the laptop.

It was now dark, but after the rollercoaster of a day she'd had, she had no appetite, so dismissed the idea of making dinner. Instead, she reached for her earbuds and downloaded a random mix of 1960s classics.

And fell asleep on the sofa before the last one had played.

14

The next day, Jonas was in the office bright and early and had barely settled down to work when his intercom buzzed, and he was informed that his security chief wanted a word.

The businessman felt a slight quiver of alarm ripple through him, and he silently cursed Elizabeth Grainger and Lyssa Moore. Although he was reasonably sure that their threat to him was negligible, the fact that every time Ian Gorman now asked to see him made him feel uneasy was enough to rouse his temper.

Damn it, why couldn't life get back to the smooth running of before? He resented, bitterly, being made to feel unsettled like this all the time.

'Tell him to come in,' he said gruffly into the speaker, then sat back and watched as the former soldier, walking neatly and swiftly – as was his habit – came to stand before the desk.

'Just to let you know. My people have now been able to go through the contents of the Moore woman's laptop, and it doesn't contain any nasty surprises. As you know, we were able to tap into her phone conversations almost right away, even before we had to visit the flat, and so far she seems to be doing nothing more than tracking down the people involved in Amelia Montrose's life and times – or their relatives, since most of the people concerned are now dead and gone. In some cases, long gone. A case in point . . .'

He paused to consult his notebook. 'She telephoned a Mr Jack Flynn. It seems he's a relative of Deborah Simmonds, who . . .'

'*He's what?*' Jonas yelped, surprising his usually imperturbable security chief considerably by jumping to his feet and turning very pale.

Ian Gorman regarded his employer thoughtfully for a moment. 'I take it that's a significant development – and not a very welcome one?'

'Of course it is! What passed between them? Tell me exactly.'

Ian Gorman pulled up the transcript of the telephone conversation between Mrs Moore and Jack Flynn and read it back verbatim.

As he did so, Jonas sank down on to his chair, sweating profusely. When Gorman had finished speaking, he took an unsteady breath. 'I want you to track down this Flynn man at once and find out where he lives. Then I want a search made of both his place and that of his dead mother – have your men remove any old papers and documents, no matter what they are.'

'Anything else, sir?'

'Yes, find out all you can about Jack Flynn. His circumstances, his background, anything.'

The security chief nodded. 'Am I looking for anything in particular?'

'Anything we can use again him, if need be,' Jonas said bitterly. And added softly, 'I'm almost sure she wouldn't have kept anything . . . she wasn't stupid. But you never know . . . Dad never trusted her . . .'

'Sir?'

Aware that he was mumbling, Jonas shook his head. 'Nothing. Just do what I said – as fast as you can.'

Without another word, the former soldier departed.

In her apartment, Lyssa was up and dressed, and busily transcribing her notes. She was interrupted by a phone call not quite half an hour into the task.

Absently she reached for it and answered. She recognised a broad Scottish accent at once and assumed it belonged to Alison Jameson's nephew.

'Hello, Mrs Moore? You spoke before to Nanna, when she agreed to look up Grand-da's files for yer book?'

'Hello, yes, thanks for keeping in touch. How's it going?'

'That's why I'm calling. Nanna wants to talk to yez, if you've a laptop handy?'

'I certainly do,' she said eagerly, quickly saving her notes, and then calling up the menu.

'Fine – I'm setting it up now. What would we do wi'hout Zoom, eh?' he muttered, as over the line Lyssa could hear him busily tapping on keys.

Within minutes all the necessary data was shared, and she and Alison Jameson were looking at one another on the screen. Lyssa saw a small woman with a white cap of hair and sparkling brown eyes in a very wrinkled but pleasant face.

'Lyssa, is it? So nice to meet you in person – well, almost,' the woman said. Her accent wasn't so broadly Scottish as her nephew's.

'Hello, Alison, and thank you so much for helping me,' Lyssa began, with a friendly smile.

'Oh, it was nae trouble. I love talking about Derek anytime, even now, and it's brought back a lot of good memories. After I heard you were writing a book about that poor lassie that died in her pond, I got to thinking back. It was a big case, right enough, and one of Derek's most famous, and I remember him talking about it all the time – once the coroner's verdict had been returned. He was tight-lipped about it before then, mind. Well, as you can imagine, him being in the police and everything.'

‘That sounds hopeful from my point of view,’ Lyssa said with another encouraging smile. ‘I’m hoping against hope that you found something about it in his papers, then?’

‘Oh aye, quite a bit, in fact,’ Alison said, making Lyssa’s happy heart skip in her chest. ‘He kept his own file – nothing official, of course, that’s against the rules, ye ken. But his old notebooks are still there, and some of his own jotted-down thoughts. I can let you have anything you need – my nephew tells me I can just swipe some little gadget or other over the papers and send them through the ether to your gadget. Hold on a mo . . .’

She leaned to one side, and another face loomed into view – that of a middle-aged, freckle-faced man with a mop of unruly sandy-coloured hair. ‘Hello there – do yez have an email address?’

Lyssa sent it to him, and after a moment, a ping sounded on her smartphone. ‘Sounds like they arrived OK,’ she said, giving him a thumbs-up. ‘I’ll download them and read them right away. But I was wondering if *you* had read them, Alison?’

‘Well o’ course I did, lassie,’ Alison said with a broad grin. ‘Curious as a cat, that’s me.’

‘What did you make of them?’ she asked. Although she now had the copies of his notes, Alison had been married to Derek and he must have spoken to her freely about the case – more so than he would have bothered writing down. And a good researcher never missed the opportunity to get someone’s take on things who had been there on the spot.

‘Oh, it brought it all back,’ Alison said at once. ‘One of his constables actually fished the poor lassie out of the water. As you probably already know, she was found by a young couple at the party who’d wandered out for a bit of a smooch, Derek always reckoned. And neither one of them thought to wade in and bring her to shore. I thought that was rather callous, but Derek said at least they didn't disturb any evidence.'

'Was there much?'

'Nae, no' really. He said there were nae signs of a struggle at the pond's edge. No footprints, nothing tangible like. Which seemed to support the theory it wuz an accident. They found an empty glass that had contained champagne or somethin' on the paving stones around the pond, which is why they thought she'd been drunk and probably just toppled in, like.'

'So, he never had any doubts about the verdict, then?' Lyssa said, feeling relieved. The thought of accidently crossing the trail of a killer had been giving her the heebie-jeebies, so she was glad to be able to put the possibility to one side once and for all.

But it was at this point that the old woman very visibly hesitated. 'Well, yez and nae,' she said, stringing the words out and making Lyssa's spirits drop. 'He said all the evidence that there was pointed to an accident, or maybe a suicide. But . . . he always told me that the case left him feeling a bit antsy.'

Lyssa bit back a sigh and, worried that the other woman might pick up on her tension, tried to keep everything sounding very casual. 'Oh? Antsy how?'

'He just didnae like the feel o' it, he said,' Alison responded with a small shrug. 'You know how it is, when something just feels off, but you can't quite put your finger on it?'

Lyssa gave a rather rueful smile. 'Yes, I know the feeling. Was that all it was, or did something in particular worry him?' she pressed.

On the screen, Alison frowned slightly, making her wrinkles multiply. 'Well, he thought there wuz a lot o' people at that party who didn't like her for one thing. And he didn't like that.'

'You mean the Bannisters – Glen's parents?' Lyssa clarified.

'Aye, them for a start. They were all set to sue her in the courts for their son's money at the time. Can't say as I blamed them for that though, neither did Derek, although he had to stay impartial. It seemed so unfair that a rich woman should get richer, when that young lad's working-class parents were left with nothing. After all, they raised him, and that's nae cheap.'

'Did he suspect them of taking more drastic action against Monty, then?' Lyssa asked, again careful to keep her voice light.

'Nae,' Alison said cautiously, elongating the word thoughtfully. 'I would nae say that. Don't forget, that chap with the camera was making a film of everything, and he caught Monty steppin' out into the garden, and Derek went over that reel of film frame by frame. He was sure the Bannisters didn't leave the party at all. Plus, he said from the witness statements that they were talking tae someone practically the whole time. Either that, or they wuz at the bar – the booze was free,' she added wryly. 'And plenty of it, according to Derek.'

Lyssa nodded slowly. 'In that case, I'm surprised he was so wary about accepting the accidental verdict.'

'Aye, well, the Bannisters were nae the only ones to have a bone to pick with the poor lassie – there were the others in the band to consider as well. He asked around, ye ken, and found out that there were serious ructions between the band and the dead lassie.'

'Yes, I know about those,' Lyssa admitted.

'And not all of the band members were in sight of the party cameraman all the time.'

'Oh?' Lyssa said, becoming tense. 'Did he know which band member was gone the longest?'

'Oh aye – the drummer for one, and the one who played lead guitar.'

Lyssa nodded casually. 'Ron Joiner – or Racey as he was popularly known, and Micky Ventriss. Did Derek question them, do you know?'

'Oh aye – he or some of his men questioned everyone at the party. The drummer and guitarist said they were in the conservatory, getting pie-eyed on brandy and probably something less legal. My Derek said the place stank of weed and not the kind that your ordinary gardener might dig out of the lawns, if ye get mae drift.'

Lyssa grinned. 'The 60s,' she said.

'Aye, the 60s,' Alison said with a fond smile. 'I hope I've been of help to ye?'

'Yes, you've been wonderful. And is it all right to use any of the images you've sent me in the book? Photographs and diary entries if there are any – that type of thing?'

'Oh aye, go right ahead,' Alison said, waving a claw-like hand vaguely in the air around her.

'You wouldn't mind signing a waiver to say as much if I email it to your nephew? And send it back to me? It's nothing to worry about – it's just a standard document, giving your permission.'

'Sure, just send it right on over. So long as I can get a copy of the book once it's written, that's all that I want to be sure of.'

'I'll send you some signed copies,' Lyssa promised. 'Will four do you?'

'That'll be nice – I can pass them round the family. To see my Derek's name in print in a book – he'd ha' been right chuffed about it.'

After the usual round of goodbyes, Lyssa ended the call and instantly downloaded the new information. Once she'd finished transcribing her notes, she would have to go through it meticulously.

The fact that the police officer on the scene and tasked with investigating the case wasn't entirely happy with the official outcome was probably going to be *the* pivotal fact of the book, and she needed to make very sure of her ground before letting anyone know what a bombshell she had.

And that included her client.

But an hour later, Lyssa had barely started looking through the pages and pages of Derek Jameson's handwritten notes before her phone pinged again, telling her she had a message on Facebook.

She almost ignored it, but habit made her check it anyway. And she was glad she did, as it was from the president of a farmers' association about her request for information on Caroline, the orphaned niece of the band's manager, Luke Raines.

The message was cautiously worded and asked for more information, and Lyssa was careful to be totally candid about who she was, and why she was seeking out Caroline. The woman said she would contact her again in a few minutes, and Lyssa promised to wait.

She knew what the other woman was doing, of course. She was googling her to see if she existed – and if she did, that she was who she said she was. Nowadays, people were beginning (perhaps a little late in the day) to seriously question the safety and security of online messages. Especially given the reluctance of the giant corporations' obscenely wealthy owners to stand up and actually take responsibility for the misuse on their platforms.

Ten minutes later though, the message icon lit up again, and a much warmer message appeared saying that Caroline was now a resident in a care home in Woodstock.

For a moment, Lyssa could only gape at the information in surprise, for Woodstock – the pretty market town that was the home of Blenheim Palace – was situated only about ten miles or so away from Oxford.

Thanking the woman farmer profusely for her help, Lyssa signed off, and googled the name of the care home mentioned – discovering photographs of a pleasant large country house, now divided into sets of 'assisted living' flatlets.

She immediately phoned the number given and asked about the protocol for visiting non-family members. The woman on the line promised to approach Caroline with her request for a visit and would let her know.

The whole conversation gave her a distinct sense of déjà vu! And if her experience of trying to get to speak to Emily Bannister in *her* care home was anything to go by, Lyssa wouldn't be holding her breath. She still hadn't heard back from them and strongly suspected that Emily had told them she didn't want to be disturbed.

And if they still stonewalled her, she'd have to give serious consideration to just turning up. She didn't like doing things like that, but very often people were flattered if you went out of your way to speak to them, and Emily Bannister might well change her mind, if the carers told her she was actually on the premises.

But all that would have to wait for another day. Right now, she had more to do than she could cope with. She was hoping that Jack Flynn, Deborah Simmonds' relative, would get back to her soon, plus she now had the Jameson papers to look through, as well as editing the Jonas Bannister interview for the choicest titbits. And her interview with Jason's Aunt Edna was scheduled for early next week.

Maybe it was her imagination, but she felt as if the whole project had just stepped up a massive gear, and that she might lose control of it.

Jonas Bannister had yet to send her any photographs of Glen Bannister and his brothers, so she'd have to keep on trying to find them from another source. She was determined to see if any of them bore a strong family resemblance to the lead singer and then to email copies to Janet Connor. If she could identify the man

Deborah Simmonds had argued with at Monty's funeral, she might stand a chance of finding out what that was all about.

With a sigh, she tried to get back to work, but she was feeling paradoxically both restless and lethargic. Inevitably, her job consisted primarily of research, reading and writing – all of which were sedentary – and sometimes she felt as if she was in danger of becoming as dry and dusty as some of the tomes that lined her bookshelves. Her eyes felt gritty with staring at a computer screen, and it was time to get out.

Once in her jogging togs, she loaded the audio file of her interview with Jonas to her device (so that she wouldn't feel so guilty about taking time out from her work) and to the sound of their voices, headed out and on to the street.

~

Downstairs in his flat, Neville saw her leave and watched her pensively but resisted the urge to follow her. Instead, he stuck to his seat by the front window, carefully watching the passing traffic and pedestrians for anyone or anything out of place. When he saw Lyssa return less than an hour later, he felt his shoulders relax, and only then realised how tense he'd been.

After fifteen minutes or so of fruitless observation, he went to the kitchen to pour himself a glass of soda and lime but then returned immediately to his vantage point. Within two minutes, he was picking up the camera that stood ready nearby and began to snap the likeness of a young man who was coming up the steps and then buzzed the intercom.

A young man who was carrying a rather heavy-looking and cumbersome tote bag over one shoulder.

~

Lyssa growled with annoyance as she was distracted from looking through Derek Jameson's notes. She'd barely stepped out of the shower after her run and had just resigned herself to getting back down to her paperwork, and then this.

'Now what?' she said out loud, as the intercom by her door buzzed.

She went over to it and snapped, 'Yes?' into it, rather shortly.

'Hello? Lyssa Moore?'

'Yes,' she admitted cautiously.

'I'm Dominic Rattle – Nick. Jase's friend?'

'Who?'

'Jase – Jason Howerd-Pitt. He said you'd been having a little, er, difficulty with some things. He said he told you he was going to call me so I could, er, check out some things in your flat for you?'

'Oh yes, of course, his IT friend. I didn't realise he'd contacted you already,' Lyssa said. 'Hold on a mo!'

She quickly slipped out of her flat and went and banged on Carter's door, and after what felt like a long while, a hair-tousled, sleepy-eyed Jason opened up and stood looking at her blearily. He looked distinctly green around the gills.

'Hangover?' she asked with callous cheerfulness.

'Have mercy! Whisper, will you?' he whispered.

'Nick Rattle's here. Says he's the friend you asked to come over and check out that I'm not being bugged and stuff?'

Even as she said it, she felt slightly ashamed – as if she was some clichéd character from a second-rate thriller novel.

'Oh yeah – yeah, he said he was going to come over this morning. Did I not say?'

'No, you didn't,' Lyssa said more or less affectionately. 'Not to sound paranoid or anything,' she continued wryly, 'but what does he look like, exactly?'

'Like an angry chipmunk,' Jason said shortly. 'Now leave me alone and let me perish in peace. I want freesias, by the way.'

'Freesias?' she echoed blankly.

'For my funeral,' he said morosely, and very carefully and quietly closed the door.

Lyssa nipped back to her flat and went to the intercom and buzzed her visitor in.

When the doorbell chimed a few minutes later she opened the door and immediately had to bite back a smile – for the man outside did indeed look uncannily like an angry chipmunk. Small and very slightly built, but with bulging cheeks, he had spiky brown hair, with two blonde stripes in it, and an agitated, jerky manner.

'Hello, love – I'm Nick. What's up, then?' he asked briskly, dropping his tote bag gently to the ground. 'Jase was a bit vague about what you needed.'

'Well – I think my apartment might be bugged,' Lyssa said, apologetically, still aware that she sounded like someone from a Bond movie. 'I've had a flat invasion, which might be burglars, or maybe not. So, I thought I'd better check there's nothing . . . well, sinister going on.'

She shrugged, aware that she must sound like a bit of an idiot, but chipmunk Nick didn't bat an eyelid. Just then, Bibbie came up and began to sniff at the bag on the floor. 'Nice cat,' her visitor said, approvingly. 'So is it just the phone, or do you want the whole works?' he asked briskly.

Lyssa blinked at him a little helplessly. Nick Rattle looked her up and down, which was rather comical, since she was a good six inches taller than he was and he had to slightly crane his neck, but she immediately recognised the appreciative male glint in his eye. She bit back a sigh, hoping that she wasn't going to have to fend off any amorous advances. She didn't think she could cope with a chipmunk with libido trouble.

'Never mind, just leave it to me, yeah?' he advised. 'Let's start with the phone. You have a landline?'

'Yes – and a mobile, of course.'

'Natch,' the chipmunk said, and went straight to the landline.

Lyssa, not sure of the etiquette in times such as these, wandered automatically to the kitchen and put on the coffee machine. 'Coffee?'

'Love one – milk and three sugars,' Nick said, opening up the bag he'd taken with him, and proceeding to attach something that looked like a baby monitor (but surely couldn't have been???) to her landline phone cradle.

He switched something on and something buzzed.

'Yup,' he said matter-of-factly. 'Someone's listening in on this right enough. That's the thing with old-fashioned landlines. The kit's pretty basic. It'll be harder to spot on the smartphone – that it?' he asked, turning to point at what was obviously her mobile phone lying on her work desk next to her laptop.

Lyssa, aware that her mouth was hanging slightly open, closed her jaws together with a snap, staggered to her sofa and dropped into it.

'The phone *is* bugged, then?' she gasped.

'Oh yeah,' the chipmunk said casually. 'Want me to see if anyone's been hacking your emails?'

'Might as well,' Lyssa said faintly.

An hour later, Nick had finished his work and had presented his findings. Both her telephones were being monitored, and her emails intercepted and copied to an unknown address. There were no actual recording devices found in the flat itself, which, Lyssa supposed half hysterically, was something, but her laptop had been investigated and all her files copied and sent to a separate unknown and untraceable address.

'So, what do you want me to do?' Nick said, sitting opposite her on one of her armchairs and drinking his sixth (yes, six – she'd begun counting them) cup of coffee. No wonder he seemed to practically vibrate with kinetic energy. She dreaded to think how much caffeine was in his system.

'Do?' she repeated now.

'Yeah – do.' He regarded her patiently. 'Do you want me to install anti-tampering gear, f'r instance?'

'Oh. I don't know. I'm not sure. I suppose so,' she said, in quick succession.

'Righty-ho. That'll cost extra, mind,' he warned.

Lyssa blinked at him, still feeling as if she was reeling from a punch to the face. Someone had been monitoring every aspect of her working life. And now she was convinced that the car she'd seen before really *had* been following her. It would fit in with the emerging pattern.

But who was doing it – and why? It baffled her.

'You know – my fee. Jase did tell you my rates, right? I am gonna get paid, yeah?' the chipmunk said, not liking her sudden silence.

Typically, Jason hadn't done any such thing, but Lyssa was not concerned about that. Elizabeth's 'expenses' would cover it.

'Yes, that's fine,' she quickly reassured him. 'I can pay by card, or you can send an invoice with bank transfer details if you prefer.'

'I prefer cash,' the chipmunk said cannily.

Lyssa just bet he did! If this young man's tax returns weren't works of fiction, she would eat her hat. 'Do what you can to make everything secure. I really need to be able to use my laptop and phone for my work. Just let me know how much it'll be and when you want to come back for it, and I'll go down to my bank and draw it out for you,' she promised.

'Fair enough,' Nick Rattle said. 'I'll get started. Couldn't have another cup of coffee, could I?'

~

Some hours later, when Nick finally left the block of flats, Neville casually sauntered out after him and crossed over to the other side of the road, where he trailed him to a nearby car park. There he took an obvious shortcut to a nearby supermarket but via a route that took him close enough to note down the young man's car registration.

15

Later that afternoon, in Gloucester, Jonas Bannister's day was about to take a decided turn for the worse, and it began with the unusual occurrence of his PA's unannounced entry to his office. Usually, Olivia Keane always checked with him via the intercom first whenever she needed to see him, so her unheralded knock on his door, followed by her slipping inside without even waiting for him to bid her to come in, took him by surprise.

A middle-aged, well-educated and normally unflappable woman, her high colour and troubled expression instantly put him on alert.

'I'm sorry to interrupt you, Mr Bannister, but there's a young man here to see you,' she began without any preamble.

'I don't believe there are any appointments scheduled in my diary for this morning,' Jonas interrupted her, frowning, but his PA was already shaking her neatly coiffured head.

'No, sir. He has none. But he's adamant that he needs to see you. He says it's urgent and imperative, and that the matter is personal. He's young and badly dressed and has a sort of knowing, supercilious way about him that . . . Well, I think he means to cause trouble, sir. He's refused to leave the outer office. Perhaps you should send someone up from security to escort him out?'

'Did he give a name?'

'Yes, sir – I'm sorry I forgot to say!' she apologised, clearly flustered. 'His name is Flynn. Mr Jack Flynn.'

Jonas drew his breath in with a hiss, further alarming his already out-of-sorts PA. 'I see. I believe it might be best if I see him after all. I have an idea . . . Once you've shown him in, please ask Mr Gorman to come up here and send him in right away. Tell him to be as quick as he can.'

'Yes, sir,' Miss Keane said, not sure whether to feel relieved or even more concerned, but departing hurriedly. A few moments later the door opened and a man in his early twenties swaggered in.

He was lean and wiry, not very tall, with bad skin and teeth. He was dressed in ragged jeans and a grubby grey T-shirt. But it was the expression on his face that instantly caught and kept Jonas' attention. As Olivia Keane said, he had a smug, almost gleeful smile that oozed confidence.

Just one look at him, and Jonas felt his mouth go dry. For a moment he quailed, but then he sat up straighter in his chair, and reached for an expensive Parker pen lying on his desk, which he made a show of casually fiddling in his hand.

'I don't believe we've met, Mr, er, Flynn, was it?' he asked curtly. He knew he needed to take control and take it quickly. Once you gave a man like this the idea that he could lord it over you, you were sunk. 'I'm afraid I don't have much time to spare, but my PA said the matter was urgent?' He gave him his best imperial glare.

In response, Jack Flynn sauntered over and sat in the chair opposite his desk, looking unhurried and unconcerned. 'No, we never met. But I reckon your dad and my great-nan had a lot to do with each other, once upon a time.'

Jonas felt his stomach lurch but hoped that he managed to keep his face blank. 'Really?' he asked, putting as much scepticism into his voice as he could manage. 'What on earth makes you think that?'

'One of the accounts ledgers that my great-nan kept, for one thing,' Jack said with a knowing grin. 'Deborah Simmonds, her name was. I'm sure that name rings a bell, don't it, Mr Bannister?' he asked, crossing his skinny arms happily across his chest. He looked around and nodded. 'Nice office. Nice business. I dare say you live in a nice house, too, right?'

Jonas' lips tightened. 'I don't see how that . . .'

'Been doing all right for yourself, ain't yah?' Jack continued, nodding. 'Nice company you've got here – I been looking you up online. Plenty of big fancy ads saying how green-minded you are, and how you're all up for helping to save the planet. All that guff about how much you're doing to help others meet government targets, and keep to green policies and all that shit. Selling yourselves as some sort of corporate super-hero good guys. Be a pity if the public finds out that it was all built on money your dad stole from some charity, wouldn't it?' he asked, still nodding in that annoying way. 'Wouldn't be so popular then, would yuh?'

He glanced out of the window at the expensive Cotswold-stone buildings lining the streets opposite. 'Fancy area, this. Nice. But I reckon your stock shares would hit the pan pretty quick, if that got out. You wouldn't be able to afford to work around here then, right? And you'd probably be voted off the board, quick as a flash, yeah?'

He leaned back and lifted his booted feet to rest them on the edge of Jonas' pristine desk. 'I seen some of them slick American shows, yah know the ones I mean, where the rich financial whizz kids live it up to begin with, then suddenly get it in the neck and go to jail for that insider trading stuff they're always banging on about. Mind you, they're all the same – bending the rules and robbing people blind – only they get away with it, 'cause they're rich, right? Until they don't,' he added with a sly, wide grin. 'Yeah, I like them kinda shows. Never thought I'd get to star in my own real-life version though.'

By now Jonas could feel himself sweating, and he almost moaned with relief when the intercom buzzed, and Olivia's voice informed him that Mr Gorman had arrived.

Ian came in quietly, shot Jonas an assessing look, and then quickly turned his attention to the young man in the chair. He recognised him at once, for he'd already begun his inquiries into Jack Flynn, and one of his men had already emailed him a photograph. He also knew the boy was not long out of a prison term – which was hardly his first. His eyes flickered disgustedly over the mud-caked boots on the desk, and then back to Jonas, elevating his eyebrows questioningly.

Feeling sick, Jonas attempted a brave smile. He could just flick a finger and know that Ian would eject Flynn like the piece of rubbish he was. But that would hardly solve the problem he now represented.

'Ah, Ian, glad you could make it. This is Mr Flynn. He seems to be something of a fantasist. I think he believes he . . . Well, what is it exactly that you *do* believe, Mr Flynn? You haven't been very clear, you know. Something about a distant relative's ledgers, was it?'

He was feeling braver now that his security chief was with him. And once he was sure about the exact nature of whatever evidence this verminous creature thought he had on him, surely Ian would be able to help deal with him.

'Oh, I know what I have all right,' Jack Flynn said, glancing at the newcomer with wary eyes. The bloke was older than him, and didn't seem to have much muscle on him, but he was giving off a vibe that he didn't like. Ex-copper, maybe? 'I got this phone call, see, from this writer woman,' he carried on, turning back to face his mark. 'She wanted to know if I had any papers belonging to a Deborah Simmonds – that would be my nan's mum. Turns out I did, see. And very interesting they were too. Diaries, and shit like that. But then I found these account ledgers. For this charity some dead rock groupie had set up. Money my great-nan very neatly nabbed for herself.'

He grinned. 'Typical of our family, you see. Crooks, the lot of us. And you gotta admire the old bird, right? She'd hit the jackpot by the looks of it. Well, she had, until your old man cottoned on to what she was doing, and muscled his way in,' Jack added, nodding in an almost friendly way at Jonas. 'Seems your family wasn't short on crooks either, was it?'

Jonas swallowed hard – not at the slur on his family, but in disbelief that Flynn could have what he claimed to have. Was it really possible? Surely the Simmonds woman would have gone out of her way to destroy the evidence of her own wrongdoing, wouldn't she? It stood to reason; she wouldn't want to leave any proof lying around as to what she'd done, especially since, back then, it would have meant a lengthy prison term. Not like nowadays, when fraudsters could get away with almost anything and walk out after a few months' jail time.

When his father retired from the business after getting dementia, his mental state had slowly deteriorated to the point where he'd started to mumble on about things he'd previously kept very quiet. But Jonas had listened all right, and some of the things Robert Bannister had said had curdled Jonas' blood. Not least, how he'd come by enough money to start the business in the first place.

The courts had finally awarded Glen's parents and each of his siblings equal shares from his estate, with Glen's parents simply putting their share in the bank and living comfortably off it for the rest of their lives. His older uncle had done much the same thing, but with the occasional added splurge, such as buying a boat and a fancy car. His aunt, when she reached the age of eighteen, had used it to go to art college and then, in later life, as top-up money for when her canvases didn't sell so well.

But his father had founded his own company, which, when Jonas came to really consider it later, must have needed far more in start-up funds than just Glen's legacy alone. The company, for its first twenty years, had been privately run and owned, so there had been no shareholders' investments to bolster it, but it had always had a very healthy bank account nevertheless, and right from the start. It was only after they got too big to stay private that his father had finally gone public.

So where had all that initial investment come from?

It had been a nasty shock when his dementia-ridden father had told him how he'd always detested Amelia Montrose and bitterly resented the poxy charity that she'd set up, especially as he always suspected that Glen had helped to fund it. And how, after Monty's death, he'd begun watching Deborah Simmonds carefully, having found out that she was the one who now had sole access to the charity's bank accounts. It hadn't been easy, but he had found out what she was up to, finally confronting her at Monty's funeral and threatening her with exposure if she didn't go halves with him. Which she had reluctantly done, giving Robert the chance to found his family business at the charity's expense.

Which was why, when Lyssa Moore had first approached him about the book, he had become so concerned. For what if, whilst digging around about the Montrose woman, she found out the ugly truth about the defrauded charity? And now, it looked as if his worst nightmare was indeed coming true.

'Hello – Earth to Mr Bannister,' he heard Jack Flynn's raised voice, followed by a nasty laugh. 'Sorry, did you just zone out there for a bit, old man? What's he like, eh?' he sneered, turning to look once more at the silent man who was watching them both like a hawk.

Jack still didn't like the look of him. And he didn't like the old geezer's stubborn silence either. It was time to stamp on any silly ideas this pair might be getting. He was in charge here. He might not look that bright, but he was smart enough to know when he was in the driving seat.

'I've got the original books for this YMT thing, yeah?' he said aggressively. 'And some diaries. I know my great-nan emptied the charity bank accounts, and then was forced to hand half of it over to your old man, Mr Bannister. Hell, she even kept proof of the bank transfers to your father's account. I reckon she was smart to do that. To hold on to proof, like. With what they had on each other, both of 'em had to keep quiet, like, or they'd both end up in the nick, wouldn't they? And now here we are, all these years later. Me, poor as a church mouse because my great-nan spent the money on wine and fancy clothes and who the hell knows what else, but you and your lot still living high on the hog. Now that's not fair, is it? I ask you? Share and share alike, that's what I say. So now we need to discuss terms.'

Jack Flynn turned and gave the still silent man behind him a swift look. 'And don't you go getting any ideas. I've already put the stuff somewhere safe – somewhere you ain't gonna find it, not even if you turn over my gaff. And just bear in mind, I got friends, see. Good friends. The sort that would take a monkey wrench to your kneecaps if I asked 'em nicely.'

At this, Jonas swallowed hard. And slowly, his eyes met those of his security chief, which were, as usual, inscrutable.

~

By a little after nine o'clock the next morning, Lyssa was already up and about to start work. Before she did, however, she supposed she needed to have a chat with her client. Things were beginning to pile up, and she wasn't sure who or what she could trust any more.

Someone had bugged her flat. And the timing of Justin Tillman's accident was looking less like a coincidence and more like something far more sinister. It seemed strange that he should have his fall just after he'd told her he was going to look for the film of Monty's last party. And if she was right about someone following *her* about, maybe the idea that someone had been watching him as well wasn't so wild after all?

But somehow, she couldn't bring herself to confide these worries to Elizabeth.

Because, when it came right down to it – how much did she trust her own client? No, best to keep her own counsel for now and just be professional about things. Make like the book was the only thing she was interested in and concentrating on. And if, a little voice piped up in her head, Elizabeth wasn't to be trusted, the last thing she wanted to do was alert her to the fact she was beginning to have her doubts and suspicions. Right?

And with that in mind, she reached for her phone. As she did so, however, she couldn't help but remember that it had once been bugged and the realisation that someone had listened in on her private calls still made her feel slightly sick. And even though, thanks to Nick Rattle, that was no longer the case, she still felt her heart flutter nervously every time she had to use the implement, and that was beginning to make her angry. If she allowed herself to become afraid of communicating with people, she knew that whoever had bugged her phone would have scored a victory over her, and that she would not tolerate. So she straightened her shoulders and determinedly punched in Elizabeth's number. With the usual greetings completed, they went on to talk about her recent conversation with the widow of Derek Jameson, the man who'd conducted the investigation into Monty's death. After which Lyssa began to sound Elizabeth out about Jameson's private doubts concerning the official verdict. She was careful to downplay it slightly, as she didn't want to come out all guns blazing about how she thought it should provide the focal point of the book. After all, Elizabeth might think that raising speculation that Monty might have been murdered would be taking things a step too far. There was also the very real possibility that the Montrose family might feel they had already endured enough publicity and scandal as far as Monty was concerned, and wouldn't have any taste for another bout of it now.

'I know it might be hard getting your head around the idea that what happened to Monty wasn't an accident, but I think we should at least raise the question, right?' Lyssa pressed gently, holding her breath a little. 'It could act as a very good selling point for the book,' she pointed out, appealing to Elizabeth's entrepreneurial spirit and literally crossing her fingers.

'Huh? Oh yeah, I can see that,' Elizabeth said vaguely. Some scuffling sounds were coming at her over the line now, and Lyssa was as sure as she could be that the other woman was in the process of lighting up a cigarette and thus might not have been paying proper attention.

She tried again. 'It might change the whole theme of the book, though?'

'Hmm? Oh, I'm not so sure about that. The whole point of the book is to do Monty justice, remember? To put right the slur on her reputation. Just concentrate for now on proving that she wrote the songs. That's what really matters, because that's what will validate her. OK?'

Lyssa swung her swivel chair from side to side, fighting back her surprise. Was she really hearing this right? She'd just phoned her client to tell her that it was possible that the subject of their biography might have been murdered, and all she could focus on was proving that Monty wrote the lyrics for the songs? All right, fair enough, she could see that was important too – but it hardly topped murder, did it?'

Just what was going on here? What was she missing?

'Lyssa?' Elizabeth's voice sounded sharply in her ear. 'You still there?'

'Yes! Yes, all right, Elizabeth, if that's what you want, I can do that. And on that subject, I've managed to track down Luke Raines' niece, and it's possible she might have some of his papers. If anyone knew how the songs came to be written, it would have been him.'

'That's fabulous,' Elizabeth said, sounding definitely pleased now. 'Let me know the instant you find anything, yeah? And remember, we really need *written* evidence that she did, not just hearsay. I mean, it'll be great if she remembers her uncle telling her that he'd just got back from Evergreen or somewhere, and that Monty was having trouble with the last lines of "Where It Hurts" or some such offhand remark like that, but it's hardly set in stone, is it?'

'No, but it would all go to building up a general picture, don't you think?' Lyssa pointed out. 'It's little remembrances like that that could really help readers build a picture of what was happening in their lives.'

'Oh yeah, sure, I'm not saying don't include it. But . . . Oh well, never mind, just do your best. Look, I gotta get down to the office – I've a client who wants everything done out in grey. I keep telling her that boat's sailed! We'll talk later, OK?'

'Yes, but,' Lyssa began, about to ask if Elizabeth wanted to see the Jameson material, but already the dial tone was sounding in her ears. With a sigh, she ended the call and sat for a moment or two, staring out of the window.

Was she imagining things, or was her client acting weirdly? Why so little excitement – or even curiosity – about the possibility that Monty was murdered? And why was she so hung up on proving Monty's authorship of the Lucky Cuckoos' song lyrics? To her, Elizabeth's priorities seemed very odd.

But then again – clients!

Philosophically, she got back to work.

It was just gone eleven, and she was beginning to get a firm outline of the shape of the coming book now.

A good biography, in her opinion, told the story of a person's life in a linear, easy-to-understand format, which nevertheless had highlights, almost like a work of fiction. She'd already gathered so much information she felt justified in setting out a very rough chapter-by-chapter synopsis and had settled on the order in which she'd present her findings and research to keep readers informed and entertained and wanting to read on, without them feeling as if they were being in any way manipulated.

She had a beginning, most of the middle, and everyone knew the ending, which was, in her opinion, a good start!

She was just beginning on the outline for Chapter One when her phone rang. For a moment, she simply sat still and looked at the smartphone, before snatching it up defiantly. She simply *had* to get over any feelings of reluctance to use it – and she would!

Besides, it might be Chloe ringing with news of her father's condition. Or even to say she had found the film.

Shaking off her sense of wariness, she abruptly answered it. And moments later, she was very glad that she had, for it was Caroline Dixon-Hayes in person. The manager of the retirement facility had passed on Lyssa's request for an interview, and Caroline was more than happy to talk about her Uncle Luke and the bands he'd represented.

'He was such a wonderful man. If he hadn't taken me in when he did, I don't know what I'd have done,' she said. 'So, I'm more than happy to talk to you about him. And it'll take me back too, which at my age is a bonus. Funny how we scorn nostalgia when we're young but dote on it when we're older! And I loved all that stuff – that world he was so much a part of. Can you imagine walking out into your back garden and finding your uncle throwing a party where there were members from the Hollies or the Troggs or the Tremeloes eating sausage rolls and riffing on guitars?'

'No, I can't,' Lyssa enthused. 'But it sounds magical, and I'd love to hear all about it. You must have known the Lucky Cuckoos particularly well?'

'Oh yes – all of them,' Caroline said matter-of-factly. 'It was so sad, how everything seemed to go wrong for them. It really upset Uncle.'

'When can I come and see you?' Lyssa asked and was totally wrong-footed by her response.

'Well, why not right now? I'm not doing anything, and you're just in Oxford, right? Oh, but I expect you're too busy . . .'

'No, no, that's fine,' Lyssa said hastily, already shooting up out of her chair and looking around her rather frantically. 'Just give me ten minutes to get myself together, and I'll be right over.'

It took her a little longer than that, for moments later Chloe Tillman finally rang back to say that her father's condition was improving and, though he had yet to regain consciousness, his doctors were much more upbeat about his chances for a good recovery.

'That's wonderful, Chloe!' Lyssa said, almost wilting in relief. 'You and your mum must be feeling so much better.'

'Yes, we are. But the main reason I'm calling is to tell you about Grandad's film.'

'Oh?' Lyssa said, her heart pounding.

'Yes. I don't quite know where to begin,' Chloe said hesitantly. 'It's all a bit odd and a little mysterious, to be honest.'

This was not what Lyssa needed right now, and she felt her heart plummet. She took a deep, fortifying breath. 'That sounds ominous,' she said, trying to keep her tone light.

'I'm not sure I'd go that far.' Chloe, too, was keeping her voice light, but underneath it, Lyssa could sense that she wasn't feeling any more nonchalant than herself. 'See, I did go through the cardboard box and found Grandad's old cine camera and lots of tin cans containing film spools. They were all well labelled, and so it didn't take me long to see that the one you wanted – with the name you gave me, Amelia Montrose, and the date of the party – wasn't amongst them.'

Lyssa felt herself wilt. Even though she'd been more than half expecting something like this, it still came as a blow to actually hear Chloe say it.

'Oh well – it was always a long shot,' she said, trying to be philosophical. 'Perhaps he lent it to someone, and they never gave it back, or it got lost in a family move to another house or something.'

'Yes, that's what I thought,' Chloe said slowly. 'But I was talking to Mum about it, and she remembers Dad bringing the box down and going through it and . . . Well, the thing is, she swears Dad found it. The film you wanted, I mean. He was quite pleased about it, in fact. He told her how much he was looking forward to watching it again, if the camera still worked, and how pleased you would be about it all.'

For a moment, Lyssa was incapable of speech. Then she finally managed to say slowly, 'I'm not sure I understand. If he found it . . .' She trailed off helplessly.

'Then where is it?' Chloe concluded for her. 'Yes, I know – I thought the same thing. But it's not there – I've gone through all the film canisters again and again and it's not in the box. Look, I'm going to have to go back into work for the rest of today, but once

I've finished, I'm going to do a quick search in Dad's man cave in case, for some reason, he put it somewhere else. You never know.'

'No, you don't,' Lyssa heard herself agree faintly, and a moment later they exchanged rather wooden goodbyes. But all the time, her mind was buzzing, imagining the scene at the Tillman residence.

Justin goes up to the roof to fix the tile. His wife would hear him fall, surely? She rushes out of the house and . . . Supposing someone had deliberately moved the ladder when Justin had started to use it. It wouldn't have been that hard, would it, to then dart into hiding, and once Mrs Tillman came out to investigate, to slip into the house and search for the film and take it.

Anyone would be too distracted by what had happened to Justin to notice if someone was moving about inside the house. Presumably neighbours would have come to help, and the ambulance would arrive, and there would be a lot of noise and consternation and to-ing and fro-ing of various people.

Someone desperate to get their hands on that film would take the risk, wouldn't they?

Or was she just losing it now, and tumbling further and further down the rabbit hole?

Making an angry *tcha* sound, she got up and vowed to pull herself together. If she kept on like this, she would become too frightened to move!

And she had better things to do than scare herself silly.

~

Neville saw Lyssa walking down the short path from the flats and then turn a sharp right on the pavement. Like most of the residents, she kept her car parked in a small private parking area opposite the narrow lane skirting the building, and he surmised that she was heading off somewhere in the car.

Grabbing his own set of car keys, he lifted a dark blue baseball-style cap off his coatrack near the front door and put it on. He was already donning his sunglasses and was jogging quickly down the side street when he saw Lyssa slip into her car and start it up.

Luckily, there were two ways into the parking area – the main entrance, which was a simple turning into the lot by which the cars entered and exited, and a narrow gap in the low box hedging, where pedestrians could slip through on the diagonal. He chose the latter and was careful to keep out of her sightline as he made his way to his own vehicle – which wasn't his own personal car, but rather one of a fleet of cars and vans that he and his colleagues could use at any given time.

These vehicles all had one thing in common – they were totally anonymous. No glaring colours, and no brand new models nor really old ones. No bumper stickers, nothing at all that made them stand out from the crowd. Most had tinted windows. All were much more powerful than they looked, and some had very interesting modifications indeed.

Neville was already behind the wheel as Lyssa was pulling out of the entrance. He followed, waited for a gap in the traffic and then settled in comfortably behind her, with four cars in between them. He had no qualms that he might lose sight of her. He already knew that she was a careful, maybe even timid driver, and never drove very fast.

He'd followed her before.

~

The residential home in Woodstock was situated on the very outskirts of the market town, overlooking a sheep-bedecked field on one side and a new-looking row of houses set on the other. Lyssa found it without any trouble. A mainly Georgian house, it had distinctly Victorian wings added on both sides and had been extended in the back during the Edwardian era. It had probably once been a country estate for a wealthy family, before urban sprawl had crept up on it. The grounds were no longer as extensive as they must once have been, but were pleasant enough, with rose borders, some perennial shrubs and well-maintained lawns. A few large cedars provided much-needed shade on hot days, and with the sun once more shining, several white-haired people sat out on terraces or on garden chairs set under the trees, reading newspapers, or scrolling on mobile phones.

Lyssa headed for the main front door that opened on to the original hall and which now housed a glassed-in reception area and desk. She wondered what the original inhabitants of the house would have made of it all.

She gave her name to the receptionist, who told her that 'Mrs D.-H.' was indeed expecting her and gave her a map showing Lyssa the way to her flat. Caroline was in 2A on the second floor, in one of the Victorian wings, and a spacious and quiet lift, situated just around the corner and a short way down a corridor, was the quickest route to it.

Lyssa wasn't quite sure what level of care Caroline needed here, and as she rang the bell and waited, she made a swift calculation in her head. Luke's niece must be in her eighties by now. It was possible that she was bedridden.

But as soon as the door was opened, it was clear to her that this was not the case, for no carer was in evidence.

The old woman confronting her with a slight smile was almost as tall as herself, but pared back to the bone, with sparse white hair and deep-set brown eyes. She rested her weight on a walking cane, but other than that and a slight tendency to stoop, she showed no other signs of infirmity.

'Lyssa Moore?' she said, her voice familiar from the phone call earlier. Slightly croaky and not strong, but somehow still pleasant on the ear.

'Yes. Mrs Dixon-Hayes?'

'A mouthful, isn't it? Call me Caroline. Come in, please. I've made us proper coffee, or there's tea if you prefer.'

She stood back for Lyssa to pass her. The door opened straight on to a large and spacious living area, with almost floor-to-ceiling windows, overlooking the grounds. The colour scheme was predominantly cream with green and neutral earth tones as accents. An open door exposed a small kitchenette area, and a closed door on the opposite side of the room probably led to her bedroom and an ensuite bathroom.

'This is lovely,' Lyssa said, glancing at the well-stocked shelves (an assortment of books, ornaments and slender vases of flowers) and then moving on to the original landscape paintings on the walls. And, scattered amongst these, some gold record discs that had been mounted and framed.

'Are those . . . ?' Lyssa began excitedly.

'. . . proof of my uncle's successful career?' Caroline finished for her with a gruff laugh. 'Yes, they are. I think one of them is a Lucky Cuckoos one too – all the others are from the other bands he managed in his later life, most from the mid-70s to early 80s.'

'Would you mind if I took a picture of it?' Lyssa asked.

'Go ahead. Can I get you that cup of coffee?'

'Yes, please,' Lyssa said, already taking out her mobile phone and heading for the wall. Finding her prize after a quick search, she leaned forward to better read the label on it. It was, of course, for 'The Frightened Heart', released in March 1963, and the band's only number one hit.

'It's a replica, I'm afraid,' Caroline called from the kitchen. 'The originals would have gone to the band.'

Lyssa didn't mind – she could see from the digital image of it that it looked good enough. But she made a quick mental note to be careful not to try and claim it was the real thing when she used the image in the book.

'So, you're interested in the Lucky Cuckoos. Writing a book about them, are you?' Caroline said, entering with a small tray containing two coffee mugs, a small bowl of sugar and a jug of milk. She had it balanced on one hand, since the walking stick was in the other, and Lyssa quickly moved to take it from her.

The old lady acknowledged her with a smile, and Lyssa followed her to the centre of the room, where a small coffee table was surrounded by two large armchairs. 'Thanks – just set it down there.'

Lyssa deposited the tray, and then accepted the chair indicated by her hostess. Caroline herself settled into the other one with just the slightest hint of a groan. 'Bloody rheumatism,' she said with a wry smile.

'My book is more about Amelia Montrose, actually,' Lyssa answered her earlier question. 'A member of her family thinks that she got a raw deal from the press, and wants a biography written that sets out a much more balanced and truthful version of Monty and Glen's love story, and their time with the Lucky Cuckoos.'

'About time too,' Caroline said uncompromisingly. 'Uncle always said she was treated so unfairly.'

16

It was an encouraging start and, quickly getting permission to record their talk, Lyssa began to draw Caroline out about what she could remember of the early 1960s, and her life with her uncle and the world of pop music.

It was good stuff, but after only half an hour, and mindful of Elizabeth's promptings, she began to steer the general conversation in the direction she wanted.

'I've listened to all the Lucky Cuckoos' music, as you can imagine, and the one thing that strikes me the most is the quality of the song's lyrics,' she began artlessly. 'I hope you won't take this the wrong way, but some of the hit songs from that period could be a bit . . .'

She hesitated deliberately, and Caroline, with a laugh, obligingly stepped in to save her blushes. 'Basic, should we say? Formulaic? Naïve and maybe lacking in finesse? Yes, I know what you mean – but there was a lot of good stuff written as well, and you're right, the Lucky Cuckoos' songs all have something, in their different way, don't they?'

'Yes, I agree. And perhaps I'm being fanciful, but I thought I could detect a connection between all the songs and the progress of Glen and Monty's relationship. The first one, for instance, "A Lovely Face", is about a man falling for a woman initially because of her looks but then seems to hint very strongly that she did the same! Now, back in 1962 that struck me as being a bit unusual. Men didn't like to think of themselves as having lovely faces, and women were certainly looked down upon for thinking too much about a man's looks.'

She paused and saw that Caroline was watching her with a rather impressed smile. 'Go on,' she urged.

Lyssa nodded. 'All right. "Lying Lips" was their next hit and was all about the lies lovers told to one another to make their relationship work. And again, that struck me as a rather sophisticated theme for a catchy pop song. And seemed almost too sensitive to have been written by a man. But it was their third hit, and their only number one, that began to really make me wonder. "The Frightened Heart" was a cry from the soul, wasn't it? The fear of losing love – no wonder it was their biggest hit. It goes straight for the jugular, doesn't it? It really gets to you. And Glen's haunting melody just gives it that extra punch.'

Caroline smiled. 'Of course, you're a writer yourself, and have a degree in Literature, I take it?'

Lyssa nodded.

'So, you would see it whereas others might not.' The older woman nodded her head and gave a slightly sad, wry smile. 'None of their fans did latch on to it, you know. That Monty wrote all their lyrics, I mean,' she stated boldly.

Lyssa felt a small wave of exultation sweep over her. *So, Elizabeth was right.*

'And the other hits, as you say, were just extensions of Monty and Glen's feelings for each other,' Caroline went on. '"Where It Hurts" and the next one, "Going Nowhere", mirrored the times when their love affair hit rough patches. "Rocks that Roll" was a reference to Monty's growing disillusionment with the drug scene, and it barely squeaked into the top twenty. And their final hit,

“Take it All”, was bitter and sad in equal measure. I often wonder, when I listen to that song, if she might not have had some premonition that things weren’t going to end well for them. And they didn’t, did they? For Glen, for her, for any of them.’

She sighed heavily. ‘It really hit Uncle hard, how things turned out, but it was Monty’s death that really broke him.’

‘Yes, I gather they were close,’ Lyssa said sympathetically. ‘She brought him and the band together, didn’t she?’

‘Yes. They were great friends – oh, not in any way romantically, I mean. He was older and just a very nice man, and I don’t think Monty really knew many properly nice, decent men. He was like a father figure to her, or a favourite uncle, you know?’

Mentally crossing her fingers, Lyssa said casually, ‘How do you know Monty wrote the songs? Did your uncle tell you as much?’

‘Sure – it was no real secret – not between the few of us who were closest to the band anyway.’

‘But on the record label, it lists only Glen as the songwriter. I’m surprised she didn’t demand equal billing.’

Caroline laughed. ‘Well, back then, women never got the credit for anything, did they? And Uncle said Monty didn’t really care – she didn’t need the royalties, did she, being so wealthy already. And she really did love Glen with a passion and was happy for him to get the kudos. And as things stood, with the press being so anti-Monty, it wouldn’t have been in anyone’s interests to come out with the truth, would it?’ she added, a shade cynically.

‘They were afraid it might affect the record sales, you mean?’ Lyssa said, sadly shaking her head.

‘I’m afraid so.’

‘So there’s no written evidence that proves Monty actually wrote the lyrics?’ Lyssa asked, already beginning to feel sad and disappointed for her client.

'Nothing official, no,' Caroline said. 'No contracts, or copyright papers or anything like that. But there *are* the letters. I know it was mentioned in quite a few of them, because I remember reading them after Uncle died, and I had to go through his papers.'

'Letters?' Lyssa asked, her heart beginning to bang in her chest. 'What letters?'

'Between Monty and Uncle. She was a great letter-writer, was Monty. Whenever she was away on holiday (and they holidayed a lot!) she would write Uncle these long, chatty letters. All about where they were, and the people, and the exotic wildlife and all that kind of thing. And I know that she would also mention stuff about how well – or otherwise – a particular song was shaping up, and how she'd just thought of this perfect line for something or was struggling to find a rhyme with something else.'

Lyssa felt her throat go dry. 'Did you keep these letters?' she asked, half fearfully, half hopefully.

'Oh yes. I have them, and all sorts of other stuff of Uncle's lodged with my solicitor. I know those glory days are long gone, but I've never quite been able to bring myself to throw them away. I kept thinking I should donate them to a rock 'n' roll museum or private collection, or something. And now, from the look on your face, it looks as if my hopeless sentimentality is going to pay off!' she said, with another happy laugh.

'You have no idea how . . . Oh blast, I thought I'd turned that off,' Lyssa said, as her mobile phone trilled annoyingly in her bag. 'Sorry about this, I'll call whoever it is back later.'

'Oh, go ahead and answer it. It might be important,' Caroline said. 'I'll make some fresh coffee – my throat is getting rather dry anyway.'

As she got up to head to the kitchen, Lyssa checked the caller ID and saw that it was Monica Farley, Ron 'Racey' Joiner's widow, and answered it. 'Hello, Monica. How are things?'

She heard Monica's familiar and slightly boozy laugh echo back down the line at her. 'Funny, that's just what I was about to ask you. How's the book going? Making any progress?'

'Yes, actually, and I have to thank you for some of that,' Lyssa said, imagining Monica leaning back on her sofa and drinking wine spritzers or whatever was her tipple of the moment. 'That tip you gave me about Luke Raines' niece has just paid off in spades. I tracked her down to Woodstock of all places, almost right on my doorstep, and what she's been telling me is pure gold!'

'I'm so glad to hear it. You'll have to buy a bottle of champagne to celebrate.'

Lyssa, who wouldn't be buying any champagne soon (but could maybe stretch to a bottle of Prosecco) grinned. 'I might just do that,' she fibbed. 'It turns out that it was Monty who wrote the lyrics for the Lucky Cuckoos, which is going to make my client's day.'

'I bet it will,' Monica agreed. 'You know, I'm not all that surprised, now I come to think of it. None of the lads were really poets, if you know what I mean?'

'I'm sorry, but I can't talk for long. I'm in the middle of the interview now,' Lyssa apologised.

'Say no more – and good luck!' Monica said and rang off.

As, over in Woodstock, Caroline returned with fresh coffee, in her own home Monica hung up and looked across at the woman lounging opposite her.

Jennifer eyed her mother balefully. 'So? What's she up to, then?'

'Don't be such a drama queen, Jen. I told you – she's writing a book, which we already know.'

'Yes, but what is it that she's *writing*, Mother? That's what matters. But obviously you couldn't care less about it, which is typical of you. Just tell me the latest.'

Monica sighed heavily, but her eyes as she regarded her only child were wary and unhappy. 'She's talking to the niece of Luke Raines, in a place called Woodstock – which isn't far from Oxford, apparently.'

'Why?' Jennifer demanded. 'Luke Raines died ages ago.'

Monica shrugged. 'He was the band's manager, so I daresay she's after any memorabilia she might have kept or titbits that she might be willing to share.'

'Such as what?'

Monica shook her head wearily. 'Jen, I do wish you'd let all this go. It's not healthy, this obsession that you have with your father's memory and his so-called legacy. I keep telling you that. You live your life in the past, and it wasn't even your past, not really. Why can't you make the most of—'

'I don't want any book coming out that bad-mouths Daddy, that's all.' Jennifer ruthlessly cut across the lecture that she'd heard from her mother many times before. 'Now what were you saying she needed to celebrate?'

'Apparently, it turns out that Monty helped write the songs. It wasn't all down to Glen, even though . . .'

'*What?*' Jennifer spat out, launching herself abruptly on to her feet. 'That's a damned lie – it was Daddy who helped Glen write the songs. He always said so,' she hissed.

Monica's temper flashed as her patience finally ran out. 'Oh, Jen, do grow up! Do you really think your father was capable of writing *anything*, let alone a hit song? He could barely put a sentence together. And even if that wasn't the case, and he had managed to cobble together a line or two, do you really think your father wouldn't have demanded his share of the royalties and made sure that he got all the credit coming to him? Because if so, you didn't know him, like I did. He was as vain as a peacock. Oh Jen,' she said, on seeing the stricken look on her face. 'Your father wasn't the saint you've made him out to be in your head. Don't you see . . . ?'

'Oh, I see all right,' Jennifer shouted at her mother. 'You never loved him, did you? It would suit you down to the ground if some book came out that belittled him, wouldn't it? As if he didn't have to put up with that sort of thing all his life, and it's still happening now that he's dead and gone and can't defend himself! Well, I'll do it, even if you won't.'

'Jen!' Monica said, but already her daughter was slamming her way out of the door.

Monica sank back against the sofa and poured herself another drink. But she was already beginning to weep – weary, helpless tears that trickled down her face and tickled as they dripped off the end of her chin.

~

'They can't see us until half past four,' Caroline said as she slipped her telephone back on to the coffee table, next to her steaming mug of coffee. She had been talking to her solicitors in town, who were fully booked up with appointments until then. 'But they say we can have a quiet room to ourselves, and someone will bring the cardboard boxes up out of storage for us. Hope that will suit you?'

'Oh sure, I don't mind waiting,' Lyssa assured her.

'Splendid. You can join me for lunch in the restaurant here while we pass the time. You can be my guest – and they do quite an extensive menu, really, considering practically none of their clientele have all their own teeth any more. It's not all pureed mush!'

Lyssa nearly choked on her coffee. It was always a bonus when the person you were interviewing had a wicked sense of humour.

'I'm sure it'll be delicious. And if you wanted to do any shopping in town before the appointment, we can do that – my car's quite comfortable and easy to get into and out of?'

'Sounds perfect,' Caroline said.

~

Neville had learned patience a long time ago and, after parking in a shady spot, he was reading the news on his tablet. Occasionally he would do a crossword puzzle or a sudoku to mix things up a bit, but he was relieved nevertheless when, two hours later, he saw Lyssa's car emerge from the entrance to the private retirement village across the road.

He noted that she had a passenger and wondered who she was talking to now about Amelia Montrose. At least her white-haired companion didn't look likely to cause him much trouble, unlike some he could think of.

He followed behind her as she toured around to find a parking space and was lucky enough to find one for himself, not too far from her own. He made sure to stick to the deeper shadows as he trailed along behind the pair on the pavement, sometimes turning into a shop doorway if it looked as if he might be spotted.

But mostly they wandered obliviously into and out of some antiques shops, a few charity shops and lastly a café, where they had tea and cakes. They were clearly killing time and when, at last, they entered a discreet building tucked away up a small alley, he sensed that the real reason for their getting together was about to be revealed.

Casually he strolled past the entrance, where a shiny brass plaque told him that a firm of solicitors resided within. He nodded.

Interesting.

Inside, Caroline was greeted with genuine warmth and respect by a man who didn't look that much younger than herself, and they were shown into a clearly little-used back room, that held a rather large table and several mismatched chairs.

Waiting on it were three large cardboard boxes. The man, who Caroline addressed as 'Bertie, sweetie', asked if they wanted tea or coffee, which they both declined, then with a gentle smile left them alone.

Caroline watched him leave with a sigh. 'Bertie's been my solicitor for years. Always had a soft spot for me, bless him.' Then she shrugged and turned to the boxes. 'Right, then,' she said firmly. 'Let's have a rootle.'

Lyssa, who was itching to get her hands on the boxes' contents, didn't demur. It didn't take her long to find the letters that Caroline had referred to, which did indeed provide proof that Monty wrote the songs – including a letter from Glen himself to the manager, saying how pleased he was with 'Monty's new verse for "Lying Lips"'. She also found some photographs of Luke Raines and the Lucky Cuckoos that had never been published before, which were a decided bonus. Fresh material was a biographer's dream!

Caroline agreed to let her use the photographs, and 'Bertie, sweetie' was even obliging enough to allow Lyssa to use their photocopier for the letters. Not surprisingly, Caroline didn't want to let the originals leave the building.

Half an hour later, Lyssa, clutching the precious photocopies in a large A4 brown envelope protectively across her chest, escorted Caroline back to her car, and then dropped her off back at the retirement community.

The worst of the rush hour towards Oxford was probably over, but Lyssa knew that it would still be clogging the main roads for a while yet, so she indicated left, and turned off down a single-track country lane that she knew was a shortcut between the two main arterial roads leading back to the city.

Here, the hedges were high and bordered deep ditches on either side of the rather potholed tarmac, and in the fields either side summer wheat and barley showed green, with the occasional splash of scarlet, where the wild poppies had grown through. She had the window down to let in the warm summer air, and she briefly heard the trilling notes of a skylark ascending as she passed by it.

Sensing movement in her rear-view mirror, she looked up and was surprised to see a large black 4x4 bearing down on her fast. Immediately, she felt a sense of panic. Did they think that they could squeeze past her and overtake her on this single lane? Or, more likely, someone was in a hurry to get home and was trying to chivvy her into going faster. She hated it when people got right on her bumper like that. She was just looking around for a flat spot on the grass verge wide enough for her to pull over to let the road hog pass when she felt the 4x4 hit her.

It nudged her back bumper hard, making her head whiplash forward and back. She cried out in pain and surprise. Then it hit her again, and this time she let out an instinctive scream and hit the brakes, expecting the driver behind her to do the same. She'd never had a prang before, but she knew the drill – you pulled over, exchanged mutual insurance information, and . . .

The 4x4 hit again, this time even harder. And then accelerated, shunting her forward. And suddenly Lyssa knew that this wasn't a simple case of a run-in with a careless driver; this was someone deliberately trying to force her off the road.

She gave a muffled sob of fear, wishing Kyle was with her to tell her what to do. But he wasn't, and she needed to do something.

Think! She had to think!

With deep ditches lining either side of the road, the last thing she wanted was to run into them and maybe overturn her car. But she didn't want to try and speed away either. She knew she wasn't any kind of a skilled driver, and knew that the more she increased her speed, the higher her chances were of sustaining a serious injury if she did indeed crash. So she began to brake even more. It was counter-intuitive, for she wanted nothing to do with the maniac in the car behind her, but what else could she do?

With the sun in her eyes and shining off the windshield of the vehicle behind her, she couldn't see who was behind the wheel, and had no idea how many people were in there. What if it were two men, or three or four, all intent on robbing her and stealing her car? Or worse? She wanted to rifle in her bag to get to her mobile and call the police, but didn't dare take her hands off the wheel as once again she was rammed, making it almost impossible for her to keep on a straight course.

The next time she was hit, it was not square on as before, but on an angle to the left side of her bumper and, with a sickening sense of inevitability, Lyssa felt her car begin to slew sideways across the road. So far, she hadn't met any oncoming cars, but if any came now, she was right across the road, and they'd be bound to crunch into her, sideways on. There was no way she could right her direction again, so instead she frantically kept turning the wheel in the direction of her spin, hoping that she might be able to get past the 4x4 and speed off back towards Woodstock before the driver chasing her could do their own turn and follow.

But even as she thought it, the 4x4 began to turn with her, and Lyssa knew that the driver meant to shunt her over into the ditch. With a sense of despair, she braced herself for the impact, hoping and praying that her car wouldn't overturn completely. She didn't think that there would be any water in the ditch, but the mere thought that there might be, and that she might end up upside down and trapped in a partly submerged car, had her once more sobbing with fear and shock.

And then suddenly there was a flash of blue and the blaring sound of an angry horn, and she could see another car coming towards her fast, flashing its lights. It must have been following on behind the 4x4, but it wasn't stopping, as she was expecting, but rather bearing right down on the vehicle that was attacking her. And because the 4x4 had followed her manoeuvre, it was now partly sideways on across the road and couldn't avoid a collision as the blue car hit it with an awful sound of crunching metal.

The blue car, not surprisingly, shuddered to an abrupt halt on the impact, and Lyssa, turning to look over her shoulder, saw a tall man starting to get out of the driver's door. As he did so, the 4x4 wrenched itself free and continued the turn to shoot past him and also Lyssa, who had now come to a full stop on the side of the road, with two of her tyres perched precariously close to the edge of the ditch. There was so little room, the 4x4 scraped its way down the whole length of her car as it went by, making sparks fly, and Lyssa clamped her head over her ears at the awful sound it made.

Then it was revving away out of sight down the narrow lane and there was an eerie period of silence. Her door was abruptly opened, and Lyssa turned to look at the man from the blue car.

'Are you all right?' he asked her urgently.

'Neville?' she said faintly.

~

The police came barely ten minutes later, as did a paramedic. Neither Neville nor Lyssa had been cut by glass so weren't actually bleeding, although Lyssa had some bruising across her chest where her seat belt had dug in during the various shunts and knocks. Neville had the same issue from ramming the 4x4.

The paramedics were satisfied that there were no head traumas or broken bones, and recommended they go to A&E if, at any point, they experienced giddiness or nausea. Lyssa was suffering from shock, and they recommended that she drink plenty of hot sweet fluids and put an electric blanket on her bed if she had one or slept with some hot water bottles if she didn't.

The police breathalysed them both – with negative results – then took their witness statements, with Neville describing the name and make of the 4x4, but when asked he claimed not to have had the presence of mind to make a note of the number plate.

Which was a lie, for he had it memorised.

The police seemed to think that the driver of the 4x4 had panicked after he'd shunted her and had wanted only to get away from the scene, and Lyssa, who was sure that there had been much more to it than that, felt too numb and shocked to explain right now. She just wanted to get home and curl up on her sofa and cry and . . . think.

When a kindly constable asked her if *she* could remember the number plate of the other vehicle, Lyssa shook her head helplessly and wearily. But all the time she was answering their questions, and submitting to the examination of the paramedics, her eyes stayed warily on Neville.

Although he'd said, whilst waiting for the emergency services to arrive, that he often used the same shortcut himself during rush hour, and it was a total coincidence that he'd been driving by, Lyssa didn't believe him. Maybe she was becoming paranoid, but she just didn't believe him.

She had called Carter once she'd got her breath back and told him what had happened and asked him if he could come and pick her up and was glad to know that he was on his way. Now she took the card of a tow-truck company that the police handed out to her and promised to call them right away. They agreed that Neville's vehicle was still roadworthy enough to drive but warned him to get it to a garage immediately he got to Oxford.

Lyssa was very relieved when she heard the familiar throaty roar of Carter's sports car approaching before the police car finally drove away. Neville, watching her, saw the play of emotions cross her face, and knew he'd lost her trust, and cursed quietly.

Now he stared in unhappy silence as Carter pulled up, dashed out and ran across to Lyssa, who was sitting sideways on the driver's seat of her beaten-up car, leaning out with her feet on the road, and staring shakily down at her shoes. He squatted down in front of her, and for a few minutes, Neville could hear only the quiet murmuring of their voices.

Once or twice, Carter turned to look at Neville. Suspicion was written clearly on his open face. Grimly, Neville waited. Eventually, Carter walked over to him. Before he could speak, Neville said quietly, 'I'll wait here for the tow truck, shall I? Have you called them yet?'

'I'll do it in a minute,' Carter said, glancing at the card Lyssa had passed on to him. 'I'll take her home now. I'm going to call Freida – she'll come over and stay the night with her. I'll probably sleep on the sofa too.'

It was a definite warning. Neville sighed inwardly but nodded his head, trying to look and sound as non-threatening as possible. 'Sure. The paramedics said if she got dizzy or felt sick that she should go to A&E. Other than that, paracetamol and plenty of hot drinks. No alcohol.'

Carter met his gaze unflinchingly. 'Right – we'll see to it.'

He turned and went back to Lyssa, picking up her bag and then walking her solicitously to his car and helping her into the low-slung seat. Then he locked up her now abandoned car, and handed the keys wordlessly to Neville.

Neville watched as the sports car turned around and roared off. Then he swore graphically and reached for his mobile. He scrolled down and speed-dialled a number. 'We need to meet. You have to come to Oxford right now. There have been developments.'

He checked both ways to make sure that there were no cars approaching, then walked over to Lyssa's car and used the keys to open it. The first thing he saw was the A4 envelope that had fallen off the passenger seat and into the floor well, and he knew that Lyssa must have been very shocked indeed to have forgotten all about this, and definitely not thinking straight.

Quietly he reached forward and picked it up, folding it carefully in half, and slipping it into the large pocket on the right-hand side of his jacket. After searching the rest of the car, and finding nothing more of interest, he carefully locked it up and returned to his own car to wait for the tow truck.

17

At a quarter past seven that evening, Lyssa's doorbell rang. Freida, Carter and Jason, who were all sitting around the small table in Lyssa's kitchen area, ceased their quiet talking, and Carter got up to answer it.

Lyssa was lying on the sofa in the living area pretending to doze but sat up when she heard her client's voice. Bibbie was snuggled up protectively against her. It was as if he sensed she was hurt and in shock and wanted to offer his body warmth, as he'd never left her side since she'd returned.

'Hello – I'm Elizabeth Grainger. I was hoping to speak to Lyssa?'

'Ummm, just let me check,' Carter said, but Lyssa was already swinging her feet to the floor and putting a hand up to check that her long ponytail wasn't too hopelessly tangled.

'It's OK, let her in, please,' Lyssa called over.

'She isn't alone,' Carter said quickly. 'Neville's with her.'

At this, the other two left the kitchen area and came forward, providing a protective phalanx around her as Neville shut the door behind him, and gave the room a general, wary smile.

'What are you doing here?' Jason challenged him flatly.

'He's with me,' Elizabeth said, coming towards Lyssa and then sitting beside her on the sofa. She looked at Lyssa anxiously. 'Are you really all right? When Nev told me about the car accident I nearly had kittens. No cracked ribs or anything? You can breathe all right?'

'Yes,' Lyssa said, looking from her downstairs neighbour to her client then back again. 'You know Neville?'

'Yeah – well, sort of. My fella knows him, and he introduced us recently, and since Nev was just ideal for what I needed, I asked him if he'd take me on as a client of his,' Elizabeth said, then grimaced. 'Sorry – that sounds a bit confusing, right?'

Carter gave a brief laugh. 'Just a bit. You're the relative of Amelia Montrose, I take it? You've commissioned Lyssa to write her biography?'

'Right. Nev told me what happened this afternoon and said things had gone on long enough and that we needed to come clean and have some kind of council of war, and I agree. Lyssa, I'm so sorry things have got out of control like this. Really, I had no idea you might be in any danger,' Elizabeth said, putting a gentle hand on her forearm.

Today, the petite woman was dressed in sapphire-coloured trousers and jacket, with a cream-lace semi-see-through blouse. And although her make-up was immaculate, as ever, Lyssa could see that underneath it she looked pale and strained. And genuinely contrite.

'Elizabeth, just what is going on?' she asked, too tired to be angry, but beginning to feel indignant. She'd had a feeling all along her client was holding out on her, and now it seemed she was right.

'It's sort of a long story,' Elizabeth began, then paused and frowned. 'Well, not long, maybe, but complicated. And involved. And, to coin a cliché, it's hard to know where to begin.'

Lyssa's three friends exchanged looks, and by unspoken mutual consent, settled down around her. Jason simply sat on the floor by the sofa in front of her, whilst Freida took the last seat on the sofa the other side of her. Carter pulled a kitchen chair up close and all four of them turned questioning, uncompromising looks at the newcomers.

Neville leaned nonchalantly against the nearest wall, taking himself a little out of the way and trying his best to look harmless.

'Well, to coin another cliché,' Lyssa responded dryly, 'just start at the beginning and keep on going until you get to the end.'

Elizabeth nodded. 'Yes. OK – well, it's sort of simple, in a way. One of my aunts always said that Monty wrote the lyrics for the Lucky Cuckoos, but I didn't think much of it – not really. Growing up, my wicked "aunty" Monty and her wild-child ways were just one more example of family lore, along with a famous Montrose beauty in the 1600s who had an affair with a duke, giving him several bastards, and securing a lot of the family land. That and the ghost of the headless monk in the wine cellar. You know the sort of thing.'

Freida couldn't help but give a quick snort of genuine laughter. 'Oh sure – we all have those stories in our families, right, guys?'

'Actually,' Jason began, but was quickly told to shut up by his beloved.

'So, like I said, I didn't really pay that much mind to things, growing up,' Elizabeth said. 'I just got on with life and did the usual things – college, married, divorced, started up my own interior design company, married, divorced again, so far yawn, yawn, right? But then I met this fella . . .'

'Oh, here we go,' Freida drawled knowingly, and Elizabeth laughed.

'No, nothing like that. He's smashing. Good-looking, sexy, smart, wealthy and a film producer.'

'Oh, here we still go,' Freida repeated, rolling her eyes. 'Don't tell me – he promised to make you a star?'

'Hell no,' Elizabeth said, sounding appalled. 'I can't act for toffee. No, he's the real deal, honestly. Spends half his time in LA.

Don't worry, I checked him out up and down before we got really involved. I'm no mug. And before you ask, no, he didn't want me to invest in his latest film!' She grinned at Freida, who grinned back. 'I wouldn't have been able to anyway,' Elizabeth grumbled. 'I plough all I make back into my business. That's the thing about coming from a family like mine – everyone always assumes I'm loaded. But I'm not. I do OK, but it's not as if I have cash coming out of my ears or anything. Traditionally, all the family wealth stayed with the men, and by the time the law changed – well, the Montroses weren't the force they once were. I know from Lyssa's research how everyone thought of Monty as the villain of the piece because of Glen's Will, and his leaving everything to her and all. And how smug they felt when the courts sided with the Bannisters, and overturned the Will, giving all Glen's legacy to the Bannister family. Nobody ever thinks about how the Montrose family was cheated.'

'Oh boo-hoo,' Jason said, faking a bored yawn. 'Poor little rich girl is actually poor, is she? Well, that's a twist.'

Again, Elizabeth gave a wide grin, showing she could at least take a joke at her own expense. 'OK, OK, have it your way. But the thing is, I need capital to boost my business just like anyone else, so when my fella tells me there's going to be this surefire big film going into production soon, with American and European backing, and that it's going to be set in the 1960s, and they're looking for a "mood soundtrack" for that era . . . well, of course, it made me sit up and take notice. I told my fella all about Monty, and the Lucky Cuckoos, and played him their hits and he was well impressed. He said their sound and songs and especially the lyrics were just ideal for the film's plot line, and, being a producer, he has some pull, and he was sure he could swing it their way.'

'Hold on,' Lyssa said, seeing at once where this was all going. 'Big hit movies tend to give a real boost to old song tracks, don't they? Introducing old songs to a whole new generation of listeners – they go viral or get downloaded by the bucketload and make a mint in royalties for those responsible for originally producing them, right? So if you can prove that Monty wrote the lyrics, you and your family would be in line for a sizeable chunk of money. Yes?'

Elizabeth nodded. 'Exactly. And it would have nothing to do with the Bannisters and Glen's estate or his inheritance either. Monty would have been entitled to those royalties in her own right.'

'So that's why you wanted me on board? Not to write the book, but to find proof of her authorship!' Lyssa yelped. 'Elizabeth, why couldn't you just have been straight with me in the first place?' At her sharp tone, Bibbie growled a little, so she reached down and gently began to stroke his head.

'Yeah – that's not on,' Carter said as all the others glared at her.

'Oh now, just hold on a minute,' Elizabeth said, beginning to flush with temper. 'I want you to write the book as well – I mean it when I say I want you to put the record straight on Monty. You yourself could see that she'd had a raw deal in the press, right? And you found out about the charity she started and all that. You can't tell me that she doesn't deserve to have her reputation re-evaluated, can you?' she challenged.

'I think you're gonna have to 'fess up, girl,' Freida put in. 'You wanted the money, plain and simple.'

Again Elizabeth flushed, not liking being put on the spot like that. 'Sure, I did,' she acknowledged reluctantly, but then flashed, 'and what's wrong with that? For over sixty years Monty's real role in the band's success has never been acknowledged. And if it had been, she'd have had the royalties due her, and at least they would have gone on to be handed down to *her* family, as is only right. We were robbed of that money – so why shouldn't we fight to get it back?'

'And by we, you mean mainly you?' Carter said quietly.

'Well, since I'm the one funding the book, and it's my lover who's setting up the film deal, I think I deserve the lion's share. Don't you?' Elizabeth fought her corner ferociously.

'You don't seem very concerned about whoever's been making Lyssa's life hell recently.' It was Carter's calm accusations that once again put Elizabeth on the defensive.

'Hah! Now that's where you're wrong,' she said triumphantly. 'That's where Nev comes into this. Right, Nev?' Elizabeth said, looking across at him.

Neville sighed. 'Yes, I suppose so.'

'There's no suppose about it,' Elizabeth insisted. 'Nev's been looking out for you all this time. That's what he does.'

'Huh?' Jason asked, blinking. 'What do you mean – what he does?'

'Nev is a security expert,' Elizabeth said. 'A sort of cross between a private eye and a bodyguard.'

Neville grimaced. 'Actually, I own and run a very large, legitimate and well-respected inquiry agency that also advises on security matters,' he corrected her.

'That's right – that's how my fella knew him,' Elizabeth explained. 'One of the film production companies he was working with hired Nev and his staff for security at one of their shoots. He provided bodyguards for the stars, and his men patrolled the shoots to keep away looters and thieves and whatnot. So when I told him I wanted somebody to . . . er . . . look after Lyssa, my bloke suggested Nev. I couldn't believe it when he told me that Nev actually lived right here in the same building as you, Lyssa,' Elizabeth said, turning to give her a brief smile. 'It just felt as if it was meant to be, you know? Fate – the stars aligning and all that. He was right here on the spot already.'

'So I wouldn't suspect a thing when he started spying on me, you mean?' Lyssa said bitterly. 'It was you who bugged my phone and laptop and hacked my emails, right?' she shot at Neville.

'Wrong,' he told her. 'That was all down to Jonas Bannister.'

For a moment, a stunned silence fell upon the group of four friends. It was, inevitably, Jason who broke it. 'Who the hell is this Jonas Bannister exactly?'

'He was one of the people I interviewed for the book,' Lyssa explained, looking at Neville with troubled eyes. 'His father was Glen Bannister's younger brother.'

'Why would he bug your flat?' Carter asked sceptically.

'Probably because he had things of his going on that he wanted to keep a tight lid on, and wanted to make sure Lyssa wouldn't unearth them and drag them out into the light of day,' Neville said, looking at Elizabeth, who was nodding eagerly, giving him permission to tell what he knew. 'I traced the two men who came to your flat via their car registration number, and it turned out to be a company vehicle which led me back to him. They work for his security man. I haven't found out yet exactly what he's worried about but . . .'

'Actually,' Lyssa said, nodding thoughtfully, 'I think I might be able to help there. I suspect that a woman called Deborah Simmonds looted Monty's charity funds after Monty died. And I began to wonder if Jonas' father had discovered this. Especially when I noticed in my research that Bannister BioSolutions was founded not long after Monty's death, and I couldn't track down the source of his initial funding to any bank loans. The coincidence is quite striking, don't you think?' Briefly she told them about Janet Connor and what she had witnessed at Monty's funeral. 'It might be a bit of a leap, and I might be wrong, but . . .'

'It makes sense,' Neville said, giving her a gentle smile. 'You've really been digging deep, haven't you? And since his two goons put him so firmly on my radar, I've had my research department checking into him as well. And believe me, the provenance of the early financing of that company of his is ambiguous, to say the least.'

'See!' Elizabeth shot out. 'Everybody was bad-mouthing poor Monty, but the Bannisters were no angels either! Blackmail and fraud! Hah!'

'Well, if it's any consolation,' Neville said dryly, 'he's probably getting his comeuppance now. I've had people watching him ever since the raid on your flat' – he nodded at Lyssa – 'and he's recently had a visit from a young villain called Jack Flynn.'

'I know him too,' Lyssa said quickly. 'He's a relative of Deborah Simmonds. I phoned and asked him if he had any papers about Deborah or the Young Mothers' Trust that Monty set up. He hasn't got back to me yet.'

'Well, I think you can take it that he must have found some,' Neville said, raising one eyebrow. 'Because he's turned up at Jonas' offices. And I'll give you three guesses as to what was on his mind.'

'Blackmail,' Elizabeth said. 'Has to be. Because if it gets out that Bannister's company was founded on stolen charity money, their share price will drop like a ton of bricks.' She sounded very happy about it, but nobody had the heart to chide her.

'No wonder this Jonas character wasn't happy when he heard that you'd started to research a book on Amelia Montrose, then,' Carter said, giving Lyssa a wink. 'Especially as you're so good at discovering everyone's secrets.' Then he turned and looked at Elizabeth. 'Is that why you hired Neville? Because you suspected Jonas might get rough?' he asked accusingly.

'Oh no, that wasn't it at all, was it?' It was Lyssa who answered his question, whilst looking at her client with knowing, angry eyes. 'You just wanted somebody on the spot to make sure that if I *did* find proof that Monty wrote the songs, I'd turn it straight over to you, right?'

Elizabeth bit her lip. 'That's putting it rather strong,' she temporised. 'Let's just say that I wanted to make extra sure. Once word got out about the new film, and the soundtrack, well . . . you might have got certain ideas.'

'Like selling the proof that Monty co-wrote the songs to the remaining Bannister family members, you mean, so that they could destroy the evidence and continue to claim all the royalties for themselves once the film made the Lucky Cuckoos a big name again?' Lyssa said flatly. 'Well, thanks a lot.'

'Of course, I don't think that now,' Elizabeth wailed, putting a conciliatory hand on Lyssa's arm again. 'I mean, once I'd got to know you and everything,' she trailed off miserably. Then, typically, rallied almost at once. Lyssa had to hand it to her – her client was nothing if not a fighter. 'And it was a good thing I did have Nev watching over you, isn't it? After all, he saved your bacon today, didn't he?'

'Yes, he did most certainly do that,' Lyssa said, looking at Neville with wide, troubled eyes. 'I suppose that Jonas Bannister was behind that too, was he? The attack on me today?'

But Neville was already shaking his head. 'No, as a matter of fact, he wasn't. I memorised the number plate of the 4x4 and whilst I was waiting for the tow truck to arrive I got my people to track down the owner.'

Lyssa blinked at him for a moment and went rather pale.

'Who was it, then?' she asked quietly, feeling a momentary sense of despair. Just how many people wanted her dead?

Neville said softly, 'I'm afraid it was Jennifer Joiner.'

Everyone seemed to take a deep breath. Lyssa, after the initial wave of shock had swept over her, slowly began to nod her head. 'I think I understand now,' she said, her voice rather uneven. 'When Monica Farley phoned me and I told her where I was, and all about finding proof that Monty had written the songs, she must have told her daughter. And Jennifer then drove straight up from

London – but who could have imagined that she'd do something so drastic?'

Neville shrugged. 'Personally, I think she must be a bit unhinged. I noticed the 4x4 pulling out after you left Caroline's care home. I didn't make anything of it at the time though, until she tried to run you off the road.'

'She was after the letters,' Lyssa said sadly. 'She's got some kind of father fixation, and "Racey" Joiner hated Monty with a passion. The last thing she'd have wanted was a book coming out giving Monty the credit she deserved for helping write the songs. Poor Monica . . . Oh! *The letters!* She gave a yelp of despair. 'I left them in my car . . .' She tried to struggle to her feet, but Jason gently pushed her back down.

'It's OK,' Neville said, hastily pulling the A4 envelope out of his pocket and handing it over to her. 'I saw it in your car after you'd left with Carter and thought you must have forgotten about it.'

'You had them all this time?' Elizabeth squeaked. 'Why didn't you show them to me?'

Neville shot her a quelling look, and again Elizabeth flushed in shame. 'Sorry. But can I see them?' She looked appealingly at Lyssa. Wordlessly, Lyssa handed them over and watched as her client read them avidly. 'These are perfect. I'll get on to my solicitors right away.'

'Bully for you,' Jason said snidely.

'What do you want to do about Jennifer Joiner?' Neville asked Lyssa, and everyone went suddenly quiet. 'We can call the police. I can say that the number plate registration has just come back to me. They'll find out who it belongs to and check out the damage done to her 4x4. And if we tell them what we know, once they learn it wasn't a random accident, she's bound to face serious charges.'

Lyssa closed her eyes and shook her head wearily. 'I don't know. I'll have to think it over. It's Monica I feel sorry for . . .'

'Well, at least you can get a good night's sleep now,' Freida pointed out. 'We were wondering if Monty might have been murdered, and that all the things that were happening to you were because of that, weren't we? But now we know that's not the case. Monty must have died accidentally after all.'

'At least our case is now solved,' Jason said, raising his hand in a high-five gesture to Carter. 'The Oxford Detective Society scores its first ever victory!'

'Huh? Who?' Neville asked, looking bewildered.

'Oh, just ignore him,' Freida advised. 'We all do.'

Carter sighed rather heavily but slapped his hand against Jason's to show willing. 'At least he's right about it all being over now,' he acceded.

Lyssa opened her mouth to say something, then slowly closed it again. She had her own thoughts about that, but right now she was too tired to get into it.

'Yes, we should leave you to get some rest,' Neville said, wilting with fatigue. 'Perhaps we can talk again tomorrow?'

Lyssa met his kind, concerned eyes and found herself nodding. 'All right. Tomorrow,' she promised.

Lyssa had just taken a long bath and slipped into a pair of leggings and one of Kyle's over-sized T-shirts that came down to her knees when the doorbell rang. With a suppressed groan, she trooped to her door. Her bed felt as if it was calling to her to come back, ignore the summons and slip between its sheets instead, and she almost answered the siren call.

Moments later, however, she was glad she hadn't. Opening the door, she saw a small, elfin-faced woman in her mid-thirties, with short golden brown hair and wide hazel eyes looking at her. She looked pale, but smiled a little tremulously when Lyssa said, 'Hello?'

'Hi – Lyssa, right? I'm Chloe. Is it OK that I came over? Only I just . . .'

Lyssa didn't let her finish, but reached out warmly and took her hand. 'Chloe! No, of course it's fine that you came. How's your father?'

She gently tugged on her hand, leading Chloe inside.

'He's doing much better, and he's awake at last. He can't remember much, but the doctors now seem to think he might have had a very slight heart attack, which would explain why he fell.'

'Oh no. Can I get you something to drink? Tea, coffee, or something stronger?'

'Oh no, I'm driving, and I had coffee before I came out, thanks,' Chloe said with a smile, but the dark smudges under her eyes provided evidence of some sleepless nights.

'Please, sit down,' Lyssa urged, indicating the sofa. 'You must be exhausted after the last couple of days.'

'I am a bit – but I'm so glad to meet you in the flesh at last. And I just thought you'd like to know – I found it!' And so saying, she reached into her large shoulder bag and brought out a big rusting tin, the kind used to store old cine-camera film.

Lyssa felt her knees go weak. 'You found it?' she repeated, astonished. So much for her theory that someone had stolen it from the Tillman residence, then! She was so glad now that she hadn't told anyone about her suspicions concerning that. She would have sounded like a conspiracy nut!

Chloe grinned happily. 'I eventually dug it out of an old biscuit tin that was in the front room sideboard, of all places. He must have kept it there for safekeeping. In case of fire, or something, knowing Dad! That's just the way his mind works! Anyway, I've been busy. You'll be pleased to know I've had this' – she gave the round tin a little shake – 'digitalised. I've now got the whole thing as a video on my laptop. I thought you might like to see it.'

Lyssa almost did a little jig. 'You have no idea how much!' she said, moving to sit beside her.

Chloe called the footage up on her laptop, and the two women watched it in silence. The audio wasn't that great, but it was all there.

After thinking about her and writing about her for so long, it felt almost magical to watch the real Amelia Montrose moving and talking. She'd worn one of the iconic 60s midi-dresses for her birthday bash, and looked as ethereal as a fairy or a wood nymph. She drank, and sat smoking a cigarette on a hanging wickerwork chair, looking tired and faded, almost as if she were already a ghost. Several partygoers were smooching and dancing, and once or twice Lyssa caught sight of an older middle-aged couple who looked very uncomfortable and out of place – presumably Glen Bannister's parents.

It felt a little weird to see Monty's Mansion – Evergreen – through the filter of more than half a century ago, and Lyssa noted the antique furniture and traditional landscape paintings on the wall. Somehow, she'd imagined Evergreen as ultra-modern, with lava lamps, bright colours and chairs shaped like eggs. But the music playing was pure 60s gold.

'And here's the last time we see Amelia, before she goes out into the garden,' Chloe, who'd watched the film twice through already, pointed out helpfully. Lyssa watched, sad and fascinated, as the young woman weaved her way out of frame, turning to blow a kiss to someone out of shot. 'We don't see her actually leave the house, but my grandad does catch sight of her through the window – here, coming up, you can just see her pale blonde hair showing up in the darkness as she moves away . . . see?' She tapped the point on the screen and Lyssa nodded. Yes, she could just make out the pale figure, moving away, like a ghost in the reflected-back image of the densely populated living room.

'The police were right – neither of the Bannisters left after she did,' Lyssa mused, 'and they were still there when Monty's body was discovered. You can tell when that happens because everyone's body language changes and a lot of people leave and wander out on to the patio.'

'I hope, after all this, Grandad's film isn't a disappointment?' Chloe asked.

'Oh, not at all. And I know Elizabeth, my client, will be happy to pay good money to have a copy of this. I'll give her your email address, shall I, so you two can set something up?'

'Yes, please – with Dad laid up, I'll be seeing to all that. And a little windfall will be doubly welcome just now.'

Lyssa nodded, still watching the small moving pictures on Chloe's laptop. And that's when she saw it.

She wasn't surprised that the police had missed it – or that Chloe and her father had either. The image was only there for a second and even if it had registered with the investigators at the time, they'd probably have dismissed it as irrelevant.

But Lyssa felt her heart miss a beat and then begin to pound.

~

The next morning, Lyssa left the flat early, having fully filled Bibbie's bowl and put down fresh water for him. Although she felt a bit bruised and stiff, she had too much on her mind to hang around and take it easy all day. So, after taking some paracetamol, she treated herself to a taxi to the railway station. She spent the train journey wondering if she was mad, or if she really was about to find out just what had happened on the night of Monty's birthday party, all those years ago.

For some time now she'd begun to seriously consider how and why Monty had died, and one idea had begun to take root and continue to grow. The only thing that hadn't fitted with her theory was all the weird things that had been happening to her recently. But now that last night's series of revelations had cleared away all that extraneous baggage about Jonas and Jennifer, she was more determined than ever to find out if she was right.

After getting off the train she took another taxi to her ultimate destination (after all, Elizabeth was paying her expenses, and right now she wasn't feeling so kindly towards her client that she felt inclined to skimp) and it wasn't until she was in the foyer of the nursing home, and asking to speak to Emily Bannister that she wondered what she'd do if they actually turned her away.

But after a brief telephone conversation with the woman in reception, someone came and escorted her to a large and pleasant light-filled room overlooking a flower-filled courtyard garden. The room contained a double bed at one end, and a comfortable couch and a couple of armchairs at the other, but the occupant was sitting in a straight-backed chair by the window. As Lyssa approached, she could see that Emily appeared to be watching the antics of a robin, bobbing about and looking for food in one of the flower borders.

She only turned her head to look at her visitor when the carer gently said her name and then introduced Lyssa. After asking the old lady if she wanted some more tea and biscuits, and inquiring of Lyssa if she wanted some herself, she left them alone with a gentle smile.

Emily Bannister, Glen's youngest sibling, was now painfully thin, with the skull beneath her nearly translucent skin clearly showing. Her eyes were deep set and looked full of dull pain, and she was wrapped up in a thick housecoat, despite the warm day. Lyssa didn't need to be told that whatever the nature of Emily's illness, the old woman was dying from it.

And for a moment, she faltered. Perhaps her coming here wasn't such a good idea after all? Especially if she had got things very wrong.

But then Emily spoke.

'So you came,' she said. Her voice was faint but audible and sounded as tired as she looked. 'I did wonder if you would.' She nodded, as if to herself. 'When they told me someone wanted to talk to me about Amelia Montrose, I wasn't the least bit surprised. I think I've always been expecting something like that to happen. Strange, it's taken so long.'

She tried to wave Lyssa to a chair but could only manage a weak flutter of her fingers. Lyssa nervously sat in the nearest armchair to her and automatically took out her digital recorder. 'Do you mind if I record our conversation?'

For a moment, Emily merely looked at her, and then her thin, colourless lips twisted. 'Oh, I think not. Unless you just want bland, vague remembrances about the old days. Then by all means, go ahead and turn that thing on.' She paused to take a long, dreary breath. 'But if you want to know the truth, as I suspect and hope you do, then . . . leave it off. I've kept my silence too long to make any dying declarations now.'

She took another breath, as if it was a chore that seemed barely worth the effort, but the deep-set and suffering eyes still had a spark of fire behind them. A spark that, despite the warmth of the room, made Lyssa shiver a little.

For a moment, the two women simply looked at one another; they were so utterly unalike, with each regarding the other from such vastly different moments in their lives, that it seemed impossible that they could have anything in common. And yet, on just one single point, they were in perfectly harmony.

Emily Bannister wanted to talk.

And Lyssa Moore wanted to listen.

Lyssa made a show of putting the recorder away, but once it was out of sight in her bag, she pressed the record button before withdrawing her hand. It broke her own self-imposed rules of ethics to do this, but if she was right, and she was about to hear the confessions of a killer, surely she could not justify her failure to provide evidence of such an awful crime? And if, after all, she was wrong, she could easily delete it.

Emily sighed faintly. Whether her sigh was one of relief or resignation, Lyssa wasn't quite sure.

The old woman turned to stare back out of the window, deliberately breaking eye contact.

'I never thought I would speak these words to another living – or even dead – soul,' Emily said simply. 'But I killed her.'

For a moment, Lyssa thought and felt nothing – not even satisfaction that she'd got it right. For, ever since she'd started to question the accident or suicide version of Monty's death, she'd gone over that night, running the suspects through her mind, and kept coming back to the same answer.

Glen's parents had the most obvious motive, but both the cine-camera footage and the police investigations had proved that they'd never left the party once Monty had gone into the garden. And whilst Racey Joiner and even some of the other band members might have resented Monty, their motive was relatively weak.

Only Emily Bannister had never come under suspicion – because of her young age, and because she was presumed to be in bed, and no one had noticed her sneaking out. Which, given the state of the majority of the rather drunken and drug-fuelled guests, was probably not that surprising.

But children *did* kill, as had become sadly only too clear over the intervening decades. And when she'd viewed the cine film of Amelia's birthday party last night, and seen the image of a young child, peering through the crack in the half-open door, gazing in at the grown-up party taking place beyond, things began to add up.

If Emily had been awake and spying on the party, who was to say she might not have spotted Amelia leaving, and followed her into the garden?

Children picked up on a lot more about tensions within a family than adults liked to admit. It wasn't hard to believe that she knew how her parents and older siblings resented Monty and blamed her for what they must have thought of as Glen's betrayal in leaving her his fortune, instead of themselves. And children could be very protective of their parents . . .

Suddenly, the moment of numbness evaporated, and Lyssa felt herself go cold in shock. The thought of a child being responsible for Monty's death made her feel rather ill, and for a moment her vision seemed to recede in black spots, before coming back.

She took a long, slow, deep breath. But her hands were icy, and she was sure she had started to shiver a little.

Lyssa realised that the seconds were passing by, and that Emily remained ominously silent. She was just beginning to wonder if she was going to say anything more at all, when the old woman stirred herself once more.

'I was eleven years old. I didn't understand death. And what happened never seemed real.' Still staring out of the window but probably seeing a very different garden in her mind's eye – one that was illuminated only by moonlight – Emily shook her head. 'I remember that I just couldn't get to sleep, with the sound of the party and music and everything. It was easy to sneak down the stairs and through the kitchen. I peeped in through a door to watch them all dancing, then I slipped out the back door and into the garden. I was in my pyjamas and slippers. I just wanted to see the water lilies, of all things.'

At this she turned briefly to look at Lyssa and then quickly away again – as if human contact was the last thing she could withstand.

Watching the reflection of Emily's face in the glass, Lyssa saw the old woman's lips tug up into what might have been called a smile. 'I'd never seen water lilies before, you see – there weren't exactly a lot of them floating around the estate! But they were everywhere in my fairy-story books – with a fairy sitting on them, or a frog prince, or what have you. They looked so beautiful and magical – I never thought that they might exist in real life. But on the drive over to the party, I heard my parents talking about the fancy garden Glen had been going on about, and how he'd had a fountain put in the pond and added more water lilies in case the ones already there died.'

The old woman shifted a little on her seat, and Lyssa instinctively knew that she couldn't sit in any position without being in pain.

'I became so excited at the thought of seeing them, but when we arrived Mum made me take a bath and go to bed instead. I was so disappointed. And after lying in bed for what felt like ages, I decided I would sneak out and go and find them anyway.'

Emily Bannister sighed. 'Strange, isn't it, how something so . . . innocent, could lead to something so evil. But there was a full moon and party lights strung up all over the place as well, so I found the pond all right, and that's when I saw her – sitting at the edge of the pond, dangling her feet in the water, swaying a bit, and drinking from a glass. Monty. Oh, how we all hated her. Me especially. Do you know why?'

She glanced briefly at Lyssa, who nodded.

'You wanted to be an artist,' Lyssa all but whispered. She was still feeling a little bit disembodied. It had been one thing to come here with a vague theory that Emily might have had something to do with Monty's death, but deep down she hadn't *really* believed it. Had she? But here she was, calmly listening to a killer's confession.

It was all rather surreal.

Emily nodded, looking almost pleased. It was as if, somehow, Lyssa's presence here and now was some sort of vindication. 'So you *do* know. Somehow, I thought you would.' She gave a little smile, then shrugged painfully. 'Yes, I wanted to paint,' she admitted quietly. 'My first real memory was of drawing our house with our neighbour's cat sat on the doorstep. I used to scrawl on any scrap of paper I could find and made sure that everyone knew what I wanted for birthdays and Christmas – paint sets, sketch books, inks, pens, anything like that. I never felt truly real, you see, unless I was working on something. Even as a kid. It was all-consuming. I *needed* to paint – to become a great artist. I never wanted to marry, never wanted children, didn't play with dolls, nothing like that. All I wanted was to go to art school and be shown how to make what was in my head appear on canvas. It was like torture, not being able to do that. No matter how much I practised, and got better, I needed to do more, always more . . . To make the images that I saw become real . . .'

She slumped back in the chair, exhausted by her sudden outburst of emotion, and gave a little shake of her head. 'Ah, but what does it matter whether I can make you understand or not?' She began to cough and wheeze, and for a while struggled to regain her breath.

Lyssa sat very still and waited, sensing that any attempt to help her would be unwelcome. And she understood why. For six decades this woman had lived with her terrible secret and had chosen Lyssa for her confessor.

Painfully, slowly, Emily began to rally strength from her fragile frame. Her voice, though, was little more than a scratchy whisper now.

'And suddenly, there she was – this woman who stood between me and what I needed. I hated my brother for leaving her his money, and couldn't understand why he'd done it. It was as if he loved her more than us. I felt so resentful and angry that I just sneaked up behind her and shoved her hard in the back.'

She sighed. 'Even as she hit the water, I expected her to come up spluttering right away, and be mad as hell at me and chase me around the garden and tan my hide for me. But she didn't,' Emily said simply, her voice full of remembered wonderment. 'She sort of floundered around for a bit in the water and then just . . . slowly sank down. I watched it happening but didn't really understand what it all meant. I was eleven – I'd never seen death before. I didn't know what it was . . .'

The robin suddenly hopped up on to the windowsill, cocked his head in that way that all avian creatures seemed to have, looked at her, then hopped back down out of sight again. Emily watched it avidly. 'Once I could have painted that bird. But not now.' She looked down at her hands, which Lyssa saw were twisted cruelly with arthritis, and again shook her head.

Then there was another silence, which went on so long that Lyssa concluded the other woman had now said all that she wanted to say. In a way, it was a relief not to have to listen to anything more, but another part of her, a small voice in the back of her head, insisted that she couldn't leave it quite at that. 'I understand you've had a long and fairly successful career painting,' Lyssa said gently. 'Would you mind if I asked . . . I just wondered . . . did you ever regret what happened that night?'

For a moment, Lyssa didn't think Emily Bannister would answer her, but then, slowly, she turned her skull's head towards her and that strange spark of dark fire in her eyes gleamed once again.

'I painted and sold a lot of canvases. I won a few prizes. A few patrons collected me avidly. I was regarded as a good, solid painter. But you know what I was never able to do?'

Lyssa held the old woman's dying gaze for a long, sad moment, and asked quietly. 'No, Emily. What couldn't you do?'

'I could never transfer on to canvas the image that was in my mind.'

Emily Bannister's lips twitched. 'Do you see, what a joke the universe played on me? Oh, sometimes I came close. Sometimes it almost seemed that greatness came within reach, and that divine spark of genius every artist craves was about to burn in me, but with my next brushstroke . . . I was back to being a superior mediocrity again. And do you know – to this day, I sometimes wonder if it was because I could never *let* myself become really great? Because, subconsciously, I was afraid that if I were ever to reach my full potential, something terrible would happen to me. Either that, or perhaps my soul had already decided failure was a just punishment for what I did that night.'

Once more she turned to look up at the blue sky. 'I don't suppose it will be too long now before I find out.'

Again, Lyssa waited, hoping for a little more, but after a while Emily Bannister dozed off, and to the sound of her quiet, shallow breathing, Lyssa finally tiptoed away.

EPILOGUE

Neville saw the old wooden country signpost just in time, and indicated left, down a tree-lined lane. All around them, the glorious English countryside was bathed in late summer sunshine, and he felt his mood lift.

He turned to look at the woman in the passenger seat beside him. Lyssa, sensing the movement, glanced at him and smiled.

'Thanks again for driving me here,' she said. 'I know I'll have to get back behind the wheel at some point, and I will, but right now . . .' She shrugged.

'Take your time. And I really don't mind a drive in the country.' He might have added, *especially with you beside me*, but knew the timing was not yet right.

Lyssa, gazing out of the window, wondered how Jennifer Joiner was doing at the mental health clinic, and hoped that she was getting all the help she needed.

When Monica had turned up at her flat the evening after the accident, in tears and so distraught that she was on the verge of collapse, it had all come pouring out of her. How her daughter, white-faced and appalled at what she'd done, had gone back to her mother and confessed all. And how Monica had finally used her daughter's moment of madness to get Jennifer to admit that she needed proper, psychiatric help. And after buckets of tears, hours of exhaustive talking and many gin and tonics ('that was just me, Lyssa, honey, Jenny doesn't drink'), they had made a plan.

Jennifer would voluntarily admit herself to a mental health facility and would do everything she could to let go of this obsession with her father. But all of this, of course, had to depend on what Lyssa intended to do.

And then Monica had literally begged Lyssa not to press charges, and Lyssa had agreed. In the end, it hadn't really been a hard decision for her to make. She was not naturally vindictive, and besides, what would sending Jennifer to prison achieve? The poor girl's life was already blighted enough. And as Monica had said, having Monty's biography come out for all to read could only be a good thing, and force Jennifer to face the reality of her father's life, as opposed to her rosily tinted view of it.

Wild Thing, when it was published, would be a revelation to a lot of people – not just to Jennifer. It would highlight how Monty had funded the Lucky Cuckoos extensively in the early days, and had been instrumental in finding them a decent manager. How she had used her money to set up such a worthy charity, the Young Mothers' Trust, and most of all, that she co-wrote the songs, and was a formidable talent in her own right.

And then there was the bombshell ending – about how, even in death, life had treated her unfairly, with Deborah Simmonds and Jonas Bannister looting the charity's funds for their own personal gain.

But the book, despite its many dark passages, would have plenty of warmth and humour in it too, thanks mainly to Jason's Aunt Edna. Once Lyssa had finally got around to interviewing her, the old lady had provided a fund of funny anecdotes about Monty – some of which had made Elizabeth snort with laughter when she'd read Lyssa's notes on them.

So she was feeling confident that she had got the balance and 'feel' of the book just right, and—

Lyssa's thoughts were interrupted as the first cottages of a small village came into view, and she glanced down at the satnav image on her phone. 'Church Lane should be just up here, on the right,' she murmured helpfully.

Amelia Montrose's family home was a large Georgian house, situated barely a mile away, and all her family had been buried in the churchyard here. The church itself was Norman (as was the family itself) but parts of it dated back even earlier. The Montroses of the first five hundred years or so had all been buried within its crypts, but in the later centuries, their tombs and burial sites had been forced to migrate outside into the open air, as she knew from her research.

Neville parked beside a low dry-stone wall, which was covered in ivy-leaved toadflax and other self-seeded wildflowers. He switched off the engine, and in the resulting silence again looked across at her.

'Do you want me to come with you?' he offered.

But Lyssa, already reaching behind her for the bunch of freesias and daisies on the back seat, shook her head. 'No, that's all right. We know there's no one stalking me now.'

Which was true enough, she mused. Jonas Bannister and his security chief had made the mistake of frightening the greedy Jack Flynn too much when he had tried to blackmail them with his knowledge of where the money had come from to start up Jonas' business.

As payback, Flynn had posted all the evidence to Lyssa, who had promptly turned it over to the authorities, with the result that Jonas and his company were now under investigation by the police – and jail time was definitely on the menu for both men. Already the company shares had fallen to an all-time low, and everyone was expecting the business to be declared bankrupt any day now.

Neville watched Lyssa in silence as she got out and walked to the side gate set into the newer part of the churchyard. She was dressed in respectful black trousers with a black-and-white top, and her long black ponytail bounced around the lower part of her back as she walked. He thought he'd never seen a woman walk so gracefully.

With a sigh, he wound down the window and rested his arm along the opening it created, letting his mind drift back.

He'd felt himself pulled towards her from the moment he met her on moving into his flat, but then she'd been married to Kyle and thus forbidden to him. And when she'd lost her husband so suddenly and unexpectedly, she'd been knocked for six and clearly broken. Which meant that she had still been forbidden to him. And now that this bloody affair of Elizabeth's had backfired on him so roundly, he had to wonder if she would ever be able, in time, to look at him in the way he wanted her to.

But he was a patient man. He would wait. She wouldn't grieve forever. And with gentleness and kindness . . . As she disappeared amongst the gravestones, searching for Amelia, he knew that he was not about to give up anytime soon.

Oblivious to the thoughts of the man waiting for her in the car, Lyssa began to inspect the gravestones, looking for the name that had become so familiar to her over the past few months. She knew from her research that Monty had wanted to be buried with Glen, who now rested in the churchyard of the village where they'd lived together at Evergreen. But the Montrose family had over-ridden her preferences, as they had tried to do so unsuccessfully in her lifetime, and had finally managed to get their way, and Monty had been buried instead alongside her ancestors here.

When she finally found Amelia's simple stone and knelt beside it, she couldn't help but wonder what she would have made of it all. Perhaps she'd have been furious, or maybe just sad. Or maybe amused? How could she, Lyssa, possibly know?

Although she'd spent so much time researching and then writing Amelia's life story and had got to know and understand many things about her well enough, not even those who had been closest to you could always know the innermost workings of your mind and heart. Everyone had, and kept, some secrets.

The grave had one of those inset wells for flowers, and she could see that it still had some water left in it from the last rains. So, carefully taking her time to make them look attractive, she arranged the flowers in front of the fading lettering.

'There you are, Monty,' she said quietly, when she had finished. 'I hope you don't mind me calling you Monty? I feel as if we're friends now, in a weird sort of way.'

The sunny churchyard was deserted of all but birdsong, and as Lyssa looked around at the quiet, peaceful place, she felt a gentle warmth steal over her. 'I feel as if you've been looking over my shoulder sometimes, as I've been writing *Wild Thing*, and I swear I could feel your approval. At least, I hope so,' she said, looking at the name carved into the marble. 'I tried to do you justice – no fudging, no lies, the good times and the bad. I recorded it all. I thought you'd appreciate honesty above all.'

The warm feeling persisted, and it made Lyssa feel good. It was probably just the late summer sunshine, but then again . . .

'You know that Emily died last week,' she went on. Then gave a rueful smile. 'Well, of course you would know all about that.' She shook her head at her own folly of talking to a dead woman about another dead woman. 'I couldn't help but wonder though, when she talked about never being able to paint how she really wanted to, if you might have been haunting her? Just to make sure that she didn't gain anything from killing you. But now . . .'

Lyssa sighed, looking around at her peaceful surroundings again. 'Somehow, I don't think you did. I think Emily was right – her own sense of guilt wouldn't let her become what she so desperately wanted and needed to become. And that brings me to why I'm here.'

Reaching forward, Lyssa slightly rearranged one of the daisies that had fallen out of place. 'Before I started this project, it never occurred to me that I would want to do anything other than write the truth, whatever that might be. I was always so sure about the ethics involved in what I do, but this time . . . Perhaps it serves me right for being so complacent!' She gave a little self-mocking laugh.

'You see, I need to know what *you* want me to do about what happened to you that night – and about Emily,' she said softly. 'All the rest of the book is finished. Soon everyone will know how your charity helped Janet Connor and her son so much and would have gone on to help so many others, if you'd lived. And your name will finally be added to that of Glen's as co-songwriter of the band's hits. And I think, in this more modern era, everyone's going to admit that you got a raw deal in the press. Elizabeth's pleased with the first draft, anyway. But then, she would be, right?'

Somehow, she thought Monty would have approved and applauded Elizabeth for fighting to get her hands on the long overdue royalties due to her heirs. 'I think you and Elizabeth would have got on like a house on fire. She knows what she wants and is determined to get it. But she's left me in the lurch a bit, in that she's leaving it to me to decide how to tackle what happened on the night of your death . . . and that's where I find myself a bit stuck.'

A blackbird landed close by and began to rootle through some tall grass. It reminded Lyssa of the robin that had so enchanted Emily Bannister, that day, looking out of her window.

'I just don't know what to do about Emily, Monty. Obviously, I have the recorded proof of her confession, but I can't help but wonder if you'd want me to make it public. I know how much you loved Glen, you see. And she was his little sister. He wouldn't have wanted her branded a murderer, would he? And she was so young. But you . . . Monty – I don't know what *you* want me to do.'

She was genuinely pleading now. 'All your short life, your achievements and accomplishments were hidden or trampled on or considered unworthy of acknowledgement. So now, as your biographer, am I supposed to just follow on in the same way? Is even the manner of your death to be kept in the dark and misunderstood? But if *you* wouldn't have wanted the truth to come out . . . I don't suppose you could help me out and give me a sign, could you?' she asked, half laughing, half serious.

But, of course, the dead were the dead, and the only thing she could hear in the churchyard was the slight rustling of the industrious blackbird. With a wry smile, Lyssa got up and stood looking down at the green grass and headstone of Amelia Montrose.

Then, with a sigh, she turned and walked away, knowing she still had to resolve a major issue.

Should she tell Elizabeth about Emily? So far, she hadn't let anyone know about, or hear, the recording of Emily's confession. And to keep such a massive secret from a client went deeply against the grain. But was Elizabeth her only client? Wasn't Monty her client too? And if she did tell Elizabeth, how would it affect how her family thought about Emily? There would be pain and shock and a deep sense of betrayal.

And hadn't there already been enough of that?

But did she have a right to keep it from them?

If only something would happen to tell her what to do and stop all this vacillating! It was driving her mad.

As she approached the car, she saw Neville glance up and smile at her, and she felt something stir, very faintly, within her. As if something chilled and withered was faintly coming to life again.

Mentally, she shook her head. She really was losing it now! Talking to a dead woman and acting like some heroine out of a cheesy rom-com.

She slipped into the passenger seat and did up her seat belt. Neville started the car and then turned it around, and, as they headed back out of the village, reached for the radio. 'A little music to lighten the mood?'

'Why not?' Lyssa said. The visit to Monty's grave had been cathartic, but it hadn't solved her very real dilemma. She'd had no trouble writing about Amelia Montrose's life and times, but just what should she write about her death?

The radio finished playing a Human League number, and the DJ reminded his listeners that this was the 'golden' hour, and the remaining forty minutes were dedicated to the 60s, 70s and 80s.

And then a familiar tune began to play.

It was a Lucky Cuckoos song – not one of their bigger hits, but a track from one of their albums. And as the opening lines began, and Lyssa heard Glen Bannister's familiar and distinctive deep voice singing his lover's words, she felt the tears fill her eyes.

For she knew she had just been given the answer to all her questions.

We found our love,

And who can say how?

And all the sins of our past,

What can they matter now?

And she murmured, 'Thank you, Monty.'

ABOUT THE AUTHOR

Faith Martin is one of the top ten most-read authors of the last decade on Amazon Kindle. She is the bestselling crime writer of the DI Hillary Greene, Ryder & Loveday and Val & Arbie crime series. Faith has been writing for over thirty years and has sold more than four million books. She lives in Oxfordshire, enjoys calligraphy and is a countryside and nature enthusiast.

Follow the Author on Amazon

If you enjoyed this book, follow Faith Martin on Amazon to be notified when the author releases a new book!
To do this, please follow these instructions:

Desktop:

1) Search for the author's name on Amazon or in the Amazon App.
2) Click on the author's name to arrive on their Amazon page.
3) Click the 'Follow' button.

Mobile and Tablet:

1) Search for the author's name on Amazon or in the Amazon App.
2) Click on one of the author's books.
3) Click on the author's name to arrive on their Amazon page.
4) Click the 'Follow' button.

Kindle eReader and Kindle App:

If you enjoyed this book on a Kindle eReader or in the Kindle App, you will find the author 'Follow' button after the last page.